COLD WARRIORS

A Special Agent Dylan Kane Thriller

By
J. Robert Kennedy

James Acton Thrillers
The Protocol
Brass Monkey
Broken Dove
The Templar's Relic
Flags of Sin
The Arab Fall
The Circle of Eight
The Venice Code

Detective Shakespeare Mysteries
Depraved Difference
Tick Tock
The Redeemer

Special Agent Dylan Kane Thrillers
Rogue Operator
Containment Failure
Cold Warriors

Zander Varga, Vampire Detective
The Turned

COLD WARRIORS

A Special Agent Dylan Kane Thriller

J. ROBERT KENNEDY

ISBN-10: 149378904X

ISBN-13: 978-1493789047

First Edition

10 9 8 7 6 5 4 3 2 1

For Hermann, Erica and Michaela Kapp, my German "Granddad",
"Grandma" and "sister".

Für Hermann, Erica und Michaela Kapp, meinem deutschen "Opa",
meiner deutschen "Oma" und "Schwester".

COLD WARRIORS

A Special Agent Dylan Kane Thriller

"Those who cannot remember the past are condemned to repeat it."

George Santayana, The Life of Reason, Volume 1, 1905

"Chronic wrongdoing, or an impotence which results in a general loosening of the ties of civilized society, may ultimately require intervention by some civilized nation, and in the western hemisphere the adherence of the United States to the Monroe Doctrine may force the United States, however reluctantly, in flagrant cases of such wrongdoing or impotence, to the exercise of an international police power."

President Theodore Roosevelt, 1904

PREFACE

The weapon referred to in this novel exists. What isn't known is how many were manufactured, and how many were smuggled into the United States and other NATO countries by the Soviet Union. Some estimates have Soviet scientists building over one thousand of these weapons over nearly thirty years. And if just one had been successfully deployed, it could be devastating.

The author will leave it to the reader to decide whether a country hell-bent on the elimination of our way of life would have even attempted such a thing, and whether or not they would have been successful.

Checkpoint Charlie
West Berlin, West Germany
February 12, 1982

"You failed."

Alex West frowned at his handler, Gord Justice. He had always been a cold bastard of few words when on the job. Loosen his lips with a good scotch and he had one of the raunchiest senses of humor West had encountered in his travels.

No bottle of scotch was in sight.

"Nice to see you too."

Justice grunted, motioning with his head that they should go, the Soviet spy exchanged for West now reaching his own handler. The traditional Berlin fog was heavy at this time of night, but the checkpoint was well lit on both sides, this far from a shadowy exchange usually executed at the Glienicke Bridge under the cover of a sparsely populated area, its most famous pedestrian U2 pilot Frances Gary Powers in 1962.

Checkpoint C or as it had come to be known, Checkpoint Charlie, was established as one of the few controlled crossing points between East and West Berlin after the Berlin Wall was erected to stop the flood of East Germans, over 3.5 million of their best and brightest, to the West. After the wall was completed, this slowed to a trickle. Checkpoint Charlie was probably the most famous crossing point between the East and West in this divided city buried in the middle of a divided country, the Iron Curtain as Churchill named it unforgiving when it came to families and borders. When the wall had gone up as a barbwire fence in a single day on August 13, 1961, families had been cutoff overnight, those fortunate enough to be on the west side of the line of troops and barbwire blessed to live out a life of freedom, those on the east, doomed to life in a communist state, in one of the Soviet Union's staunchest allies.

"Control wants to see you immediately."

West nodded. "I should hope so," he said, following Justice to a waiting car. Control had no sense of humor. He had never met Control in all his years of spying for his country. Sometimes he was certain the voice at the other end of the speaker was a different person, and it probably was. There were too many missions for Control to directly oversee them all. Then again his missions were usually critical, not the casual photography job of Red Square that most embassy staff were asked to perform. His were much more cloak and dagger, far more life and death than most operatives were faced with.

And in this case he knew the only reason he was walking across the border was that killing him would acknowledge what he had found out was true. He knew the Soviets were betting on him failing to convince his handlers of the truth. But if he failed, the potential devastation that could be wrought upon America was incalculable. It could mean the end of Western civilization, and a planet doomed to a post-apocalyptic horror dominated by an uncontested communist Soviet Union.

"You realize how much shit you're in?"

West did. He was in it up to his nostrils. He had gone against orders, created an international incident that had required his side to hand over a valuable captured asset, and because he had been caught, he had none of the evidence he had accumulated. He was barely treading water in the cesspool he now found himself in.

"When Control hears why I did what I did, something tells me he'll have bigger things to worry about."

"You seem pretty confident."

2

"With reason."

"Why? Why did you do it?"

West realized nobody on this side of the Curtain knew what was going on. They only knew one of their top men had gone cold, then through unacknowledged diplomatic channels had requested an exchange. It was almost unheard of; usually when captured, covert agents would simply endure their torture, then wait in a cell for an exchange—if they were still alive.

But in rare cases when they felt their intel was far too valuable to wait, and if the other side holding them felt they knew nothing of importance, or could prove nothing if it were, they'd make an exchange for one or more of their assets who were being held in accommodations usually just as pleasant.

West had nearly shit his pants in surprise when he had seen who he had been exchanged for. Viktor Zorkin, a master spy if there ever was one. They had exchanged fists and bullets and tails for years, and over their years of thrust and parry they had both been responsible for each other's capture and defeats.

But this was insane.

How the hell did he get captured so quickly? I just saw him not even a week ago!

They were warriors who respected each other, and as part of that unwritten code, certain leeway was cut by both, a leeway that had saved both their lives over the years, including this most recent mission. Their rivalry was old, going back to the start of both of their careers, and he found whenever he saw Zorkin in some other part of the world, he smiled slightly and gave the man a nod, it always returned if possible. It was almost a friendship, a friendship that reminded him of the old cartoon characters Ralph E. Wolf and Sam Sheepdog, Sam defeating Ralph mercilessly while at the job, but at the sound of the steam whistle, they would return home the friends they were.

Old warriors.

He felt old. He wasn't, not by anybody's standards but the young whippersnappers coming out of training, desperate to jump in and defeat the evil Soviet Union in one single, movie-inspiring stroke, their names forever to go down in history.

More likely they'd end up on the Memorial Wall at Langley, an anonymous star to be remembered and eventually forgotten to all but their families.

It was a brutal business.

And he loved it.

He climbed in the back of the car with Justice.

"If Control clears you, I'll tell you all about it," he said.

Justice's eyebrows shot up.

"Christ, Alex, it's me, Gord. How long have we known each other?"

West gave him half a smile.

"Long enough to know you'd give me up in a heartbeat to save yourself."

"Uh huh." Justice wasn't happy with the remark, but didn't protest it because he knew damned well it was true. West had read his record before agreeing for the man to be his handler. He didn't mind the fact that the man would sell him out to save himself, all he cared about was to what side. Justice was a patriot, through and through, and would never betray him to the Soviets, but to his own people, he'd sing like a damned canary if it were demanded of him, but only if it meant saving himself from some blemish on his immaculate career jacket sitting in a cabinet in a file room at Langley.

He was a career man willing to step on anyone to get ahead.

But he was definitely not a field operative.

And unfortunately he was the closest thing to a friend West had.

"I'm sorry," he said. "I'm just grumpy. You know I can't tell you, but if Control agrees, I'll ask you sit in."

This seemed to placate the wounded Justice, and the rest of the short ride was filled with talk of baseball, West's beloved Cleveland Indian's seemingly always a disappointment to Justice's glee, he being a Yankee's man himself. What Justice didn't realize was that the Indian's weren't West's home team. He had been forced to give them up, Cleveland instead part of his cover. Home teams gave away your home, something you didn't want anyone finding out about in this business.

They arrived at "The Exchange", a secret underground complex in the American sector of West Berlin where underground tunnels could lead them pretty much anywhere in the sector they needed to go, away from prying eyes, including those of the KGB agents that had been following them from the moment they had left Checkpoint Charlie. They were tolerated because they were known. It was better to leave a spy in place as long as he was doing no harm. If you arrested them every time you identified one, you'd be spending more time trying to find his replacement than you'd save by keeping the known man in play.

It was a game with rules, that men of honor played by.

Unfortunately not every man playing the game was honorable.

They exited the vehicle, switching to another that would bring them to their final destination, their original car now headed back outside with two stand-ins in the rear to play a little wild goose chase with their KGB shadows.

"You know, this is probably going to end your career, my friend."

West nodded.

"If I go out on this one, then it will have been worth it. As long as somebody listens."

5

Justice made a disgruntled sound.

"No guarantee on that," he said as they pulled up to the underground entrance to one of several CIA outposts in the city. Within moments West was in a room, a light shining on him, ashtray in front of him, still half-full from the previous debriefing.

He didn't smoke.

At least not any more. He found it made him too jumpy if he was without. Which was something that could get you killed in the field.

He pushed it aside, the thought of taking a long drag now disgusting to him.

Chairs scraped in the darkness on the other side of the light, and several red cherries glowed in the dark as his interrogators indulged in their own bad habits, none having yet apparently conquered the addiction.

"Welcome, Mr. West," came the voice of Control. "Yet again we meet under less than auspicious circumstances."

Meet?

West would hardly call this a meeting. Meetings implied two way communications in which you could not only hear, but *see* the participants.

"I fear it's the nature of the business we're in," he replied.

"Yes, I seem to see you more than any other of my agents."

"Perhaps because I am given the more difficult assignments."

"Yet you ignored your latest mission's parameters."

"If you heard my reasoning, you would understand why."

"How would you like to proceed, Mr. West?"

"How about at the beginning?"

Shali, Chechen Republic, Russian Federation
Present Day

CIA Special Agent Dylan Kane shoved the shopkeeper aside, racing between temporary stalls set up daily by their owners, and the more permanent structures for those who had the right connections—warlords who provided protection for a price.

Which meant only the most successful vendors occupied the most desirable places in the markets. A Catch-22 if Kane had ever seen one.

"Byekhk mah beel-lahh!" he yelled, apologizing to the downed vendor, one who hadn't paid attention to the man charging through the market, instead immediately casting a watchful eye over his wares, knowing shoplifters took advantage of just these situations.

And one had, hence his darting in front of Kane necessitating the less than gentle shove.

His target was about thirty feet ahead of him, making great time, obviously familiar with the market, but Kane had the advantage. His target had to decide where he was going which took mental cycles that subtly slowed him down, and with each delay, Kane gained inches. And as long as he could rely on the crowd to stop and stare after the man who had shoved through them, he could use their momentary distraction to speed through with little interference.

A dodge into an alleyway and Kane lost sight of his man, but moments later he was in the same narrow passage just in time to see him exit the other end and head left.

Kane poured on the juice, sprinting with all his might through the alleyway, bursting through the other side and slamming headlong into a cart rushing through the back street far too fast. Kane spun but kept his footing, spotting his man a good hundred feet ahead of him, a grin on his face at Kane's pain.

Kane pushed through the ache in his thigh from where it had caught the spinning wheel and was soon back to full speed. His adversary rushed up a set of steps leading to the roofs of a row of houses lining the rear of the market and soon they were racing along slippery shingles and rooftop terraces. Kane shoved through a series of sheets hung out to dry, pushing the last one aside and gasping as he put on a burst of speed then jumped, only five feet of rooftop left between the sheets and the street below.

He pushed off the ledge, his philosophy of 'assume you're already dead' paying off as he saw the roof across the street, about one story below, rapidly nearing as his feet and arms waved in the air.

"Not gonna make it!" he cursed as he approached the other side, the gravity end of the curve finally coming into play as he sunk, smacking into the wall with his body, his arms stretched out above him, grasping the ledge. As his fingers began to slip he raised his feet, pushing the toes against the side, creating some traction to push himself up slightly, his right toe finally catching on something large enough to halt his descent. He let go with his left hand and flung his entire left side up as hard as he could, grabbing onto the other side of the ledge, then pulled himself over the side, dropping unceremoniously to a rooftop patio, gasping for breath.

Voices had him shoving himself up on his elbows. Two women were looking over the edge he had just climbed, one pointing below. The one pointing was older, the other younger, perhaps early twenties. A mother-daughter pairing if he had ever seen one. The daughter looked at him, smiling shyly. He scrambled to his feet as he surveyed his surroundings.

His target was gone.

Shit!

It had taken him two weeks to find the man, Aslan Islamov, a known Chechen terrorist, or rebel as they preferred to call themselves. Anti-Russian all the way, and responsible for an extensive drug network that had its tendrils deep into the United States, distributing massive amounts of narcotics to the American public.

And they were brutal.

They put the Mexican gangs to shame.

His assignment was to track and observe, see who his contacts were, and to then capture him if possible, take him out if not.

But one week ago Kane had witnessed something he wasn't supposed to. A meeting between Islamov and a man who was clearly Russian, his white skin and prominent nose a dead giveaway in this area. Kane had sent the photos back to Langley via satellite link as the meeting progressed, and he soon had IDs on the men. The guards were all former Russian Special Forces, Spetsnaz, and the main man himself was former Major General Yuri Levkin, once responsible for the entire Soviet nuclear arsenal.

A staunch opponent of the new Russia, but fiercely patriotic—Levkin was a man who wanted the Soviet Union to return, in all its former glory, with an iron fist at its head. He was a tacit supporter of Putin, especially since Putin had begun to remove most of the freedoms Russians had gained, turning elections into a farce, crushing any opposition on the streets and in the press, and rebuilding the armed forces to once again rival that of their traditional enemy, the United States.

But Levkin was one who felt that was just a start.

He wanted the hammer and sickle to fly once again over the Kremlin, for the once proud CCCP acronym to adorn their military hardware, and for the world to tremble when Soviet armor redeployed, even if only on an exercise.

So when this man met with Islamov, Kane immediately took notice. What appeared to be a massive amount of cash was handed over to Levkin by Islamov's people, then computers were employed for about five minutes to most likely conduct wire transfers, and then the meeting was over.

With Islamov apparently receiving nothing but a memory stick.

When Levkin had left, Islamov had immediately plugged the stick into his laptop, then minutes later pulled it, destroying it with a rock and tossing it into a cooking pit with a flame substantial enough to melt anything exposed to it in time.

Kane had retrieved it, but didn't hold out much hope of anything being recovered.

He had called in a satellite trace of Levkin in case they needed to pick him up, then awaited orders from Langley on what to do. They had come in just minutes ago.

Take Islamov alive.

Which was why he hadn't just shot him in the market. Instead he had shot his four man security detail, all amateurs and barely trained from what he could see, but during this brief moment, the bastard had been able to escape on foot.

And now was nowhere to be seen.

He approached where the two women were, the young one blushing as she held her veil up, covering her face, but leaving a stunning pair of eyes to gaze out at him.

"What is it?" he asked in Chechen.

"Look for yourself," was the response of the older woman, none too pleased to see him on her rooftop. She glanced at her daughter then yelled, the poor girl crying out in anger and embarrassment, then running toward the door leading to downstairs, casting one last glance, and with a drop of her veil, a smile at Kane.

Kane returned it, hating to break a young girl's heart, then looked over the edge.

And found his target, Islamov, lying on the ground, barely moving, he obviously not as successful at clearing the alleyway as Kane had thought. Kane looked for a way down, but found none, instead running toward the door the young woman had just entered.

He pushed the door open and wound himself down several flights of steps until the bottom, coming out into a common area where the girl was sitting on the floor, preparing a meal. She jumped up, her eyes full of hope as her mother burst from the stairs, yelling at him to get out.

Kane gave the girl a wink, she blushed, and he stepped out into the alleyway and over to his target. He quickly checked the man's vitals. He was weak, and judging from the piece of rebar shoved through his abdomen, he would have a few minutes of slow, agonizing dying before he'd be of no more use to Kane.

Kane smacked him on the cheek, reviving the man. Groans were the response, then fluttering eyes.

"Help me," he muttered.

"I will if you answer some questions."

"Help me."

"Why were you meeting with Levkin?"

The man shook his head.

Kane grabbed the rebar and gave it a push.

The man winced, paling even more, but now a little more alert, the sharp pain having sent a surge of adrenaline through his system.

"Don't make me hurt you. Why were you meeting with him?"

"Codes."

"Codes for what?"

"I don't know."

Another jerk on the bar.

"I don't know!" gasped the man. "I swear."

"You paid a fortune for codes you know nothing about?"

"I'm just the middleman."

"Who are the codes meant for?"

"I don't know. I emailed them. He wired the money."

"What's the email address?"

"I don't know, I destroyed it."

The man's voice was barely a whisper.

"Your account number?"

"In my wallet."

Kane searched his pockets, pulling out a worn black leather wallet. Between several bills he found a folded piece of paper with an account number written on it.

"Do you have any idea what this is about?"

He shook his head.

"Did Levkin say anything that didn't make sense?"

"Help me."

"I will, if you tell me what I want to know."

"He said, 'Now Crimson Rush can finally proceed.' That's all."

"Crimson Rush? What's that?"

But Islamov didn't answer, finally passing out from the pain and loss of blood. A growing crowd was gathering at either end of the alley and it would only be a matter of time before this man's friends would find him.

Kane decided it was best to avoid that.

He stepped back inside the house he had just left, the mother protesting, slapping at him, the daughter smiling shyly behind her veil, as Kane thanked them in Chechen for their hospitality, climbing the stairs then racing across the roofs and away from the body that was once one of Chechnya's greatest drug lords, his mind consumed by one thought.

What the hell is Crimson Rush?

The Opera House
West Berlin, West Germany
February 5, 1982
One week before Checkpoint Charlie Exchange

Alex West sat in the high back leather chair, a luxury compared to what he was used to. One way to judge the importance of a meeting to those organizing it was how comfortable the chairs were. It was his experience that the most important meetings were in comfortable chairs like these; the most life threatening in the utmost uncomfortable imaginable.

He sat on one side, alone, about a dozen chairs surrounding the table. He sipped his coffee, black and horrid, wincing with each sip at the bitter brew that rotted his gut with each ounce he consumed.

The bastard responsible should be handed over to the Soviets.

He put the mug down, the blue NATO logo emblazoned on white facing him. He pretended to be interested in the logo as he assessed the situation. Only two weeks ago he had successfully rendezvoused with a nuclear sub in the Bering Sea with a microfilm obtained from a double-agent in Siberia that contained information he was forbidden to look at, the canister containing it apparently rigged to detect if he had.

At the time he had decided not to risk it. If it was that important he'd find out eventually if there was a need to know. Meetings like this with this many chairs were rare, which had him guessing this was about his last mission. Either a debriefing by a high-level committee, or a briefing by an equally high-level committee.

"The Opera House" as it had been nicknamed was a series of offices in the American Sector of West Berlin housing most of the CIA personnel in the zone. Top of the line security and anti-surveillance technology filled the building, but nothing beat burying everything. At the moment he was sure he was at least fifty feet underground, devices embedded in the soil to detect any digging from the Soviets.

It wouldn't be the first time a tunnel had been dug from one side to the other. In 1954 the British MI-6 and the CIA, in a joint operation, had tunneled almost 1500 feet to the Soviet side and tapped all their landlines, gathering intel for over a year before the Soviets discovered the taps.

Unfortunately the Soviets had known all along, a KGB mole inside MI-6 having tipped them off before the tunnel was even complete. To protect their mole, the Soviets left the taps in place, staging the accidental discovery. An incredible amount of intelligence was gathered, and the propaganda coup the Soviets had hoped to gain with the discovery backfired, the public in the West instead marveling at the balls displayed by their intelligence apparatus.

West looked up as the lone door opened and a stream of brass and suits entered, each taking seats as if assigned by perceived pecking order. Somebody frowned at West's apparent choice.

I'm not moving. I was on time.

Several ducklings lined the walls, apparently too junior to merit chairs, but with security clearances high enough for whatever was about to be presented. He recognized the man sitting at the head of the table. Chester Albright. He was the top CIA man in Europe. For him to be here meant this was big.

Very big.

Albright cleared his throat and an aide leaned in, activating a speaker and microphone so somebody else out of view could listen in.

Probably Control.

"Thank you for coming on such short notice," began Albright.

15

Like I had a choice?

"What you are about to hear is classified. You are not to repeat it to anyone. No notes or records will be kept, paper or electronic." Albright droned on for another minute repeating what was pretty much standard in the meetings West was involved with.

Blah blah blah, you talk you die.

A folder was placed in front of Albright by an aide. Albright opened it, flipped past a cover page, then looked around the table, his eyes settling on West for a moment, then continuing around the room.

"This is what we know. Thanks to a double-agent, now dead, one of our agents was able to obtain disturbing intelligence last week that powers far above me have decided must be taken seriously, and acted upon immediately."

West was quite certain it was his intelligence that was being referred to. He felt a twang of regret that the other agent was dead, then again, the man was a traitor of opportunity to his country, even if the enemy. Playing both sides for a profit was a dangerous game, and not looked upon favorably in the spy community. Double-agents were valuable, their information sometimes invaluable, but it said something about a man who was willing to betray his country for profit.

West could never see himself betraying his country, going against orders, or doing anything disloyal or unpatriotic.

He loved his country fervently, believed in democracy and the West's way of life, and was determined to defend it against the tyranny of Soviet Communist aggression.

So when a double-agent he had shook hands with not seven days ago died, he knew he wouldn't lose too much sleep over it.

"The intelligence was scant, but we think valuable," continued Albright. "This is what we know, and it is minimal. The Soviets have developed a new first strike weapon system, referred to as RA-155. We know it is an offensive weapon, it can apparently hit our cities with zero warning time, and if deployed, could change the balance of power overnight. Other than that, we know nothing beyond its code name."

The room seemed to lean forward in anticipation.

"Crimson Rush."

Hotel Arena City, Grozny, Chechen Republic, Russian Federation
Present Day

Kane smacked yesterday's newspaper on yet another cockroach, striding to the balcony with "city view", scraping the dead inheritor to all that is and will be on the railing, then flicking it to the street below. He looked out upon the city, half still in various states of repair, the other half rubble, the long civil war having taken its toll, including on the currently darkened power supply. Russia was pouring money in now to try and rebuild the capital to maintain the support of the ruling, pro-Moscow government, the rebel movement mostly crushed.

On the street below beaters and asses competed with Bimmers and Astons, the gap between the rich and poor in this former Soviet state far more harsh than back home. He chuckled as he saw two horses passing by below, pulling the chassis of a Jaguar XK-8 cabriolet, the harness integrated into the empty engine compartment, this apparently not a recent development.

It's probably more reliable now!

The owner sat in the driver seat, reigns in hand, flicking them gently as the odd pairing moved with traffic, his dated clothes nearly immaculate, his posture one of forced dignity, he apparently no longer the success he once was.

Suddenly the power came back on, his fan kicking in, the only state of the art piece of equipment in the room beyond the flush toilet, it at least stolen from someone who had purchased it this millennia. The TV was Soviet era, the phone would have looked at home on Stalin's desk, the light a single bulb dangling from the ceiling, now rocking back and forth in the fan's breeze.

He checked his satphone and saw it was now charging, the battery completely dead from a week in the field with no electricity available, and frequent transmission of photos and data back and forth. His solar panel meant for those situations had failed on the third day, leaving him at risk of being incommunicado. He had relayed his status, then shutdown, only turning his gear on for emergency broadcasts or his twice daily scheduled check-in.

But now back in near-civilization, he was taking the opportunity to charge up everything. He activated the satphone and dialed a now familiar number, checking his watch to see what time it was at Langley. The phone rang, picking up on the third ring.

"Hello?"

"Hey old buddy, how's it hanging?"

There was a pause as he knew his friend Chris Leroux would be trying to figure out a way to respond without giving away who it was. He had known Leroux since high school, Leroux a nerd two years his junior that had tutored Kane in his final two years, getting his grades high enough for college, and in exchange Kane had protected Leroux from the bullies. They had become friends, but lost touch after school.

Kane had only attended college for a year, dropping out in his second year, almost immediately after 9/11, joining the army after a long heart-to-heart with his archeology professor, James Acton, a man whose CIA file was over an inch thick and incredibly interesting reading. He had gone Delta eventually, then CIA Special Ops. Leroux on the other hand had completed college, then been approached by the CIA after passing some aptitude tests with flying colors. He was now one of their top analysts with the ear of the Director.

Neither had realized the other was in the CIA until a chance encounter at Langley, and their friendship had been rekindled. In fact, Kane considered Leroux one of his best friends, if not his best friend, the nature of this business making it almost impossible to make close friends. It meant constantly lying to them about what you did, where you were, how you got that cut, why you were so tanned.

It felt like a holiday with his family, forced to constantly lie.

With Leroux it was different since he knew exactly what Kane did. He could be more open with him, not hiding who he was. He didn't talk missions of course, but at least could honestly say the ringing in his left ear was due to a grenade rather than a Linkin Park concert.

"Hi, umm, it's hanging fine? Ah, you? I mean, yours?"

Kane laughed, loving the awkwardness of the still developing Leroux. He had a stunning girlfriend, CIA Agent Sherrie White who was the exact opposite of Leroux—outgoing, personable, fun. She had fallen for him and they were now living together, her personality slowly pulling Leroux out of his lonely hole of bachelorhood, self-imposed due to extreme shyness. He was a good looking kid, just never been kissed—at least not enough for a man his age.

Sherrie certainly took care of that!

"Fine. Listen, I need a favor from you. I've already sent in a secure packet for analysis, but I need the best. How's your schedule?"

He heard giggling in the background and the sounds of an embarrassed Leroux shushing Sherrie who apparently was checking the hanging status of something.

"Open enough, I guess," managed Leroux between grunts, giggles and protests.

Kane grinned.

"How about you take care of business there first otherwise you won't be able to concentrate. Get back to me through secure channels when you have something for me."

"Hey! Not while I'm on the phone!" came a muffled protest, the phone mouthpiece not properly covered. The sound of a hand uncovering the phone had Kane wondering exactly what was going on, a little jealous of the action his friend was apparently getting.

Get it while you can buddy! I've been holed up in Chechnya with nada available!

"I'll get back to you as soon as I can," said Leroux.

"Okay, thanks buddy, bye."

Kane killed the call to free up his friend and his libido, placing the phone back on the table, then dropped on the bed, the squeaking of the metal springs loud and disturbing, this being a fairly dry climate.

Within minutes he was asleep, his mind a turmoil of thoughts on what Crimson Rush might be, then turning to the cute Chechen girl, her mother nowhere to be found.

Sheremetyevo International Airport
Moscow, Union of Soviet Socialist Republics (USSR)
February 6, 1982

Alex West, CIA Special Agent, or spy for lack of a better word, shuffled along the long line of those waiting to clear customs at Moscow's Sheremetyevo International Airport, his Aeroflot Ilyushin Il-86 four engine wide body having landed about forty minutes before. He had his suitcase and carry-on with him, and his ass was killing him from the threadbare seats he had been forced to endure, the cushion flattened down to the metal frame.

Soviet superiority my ass.

Ten years ago it wouldn't have bothered him, but now in his mid-forties, he knew he was reaching the end of his useful life as a spy. He kept himself in top physical shape, that was essential, but he knew it was just a matter of time before the old bones just couldn't keep up with the young ones they were competing with.

The line shuffled forward.

His disguise was simple. Look exactly the same as he had every other time he'd been here. Trying to disguise yourself like in the movies was dangerous. Very dangerous. If you were pulled aside, explaining false mustaches, dyed eyebrows and cotton stuffed cheeks was difficult. But a well-crafted background identity, consistent mannerisms, and confidence with zero arrogance would get you through almost every time.

The KGB usually knew who you were when you came through, it was the customs guys you didn't want blowing your entry. The KGB didn't want them blowing your entry either—they wanted to know what the hell you were up to.

He reached the kiosk and handed over his papers, a perfectly forged Canadian passport and a perfectly valid Soviet Visa, a detailed itinerary showing hotel, planned meetings, etc, and a thin smile without a trace of worry on his face. He'd been here dozens of times, using this same passport, and the same cover story.

"Your purpose here in the Soviet Union, Mr. West?"

The accent was as thick as the man's mustache, and rather than answer him in Russian, which West spoke perfectly with a trace of an Odessan accent, he stuck to English, his cover unilingual.

"Business, and I hope to squeeze a little bit of pleasure in of course," he replied.

"And what type of business are you here to conduct?"

"I represent a company that sells farm equipment. I do a lot of business with your government, especially around this time of year when we're nearing planting season."

"And you feel your equipment is superior to our Soviet designs?"

West knew he was being baited. Less experienced agents quite often tripped up here, sending themselves down a path that attracted attention, too eager to avoid offending and raising suspicions.

"Absolutely. Our company is famous across the world for its farm equipment. Our latest combine is capable of clearing more acres of—"

"And what type of pleasure do you wish to 'squeeze' in while you are here?"

"Some of your fine cuisine, perhaps a visit to the ballet if possible. No one can match your dancers."

"It appears we agree on one thing, Mr. West."

And with that a large stamp was slammed against his passport and other documents, and he was waved on. West took the documents and nodded, not saying another word as he pulled his luggage through the airport and out to where a limited number of cabs waited, mostly first generation Volga GAZ-24's with an easy to hose down all vinyl interior that oozed comfort, their lime yellow paint job with heavy chrome a pale imitation of the yellow cabs of New York City. Looking about at the drab Moscow streets that greeted him, any color nature might have provided pushed south by the harsh winter, he wondered if the country even had yellow paint.

He tapped on the trunk of an idling cab and it popped, the driver staying inside the warmth of the vehicle. West placed his bags in the trunk, slammed the lid shut then climbed in the back of the vehicle, already thankful for the semi-warm interior, the heaters in these barely adequate by North American standards.

He was asked where he wanted to go in Russian, but since his cover had no clue what was said, he replied, "Do you speak English?"

"Da," replied the gruff voice, the man occupying the front seat large, bearded and weathered, his skin a thick leather from decades of lye-based soaps, inadequate insulation and a cold and lonely job.

"Berlin Hotel, please."

The man nodded, a slight smile creasing the leather as he realized he might be in for a large tip, the hotel one of the finer ones available, only used by the Party elite and foreign visitors. It used to be called the Savoy, but the Party had it renamed to cater to wealthy Germans and Austrians. The same Party members wouldn't tip him should they grace his cab rather than take an official car, but tourists and foreign businessmen were in the habit, quite often taking pity on the poor souls relegated to this side of the Iron Curtain.

"Very nice place, da?" asked the man as the cab pulled from the curb and into the barely existent traffic.

"Yes it is."

"You've been there before?"

West looked at the reflection in the rearview mirror, nodding.

"Many times."

"You important business man, da?"

West chuckled, shaking his head.

"Business man, yes. Important, no."

As they turned on to Volokolamskoye Highway the cab driver glanced in his side mirror, then his rearview and became silent for a moment, glancing between his passenger and the mirrors.

"I think you're more important than you think you are," muttered the man in Russian.

"Sorry?"

"Ah, nothing," replied the now nervous man. "We almost there, I get you there in good time."

West shifted slightly in his seat so he could see through the side mirror without making it obvious. A black sedan, standard issue KGB, was behind them, the same one he had seen pull out after them from the airport.

He had successfully acquired his tail.

Now all he had to do was lose them.

CIA analyst Chris Leroux held his right hand out, watching it shake slightly. His Red Bull habit was back with a vengeance. It had been fueling him since the New Orleans crisis, allowing him to put in extra hours on his delayed assignment to find out who The Assembly were, and what they were up to. What he did know was that The Assembly was an ultra-secret organization made up of senior corporate executives as well as government officials, including elected politicians, some voluntarily, some coerced.

They claimed to be the puppet masters pulling the strings of society, and claimed it was for a long time.

It was why he had a 24/7 security detail, and why he was working late nights. He had an accidental breakthrough during the New Orleans crisis when the President essentially suspended the Constitution, allowing all taps to be opened without warrant requirements. His automated searches had been working behind the scenes, constantly seeking out any mention of The Assembly or the few things they knew this organization had been involved with and the few people, all dead, that had ties.

The searches had produced nothing until the blocks had been lifted.

After the crisis when he examined his files he had found a single hit but hadn't opened it. He knew if he did, and it went to court, the evidence would be tossed due to the lack of a warrant.

His boss, National Clandestine Service Chief for the CIA, Leif Morrison, had told him to ignore it, fruit of the poisoned tree. He wanted to take down the network legally. Leroux hadn't said anything, his personality not one to challenge, but felt it was a mistake. It was more important to take them *out*, not take them to court.

Kane would have opened the attachment.

Leroux, hand still shaking, flipped over to his secure email and clicked on the email in question, highlighting it in the long list of false positives.

Open it!

His finger hovered over the mouse button, shaking, spasm after spasm urging him to click, fake an accidental click, do something.

Take action!

His computer beeped with a tone indicating something urgent had just arrived for him. Sighing, he flipped over to his main Inbox and saw the email containing the results of his search Kane had requested. His heart pounded a little faster as he opened it and began to read.

By the time he was finished reading the single hit found in the archival database, his heart was slamming in his chest. He leaned back in his chair, sweat having broken out on his forehead. He wiped it with the back of his hand, then his hand on his pants as he mentally processed what he had just read.

Why is Kane asking about Crimson Rush?

He knew he was on an op, and that it was classified as per usual, but he knew enough from the other intel requests he had seen that it seemed to be Chechen related, except for one group of Russian ID requests that was almost immediately followed by a reprioritization.

And now he knew why.

"Holy shit!" he muttered.

"What?"

His head spun toward the voice as his fingers instinctively raced for the keyboard to blank the screen, his brain not yet registering the voice belonged to his girlfriend. He smiled at her, his fingers still doing their job as he spun his chair toward the love of his life. In fact, she was the only woman he had ever loved. And the only woman he had ever really been "with" if you didn't count the couple of pity "dates" he had been on years ago. He was a late bloomer, and probably never would have bloomed if it weren't for this incredible woman who had taken a chance on a dork, thanks in no small part to his best friend, and perhaps his only friend, Dylan Kane.

It had been a lonely life.

He raised his chin as Agent Sherrie White leaned in for a kiss. But instead of their lips meeting, she gave him a gentle smack on his cheek, wagging a finger at him then pointing at the half-empty can of Red Bull.

"How many is that today?"

Leroux flushed.

"Do you mean since we came in this morning, or since midnight last night?"

"You mean there's been enough to actually warrant a different count?"

He shrugged.

She dropped in the spare chair in his cubicle.

"I thought you were going to stop?"

"It's a hard habit to break," he replied, his eyes bouncing around the office, finally settling on her breasts for a moment, then her face. Sherrie pointed at her breasts.

"Until you quit, this treasure chest is off limits."

His eyebrows shot up as his eyes dropped to where she was pointing, just to be certain she wasn't talking about some other chest. Then the question begged to be asked if the quarantine included other bits and pieces. He opened his mouth.

"And yes, that includes everything." She leaned over and squeezed his leg, causing a twitch. "That's all the sugar you get until you're off the energy drinks."

His shoulders slumped. He eyed the can, sleek and narrow, the grey and blue longtime friends to a lonely existence occupied in an office that fed off of people like him, willing to go above and beyond the call of duty and devote their lives to the organization not due to patriotism, but due to a lack of better options. Those doing it were mostly young, male and single.

It had sucked.

And he hadn't realized how badly it had sucked until Sherrie was in his life.

"Fine," he said, not wanting to lose the nookie over a drink. "I won't touch the stuff again."

She smiled, satisfied.

"Good." She motioned toward the locked screens with her chin.

"Same old stuff?" she asked, privy to his long term assignment.

"No, something for a friend."

She knew immediately who he was talking about.

And only nodded, knowing she wasn't cleared for the intel.

"Then I'll leave you to it," she replied, leaning in and faking him out on a kiss, instead turning her head at the last moment so his lips met her cheek. She picked up the can, wagging it at him between her thumb and forefinger. "Don't forget. You drinkie, no nookie."

He shook his head with an awkward smile, still not certain how to respond in these types of situations.

"I promise."

She bounced on her toes.

"Good!"

She winked and left him alone, his response apparently appropriate. A quick glance at his watch told him he had about two hours before the caffeine crash would hit him. Fortunately that was about the time his shift was over and they'd be heading home.

Unless Kane needs me.

He forwarded the intel to his friend, his thoughts of Sherrie pushed to the background as the intel he had just read flooded back. The implications were terrifying. The terrorist potential was massive. It was a worst case scenario type threat. The question was why were the Russians selling it to Chechen rebels? They were enemies in the post-Soviet era.

He didn't have answers, and he didn't know who knew what he now knew. It was time to see the Director.

If the Homeland Security Advisory System was still in effect, we'd be at Red for sure.

As if the world were reading his mind, an alarm sounded, a single harsh pulse of what mimicked a klaxon. He had never heard it before, and had hoped to never hear it in his lifetime. He knew what it was, they all knew what it was as the entire office stood.

The Defense Readiness Condition or DEFCON indicator on the wall at the front of the large room crammed with analysts was flashing, the blue "Normal Readiness" indicator of 5 no longer lit, the green indicator of 4 now flashing—"Above Normal Readiness".

Jesus Christ! Someone does have Crimson Rush!

Berlin Hotel (Formerly Savoy), Moscow, USSR
February 6, 1982

Alex West lay on his fairly comfortable bed, the mattress far better than many of the flea bags he had stayed in over his career. He was completely naked, his legs spread, his arms spread, as he examined the room without moving. He knew for certain there were listening devices. The question was whether or not there were cameras as well. His in the buff spread-eagle display was designed to cause those who might be observing to look away from the camera.

Men don't stare at naked men, even when ordered to.

They look away, which meant his close observation of the room from his vantage point might just not be noticed, and instead excused as a man relaxing after a long shower and an even longer journey. And a generous amount of vodka. The ceiling was plaster and solid, a white dulled into a dark cream from years of cigarette smoke, the lone light overhead, its brass fixture in need of polishing touched recently, but with one of the three bulbs shining brighter than the others, he assumed maintenance. The light was still an option, but it was such an obvious option, he felt no self-respecting spy agency would use it.

No, he was looking for something that would give coverage to the entire room, but not easily discoverable like the camera in the bathroom, his long, hot shower having revealed a difference in the fog on the mirror where the camera was hidden. A shaving cream accident covered it up for a minute while he had scanned the bathroom for listening devices with his modified transistor radio.

It had whistled at the ceiling light.

Now the game in the main room, examining everything carefully from a distance, narrowing down the list he'd have to check more closely. The advantage he had over looking for listening devices was there was no way to transmit a video signal without a device far too large to hide in small places. Audio was easily transmittable, but video? Nope.

Perhaps one day?

Which meant any video device would need a wire, and that wire meant it had to be either in the walls or close to the walls.

There was an impressive painting over the headboard which would be a prime candidate for hotel room shenanigans to be taped, but again an obvious choice. He reached down with one hand and scratched his kibbles and bits as he reached with the other arm and stretched up, pulling the painting out from the wall a bit.

Nothing.

Reaching up with the other hand, he duplicated the stretch to avoid suspicion, then turned his attention to the one other painting on the wall, a typical Soviet style piece showing a worker toiling in the field, a young child handing a water filled ladle to the man, a woman in the background hauling a bundle of hand-reaped wheat over her shoulder, all with smiles.

All for one and one for all.

He wondered if Dumas had even conceived of communism when he coined the now famous phrase that could so aptly describe the political system that by its very nature was impossible to implement.

There are always leaders, therefore some will always be more equal than others.

He stood, pouring himself a vodka, the bottle requested upon arrival. He had had a few sips to numb the damage the flight had done, then brought it into the shower with him, making a show of tipping the bottle up so any camera could see it above the shower curtain, but in reality letting it dribble out of his mouth as he rinsed.

He also let the water fill the bottle, reducing the potency of what remained. At this point his observers would assume he was three quarters of the way into their national sport, and any odd behavior, such as lying naked on the bed and scratching yourself, could be excused.

Swirling the wheat-based rather than potato-based alcohol in his crystal glass, he having opted for a finer quality his cover enjoyed, he took a swig of the now extremely weak mix, eyeing the painting with interest, focusing on the man and girl, but letting his peripheral vision do the walking of the rest of the large piece of artwork and frame.

There it is.

Upper left corner, a hole in the ornate frame, perhaps half an inch in diameter, stood out to the expert eye, the reflective surface of the lens making it even more obvious once spotted.

"I think you need wh-wh-one of my tractor's," he said to the man in the painting, his knees shaking, his body wavering back and forth as he tried to keep balance, his words slurred and stammered just enough. "That way you c-c-could shpend more time with yer faamlee." He held up his glass, toasting the man. "To Mother Russia! Pro-Pro-Prost!" He took another swig then stopped, a curious expression on his face. "Wait. Ish Prosht Ru-Ru-Russian or Ger-German?" His eyebrows narrowed. "What, you don't know?"

He stumbled into the painting, shoving it up and pulling it from the wall, dropping his glass and landing with the painting covering his upper body.

"Sh-shit!" he exclaimed, pushing the painting off, the corner of his eye catching the now dangling camera hanging from the wall. He stumbled to his feet, lifting the painting and keeping it between him and the wall at all times so anyone still watching would assume he never saw the camera. He lifted the painting higher than the hooks in the wall, then slowly lowered it until the wire snagged.

He left it crooked, the camera now behind the painting, its view completely blocked by the canvas.

"That sh-should d-do it."

He turned the light out then stumbled back to the bed, collapsing on it, and began to snore.

One obstacle down.

CIA Headquarters, Langley, Virginia
Present Day

Leif Morrison, National Clandestine Service Chief for the CIA, read the latest update on Dylan Kane's mission while one of his top analysts, Chris Leroux, sat by all outward appearances impatiently. Kane was one of the best he had, if not *the* best, that distinction in this business usually fleeting—the better you were, the more difficult the missions, the more likely to be injured with no hope of returning to active duty, or worse, killed.

For someone like Kane, he'd probably prefer death.

Kane was pure warrior and Morrison knew his jacket like the back of his hand. Tutored through high school by the younger Leroux, football scholarship to St. Paul's, then a year later 9/11. Joined the army right away, worked his way quickly to Sergeant and immediately applied to Delta, where he again excelled. He had been offered a chance—a chance jumped at—to join the Special Operations Group and their elite Special Activities Division within the CIA.

And he had excelled.

He was a loner, minimal friends, not very close with his family—not estranged, simply not the type that needed to call constantly or visit all the time.

His cover with them, insurance investigator with Shaw's of London was perfect. It had him travelling the globe, excused him with his family, and allowed him to establish his bona fides in every major city in the world.

But his current mission had stumbled on something that didn't make sense. Why would the former commander of the Soviet nuclear arsenal be involved with a Chechen drug lord? Why were massive amounts of funds transferred to this General in exchange for a memory stick? What was on that memory stick? And what the hell was Crimson Rush?

He looked at Leroux.

"What have you got for me?"

"I found out what Crimson Rush is."

And when Morrison heard his young analyst's report, he felt himself weaken noticeably as his blood pressure dropped.

"This is now your top priority. I have to contact Washington." He pointed at the door, Leroux jumping to his feet as Morrison hit the speed dial for the Director of National Intelligence.

"Lou, it's Leif. I've got something that can't wait for the President's Daily Brief. Intelligence is thin, but he's going to want to know about it now rather than tomorrow morning."

"NSA is already hot about that Crimson Rush thing your guy stumbled on. They already convinced the President to go to DEFCON Four under the assumption our ex-General just sold nuclear launch or detonation codes to Islamists. I assume this is about that?" asked Lou Tenet, the man responsible for delivering the daily report to the President covering essentially every threat known to the country.

"Yes it is. But we now know what Crimson Rush might actually be."

Three minutes later Morrison was headed to a meeting with the President.

Berlin Hotel (Formerly Savoy), Moscow, USSR
February 6, 1982

The snore erupting from Alex West's throat was steady, heavy and a perfectly controlled imitation of how he sounded when drunk and passed out. Yes, he had taped it and practiced it until perfected. And he could control the volume if necessary. He reached slowly up to his nightstand, pushing the play button on his Sony Walkman with external speakers, power source and the all-important auto-reverse. The volume was already preset, the 90 minute cassette cued up, and immediately snoring burst from the speakers at the exact same volume he had been faking.

He swung quietly from the bed and with the snoring playing smoothly from the speakers, and the tape designed to have him suffer from a little sleep apnea to cover the delays when the tape would reverse at the end of the 45 minutes, it should buy him plenty of time.

Hopefully all he'd need if he were lucky.

He quickly dressed, all in black, a pair of specially designed dress shoes with the latest soles designed for grip and retractable studs ideal for running on icy Soviet streets, leather gloves, wrap around glasses to protect from the elements, and a Russian style Ushanka hat, a patriotic hammer and sickle carefully embroidered in the center. Gun, originally hidden disassembled in his Walkman speakers, utility belt and papers completed his ensemble.

He looked down at Rozhdestvenka Street, poorly lit compared to North American standards, but typically sparse by European expectations. His escort vehicle sat across the street, the occupants not concerned about the tailpipe exhaust giving away their presence in the cold night, the vapors obvious.

37

They would be watching the front entrance, and most likely would have been told of what had just happened in his room, and the fact he was passed out drunk.

If they bought the ruse.

Having already checked the window when he first arrived for wires, he turned the knob and pushed the window out, quickly stepping onto the ledge that rimmed each floor. Shuffling aside, he closed the window, glancing down at the car.

No movement.

He glanced to his left then his right, deciding to proceed that way, there only being three rooms to pass in front of before he could climb a drainpipe to the roof. Inching along the less than foot wide row of stonework, he worked his gloved fingers into any groove or handhold he could find. The slow progress was painful, and with the cold rapidly working its way through his clothing, his fingers became numb.

The first window came far too slowly for his liking, but thankfully the curtains were closed. He shuffled past, the ledge slightly larger at the windows, and continued to the next. His toes were frozen, his fingers barely feeling the brickwork he was grabbing. He had done this before, but never on a night this cold.

It must be some sort of record cold snap.

A car door opened below just as he stepped in front of the next window. He froze, looking down to see one of his shadows rushing across the street. He pressed himself against the window, the ledge giving him some extra cover, but all it would take would be a quick glance up to curse the snow and he would be spotted.

Unless of course he was already spotted and this wasn't just a piss break.

But it was one man. Surely they both would be leaving the car to chase him down if they had spotted him.

Unless one is going to watch you from the warmth of the car until he needs to get out.

The thought had his heart pumping a little faster as his mind raced to a decision—return to his room before his KGB escort arrived, or take a chance and continue on.

Shuffling to the right, his jacket buttons scraped the window as he tried to keep out of sight.

He winced at the sound, impossibly loud in the still of the night.

A quick look down showed his escort was already inside, the car still idling quietly across the street.

Suddenly the curtains flew open, light pouring out into the near pitch black. He spun on his right toe, kicking out and flipping away from the window and onto the ledge next to it, his back pressed against the wall, his left foot finding its footing just as his right heel was about to lose its. His left hand slapped against the wall, his ice cold fingers grasping for something to hold onto while his right flipped around, trying to hold onto the corner of the stone frame of the window.

His heart slammed in his chest as he felt himself beginning to tip forward, away from the wall. He arched back as hard as he could, his left hand still grabbing for anything, when he felt something through the numbness. He squeezed his hand, grabbing whatever it was, his head spinning to see what it might be.

A cable.

His fingers grabbed hold with all the strength they had remaining as the window beside him opened. He spun around again, this time on his left heel, his right foot and arm swinging out from the wall, all that was now keeping him from falling to an ignominious death the thin wire stretching over his head to he assumed the roof.

"I know I heard something," said a man's voice in Russian.

"Come back to bed, Grigori!" protested a woman. "You're letting all the cold in!"

"But I heard something!"

West slapped against the wall, both feet now on the ledge, his right hand reaching out to the edge of the next window, his balance finally steady.

"I heard it again!" exclaimed the man.

West pressed against the wall, praying his dark clothes and the frigid night would discourage any prolonged search.

"Grigori, come in this instant or there is no sugar for you tonight!"

"Fine!" yelled the man, adding with a mutter something in Russian that couldn't be translated into English without losing the true depth of the insult. West just hoped the woman never followed through on her threat or she might find herself in a lot of pain.

West continued to pass the third window uneventfully and soon reached the drainpipe wedged into a corner. Straddling the ledge on both sides, he rubbed his gloved hands together trying to coax some feeling into them with little success.

Now or never.

He grabbed on and began to climb the two floors to the roof. The pipe seemed to hold, but a slight play had him a little concerned, and as he rested on the next ledge he saw why. The bolts holding the clamp that secured the pipe to the wall were loose above him. They hadn't been last time, he was sure of it. It made him wonder if he perhaps had loosened them by accident last time he did this, pulling them from the wall slightly, if another person in his profession had done it just as accidentally, or if they were purposefully loosened to make climbing impossible.

He wouldn't put it past the KGB to do something sneaky like that.

"Look! There he is!" yelled a voice below him. His head whipped toward the too close voice and he spotted the man from earlier, his head poking out his room window, pointing. "I told you I heard something!" A woman's head quickly followed, joining in the shouting and pointing. He looked at the car and saw a window roll down.

Shit!

He scrambled up the loose pipe, praying it would hold, when suddenly there was a creaking sound of metal bending. He thrust up with his right hand, grabbing the raised lip at the top, pulling with all his might as he heard a car door open below, the shouts continuing. With another heroic lunge he transferred his left hand to the roof, pulling himself up and flipping over onto the large, flat lip that ringed the hotel. A quick peak over the side saw his second shadow exiting his vehicle, joined by the first who had just returned, looking up at the roof. He knew there was no way they could see him up here, it too dark, but he had little time to escape them should they decide to believe the slurred shouts of a couple in post-coital bliss.

Snaking along the lip, he crawled on his belly toward the corner, rounded the bend, then looked over the side again to see no one following. He leapt to his feet and scurried to the back of the hotel, slid quickly down another drainpipe at the rear, this one still secure, and hit the ground at a run, sprinting toward the service entrance of the hotel. He skid to a halt just short of the door, the master power switch to the entire building behind a locked utility box. He quickly picked the lock, his numb fingers barely functioning, and pulled the dull grey door aside. He loosened all the old ceramic fuses he knew from past experience were for the floor lights, then yanked down the master switch.

He closed the panel then pulled open the service entrance door, plunging into the confusion inside, several voices cursing in the dark. Running blindly forward toward the door he knew was at the other side of the vast storage area, he collided headlong into a confused employee who

41

from the sounds of what West heard smacked hard onto the concrete floor, expletives erupting from his mouth as West struggled to keep his bearings. Pushing on, he reached the door without any additional encounters and pulled it open. Outside even more confusion reigned, the odd candle already lit by on-the-ball staff used to Moscow's occasional blackouts, especially during winter storms, the only sign of order.

From his vantage point he could see the front lobby and his two shadows rushing through the swinging front doors. He ran to his left, his hand trailing the wall, counting off the doors until he reached the third one. He pulled open the door and entered a completely dark stairwell, emergency lighting apparently not something required in Moscow hotels. He counted the flights until he reached his floor, the sound of the door below him opening, footfalls hammering on the stairs causing him to slow his pace the last flight lest they hear his own.

Pressing on the bar to open the door as quietly as possible, he stepped through then gently pushed the door closed. He sprinted toward his door, his key already out. Feeling around for the lock, he pushed the key inside, yanked the door open and closed it behind him with a silent push as the snoring from his tape recorder filled his ears. The sound of the stairwell door opening had his heart slamming into his chest.

He rushed toward the bed, yanking his clothes off, tossing them into a pile, stripping down naked, his numb fingers barely able to untie the laces on his shoes.

Hammering at his door began and he gave up, simply yanking them off and shoving them under the bed. He grabbed the rest of his snow covered clothes and piled them on the chair by the window, shoving it open slightly, wind and snow whistling in, hopefully explaining away the reason they weren't dry.

A shoulder slammed into the door.

He jumped for the Walkman, now running on batteries, hitting the stop button, his own snoring replacing it none-too-steadily, his chest heaving from his efforts. Rushing around the end of the bed, he dropped onto it, his knees on the floor, his ass exposed to his visitors as they burst through the door, flashlights in hand, he draped over the bed, snoring.

"He's here!" whispered one to the other.

"Impossible!"

"Look!"

"That's disgusting. Has he no shame?"

"American, what do you expect?"

West continued his snoring as the men entered the room, quickly checking the bathroom then the closets.

"Where are his clothes?" asked the first.

"By the window."

Footsteps went to the chair.

"They're wet!"

"So he *was* out!"

A gust of wind blew the drapes.

"Shit! His window is open."

"So?"

"Snow is coming in. They could be wet just from that."

"What should we do?"

"Get out of here before he wakes up."

"Should we fix the camera?"

"In the dark?"

West shifted his position, changing his snore as if he were about to wake up.

"Let's get out of here!" said the one closest to the door in a harsh whisper.

The other man didn't reply but West could hear the footsteps walk past him, then the door close behind them.

West jumped up, reactivating the Walkman then quickly got dressed. He listened at the door and heard nothing, then quietly opened it, peeking out. It appeared clear; at least of flashlight toting KGB. He made for the stairs then opened the door gently, hearing footfalls below as the KGB men cleared the last couple of flights, their voices echoing up the steps as they commented on his naked display.

"He better hope he doesn't end up in Siberia," said one. "With an ass that pretty, he's sure to be popular!"

The comedian roared in laughter at his own joke, the other joining in as the door at the bottom floor was pushed open. West waited for the door to close then burst into the stairwell, racing down the steps as fast as he dared, there still no light. He counted off the flights and as he neared the second floor he saw a light go on far above him.

They're fixing the fuses!

Floor after floor turned on above him as he cleared the last few steps. Shoving the door open he stepped into the hallway off the lobby then made for the rear exit, tipping his hat at a staff member holding a candle and the door open for him. The lobby was suddenly flooded in light as West stepped out into the cold Moscow night, free of his tail.

Crossroads Center, Falls Church, Virginia
Present Day

Chris Leroux held Sherrie's hand as she dragged him to the third shoe store in the past hour. He looked longingly at the benches occupied by men far older and far wiser than him, waiting for their wives while girl watching.

Right now I'd rather be a dirty old man.

He hated shopping. With a passion. His idea of a shopping spree was hopping on Amazon and buying half a dozen Blu-Rays, some songs off of iTunes and an Extravaganza pan pizza from dominos.com. He couldn't remember the last time he had done that. Certainly not since Sherrie had entered his life.

Between her and his security detail he no longer had any privacy. When she was off on a mission, he missed her, but didn't get his downtime since his detail was just outside, monitoring every delivery, doing God knows what with his privacy. They said they weren't monitoring his communications, but working for the CIA made him paranoid, since he knew what his own employer was capable of.

But this evening he was tired. He was coming down from his Red Bull rush and just wanted to sleep. But Sherrie was energized, heading out on an op in the middle of the night, and needing a new pair of heels for an undercover part of the operation.

I wonder if she has to romance these guys?

He felt his stomach flip at the thought of her with another man, kissing him, touching him, making love to him. He shook his head, trying to rid it of the thought.

"What's wrong?"

"Umm, nothing."

"Bullshit. Something's on your mind."

"Just your op, I guess."

"Uh huh." She didn't sound convinced. "It's the heels, isn't it?"

He looked away.

"Thought so." She stopped, pulling him toward her. "I modified my profile after we got together."

"What do you mean?"

"My profile no longer indicates I'm willing to have sex with a target."

Leroux felt his heart race slightly, his stomach doing unknown things as his mind tried to process the fact that she *had* been willing to, and that now she wasn't. His mind flashed back to that first night she had put the moves on him, testing him as an agent, he the mark.

So she would have went all the way?

Twitch.

He was happy she hadn't, or rather *he* hadn't, otherwise there was no way this current relationship could have happened. And now that he knew she had taken sex out of the spy equation, he had to admit it did make him feel better. Obviously the relationship was important to her, and she was a one man woman.

She put her hand on his cheek.

"You okay?"

He nodded, blushing slightly.

"I guess I'm just a little insecure," he muttered, looking anywhere but at her.

She pulled him down a bit and planted a loving, soft kiss on him.

"That's one of the many reasons I love you." She pointed at a vacant bench across from the store. "Now, why don't you wait there for me while I shop. I'm sure this is boring you to death."

"No, it's okay—"

"I'm a spy, trained to spot lies. Go sit."

He smiled at her and followed her orders, sitting on one side of the bench, watching her disappear amongst thousands of shoes.

"I'll never understand women's obsession with shoes."

Leroux nearly jumped, his head spinning toward the voice, finding an old man, probably seventies, sitting at the other end of the bench.

How the hell did he get there?

"Huh?"

"Women? Shoes? Obsession?" He motioned toward the store where Sherrie was, her head popping up, waving at Leroux.

The old man returned the wave.

"She's beautiful."

"Yeah," murmured Leroux, not sure what to say.

"How'd you meet her?"

It wasn't that Leroux was sure he didn't want this conversation, it was the varying degrees of how sure he was that made his response difficult. He went for his traditional route.

Complete and utter capitulation.

"Work."

"What kind of work?"

"Umm, government. Just a paper pusher."

The man frowned, looking back at the store.

"There's no way she's a paper pusher."

Leroux shrugged, not sure what to say.

"You need to work on your conversation skills, sonny. Increase the repertoire, practice in a mirror if you have to. You'll get better at it the more you get out and expose yourself to the world."

Who the hell are you?

He wanted to scream it, to demand it, but in reality he just wanted to shrink deeper into the rabbit hole that had become his life, escaping all the life he knew in the hopes he might find something better on the other side. Unfortunately he had wished that before, and realized that it always resulted in mixed blessings. His life now was completely different. He had a girlfriend who was way out of his league, but a life that was far more dangerous than it had ever been.

And old men asking him inappropriate questions and making even more inappropriate observations on his life.

"I guess you're right," he replied.

"Can I give you some advice?"

"I thought you just did."

The man smiled, turning on the bench to face him a little more.

"See, you're already getting better," smiled the man. "Let me give you some more free advice."

"What's that?"

"Tell your security detail that sunglasses inside a mall while wearing suits is so blatantly obvious that if they were working the agency in my day, the commies would have picked them out in a heartbeat."

Leroux's stomach squelched, his bladder and sphincter loosening, thankfully having nothing to let loose. He grabbed the bench with both hands, squeezing hard as he tried to keep from fainting, the sudden drop in blood pressure almost overwhelming him.

"You okay, sonny?"

Leroux ignored the words, instead focusing on the voice. He closed his eyes, then opened them, staring at a black scrape from a shoe on the tile floor as his world regained focus.

"H-how—" He cut himself off, realizing he had just confirmed to the old man that he was right. Suddenly he had his focus back. He turned to the man. "Who the hell *are* you?"

"Now that's the question you should have asked several minutes ago," replied the man. "You *are* getting better at this." He looked over at one of Leroux's shadows. "Let's just say I'm part of the Grey Network."

"What's that?"

The man chuckled, shaking his head.

"You can look that one up if you have to, but you're a smart cookie from what I've been able to find out. You should be able to put two-and-two together."

Leroux's mind raced, suddenly realizing what the man meant. He was clearly an ex-spy, and his age meant he would have been long retired from the business. *Grey as in grey hair?*

"You mean a group of retired agents working together?"

The man pointed at him.

"Bingo, kid, you got it." He leaned in. "Now you're going to help me up, and I'm going to palm you a message that I don't want you being surprised about. When you get home and out of sight of your detail, you'll look at it, understood."

Leroux nodded.

"Oh, and go ahead and show it to your pretty girl, since I know you will anyway."

Leroux looked away.

"Now stand and help an old man up."

Leroux stood and helped the man to his feet. The man shook his hand, a piece of paper in his palm. Leroux closed his hand around it, nodding and smiling as the old man thanked him, then shuffled off looking far more frail than the handshake Leroux had just received would suggest.

He shoved his hand in his pocket, depositing the paper as Sherrie exited the shop sporting a bag and a smile.

"All set?" she asked.

He nodded.

"Who was that old man you were talking to?"

"You wouldn't believe me if I told you."

Her eyes narrowed and he shook his head.

"I'll explain when we get home."

As they walked to their car, his detail now painfully obvious to him, he found he eyed every retiree with suspicion.

Just how big is this Grey Network?

Then a better question popped in his mind, one he wouldn't be able to answer until he got home.

Was he a former agent with a message for me, or was he just some old man suffering from dementia?

Leroux picked up the pace slightly, eager to find out.

United States National Security Council Meeting
The Situation Room, The White House, Washington, D.C.

The President sat quietly, apparently contemplating what he had just heard. Morrison was impressed the Commander-in-Chief had managed to stop his jaw from dropping when told what Crimson Rush could be. They had all of course heard the rumors and accusations that the weapon existed, one Senator even displaying a mockup in outrage, but little attention had been paid. Certainly during the Cold War the weapon's existence was highly classified on both sides, the West essentially dismissing it, quietly informing the Soviets that if any such weapon should exist, and were deployed, it would be considered an act of war.

And that had been the end of it.

Or so everyone had thought.

It was a relic of a bygone era, of no concern to anyone except those ranting for political points, and certainly was no threat.

But now it looked like the weapon was absolutely real, that it had been deployed, and was now about to be activated by parties unknown.

It was a needle in the proverbial haystack.

"Can we find it?" asked the President.

"The question is how many are there," replied Lou Tenet. "Intelligence gathered after the collapse of the Soviet Union indicated perhaps over one thousand of these may have been built, and nearly as many deployed. If that's the case, we could be looking at anywhere from none to a thousand located anywhere in the continental United States or any number of our allies."

51

"We'll need to notify NATO," said Jack Hodges, the National Security Advisor.

"Again, can we find it *or* them?"

"I'm not optimistic, but finding even one could save thousands of lives. But that could merely be swatting a mosquito in the bayou—there's a thousand more to replace it," replied Tenet.

"We have to try," said Hodges. "We can't just let this happen, even if it's just one. Americans were furious with 9/11 when we didn't know anything concrete beforehand. Now we have this piece of intel, solid intel. If we don't act, our heads will be on spits."

The President cleared his throat and leaned forward.

"Ladies, gentlemen," he said, pausing to ensure all attention was on him. "We are talking nothing less than our country, and our way of life. Should Crimson Rush be real, and should it have been deployed and continue to be functional, in small numbers or large, we risk complete and utter chaos should it be used. Millions could die in the initial strike, millions more in the aftermath.

"We face a dilemma. We can ignore this completely, and hope it is nothing. We can quietly look into it so as not to cause a panic, or we can publicly look into it in an active, massive search. This will mean troops on our streets, press headaches, economic turmoil, and hoarding as the public panics.

"I agree this cannot be ignored, but I am not willing to cause a very real panic that would be more devastating than the imagined threat. I need more intel before I can make a decision."

Tenet looked several shades redder than usual.

Morrison leaned forward before the man said something he'd regret.

"We should begin to look at this from a Soviet mindset. They would have wanted to cause confusion, yes, but they weren't out for mass civilian casualties. They would be targeting military and government installations, command and control, communications, power, distribution. Their goal would have been to affect our ability to fight back, to delay our response. If we think in those terms, I think we can at least begin searching military and government installations; quietly so as not to induce panic. This will at least give us a head start should it become necessary to expand our search."

The President's fingers steepled in front of him as his head slowly bobbed up and down, his eyes staring at the table in front of him.

He looked up at Morrison.

"Proceed." He then pursed his lips. "And pick up this General Levkin for questioning. I want to know what the hell he gave our Chechen 'rebel'."

Morrison resisted the urge to pop his eyebrows up his forehead.

"As far as we know he's still on Russian soil protected by a well-trained detail. We can't exactly send our own Special Forces in."

"Then call in a favor. Have the Russians pick him up."

Morrison's face didn't reveal his opinion of that option.

"I'll take care of it," he replied, deciding the President didn't need to know how many laws he might be about to break.

On Route to Leroux Residence
Fairfax Towers, Falls Church, Virginia

"What's wrong with you?"

"Nothing."

Sherrie frowned at Leroux. He was jumpy and he knew it. He had a note burning a hole in his pocket that he knew had to deal with Kane and the recent DEFCON 4 alert that barely made any news coverage. It was being attributed to North Korean sabre rattling and simply a routine response. Impressive stock footage was shown on the news channels, enough to convince an uninformed, trusting public.

But Leroux was convinced this was dealing with Crimson Rush. Especially after reading the lone report he had managed to find that suggested what it might be, the report itself dismissed at the time by the higher ups as having "insufficient intel to be reliable".

Then why would they go to DEFCON 4?

"You can tell me," said Sherrie, placing her hand on his leg and giving it a gentle squeeze. "Is it something I did?" She sounded almost regretful.

He stole a quick glance at her as they came to a stop at a light.

"No, nothing to do with you," he said, giving her a slight smile. "I'll explain when we get home, okay?"

She nodded but he could tell she wasn't satisfied by the way she looked out the passenger side window.

Man, I suck at this!

Being a boyfriend was tough. A fulltime job he hadn't realized was so much work. Single life was far easier, albeit lonelier and with few benefits that outweighed the positives of having Sherrie in his life. He reached over and fed his fingers into her hair, giving the back of her neck a squeeze, removing it as traffic started up.

"Trust me, there's nothing wrong, not with us I mean. You'll know everything in five minutes."

She seemed to brighten slightly, instead turning the conversation to her new shoes and their schedule for the evening before she left on her op. He really liked that she had scheduled over an hour for "downtime" which was their code for hitting the sheets, couch, floor, shower, kitchen counter, or whatever surface they happened to find themselves against.

Way better than being single.

He parked and they waited for the all clear from the security detail, two of them entering the apartment ahead of them to make sure everything was copasetic. His phone beeped with the all-clear message and they entered the apartment, ignoring the detail. Leroux wondered what his neighbors thought, but since he barely ever saw them, they may not have even noticed strange men entering and leaving his apartment at all hours just before he arrived home.

And every time he waited for the all-clear, he thought of how much danger they really were in, the tension building until that signal arrived, unnoticed held breaths released with a gasp, clenched fists with nails digging painfully into flesh, opened.

Today was made worse by the knowledge he had some sort of top secret message in his pocket from some old dude who might be crazy or part of the CIA secret agent retirees association. He closed the apartment door as Sherrie spun toward him, clearly desperate to know what had him so much on edge.

He reached in his pocket and pulled out the piece of paper, folded in squares.

"What's that?"

"Remember the old man on the bench?"

She nodded.

"He gave me this. Claimed he was a spy, part of something called the Grey Network."

Sherrie's eyes narrowed as if she thought the entire idea crazy.

"You're sure he wasn't just playing a joke on you?"

"He seemed to know who I was and what I did, and picked our detail out with no problem."

This seemed to concern Sherrie as she motioned with her hand for him to open the paper.

"Let's see what this is," she said, her voice serious.

He unfolded the paper and placed it on the kitchen counter so they could both see.

"What is it?" asked Sherrie.

"Coordinates?"

There were four numbers, typewritten, literally. This wasn't from a printer, this was clearly an old style typewriter generated page. And below the numbers a short, simple message:

For your friend if he's interested in Crimson Rush.

"What's Crimson Rush?"

Leroux quickly explained the search request he had received from Kane, and the lone report he had found. She paled.

"This is huge!" she whispered, looking around nervously. "Do you really think this could be real?"

Leroux shrugged. "All I know is Kane was on an op, requested intel and was almost immediately retasked. And we went to DEFCON Four. If Crimson Rush is indeed in play, life as we know it could be over until this is stopped."

"Do you think they'll call up the National Guard?" asked Sherrie as she pulled out her smartphone and entered the coordinates. She showed him the results. "Germany."

"They'll have to. I can't see them not locking down the country," whispered Leroux, still not convinced that everything they said wasn't being listened to when they were here despite the agency's assurances. "Imagine if this got out to the public? There'd be mass panic, especially in the cities."

Sherrie nodded.

"You better get that message to Dylan right away."

"Are we sure they're coordinates?"

Sherrie shook her head.

"No, but I'm sure Dylan will know what to do when he sees the message."

Hotel Arena City, Grozny, Chechen Republic, Russian Federation

"What the hell am I supposed to do with this?" asked Dylan Kane aloud as he read the secure message from Leroux. The accompanying email was equally baffling. *Grey Network? Old man on a bench? Germany? DEFCON 4?* None of it made any sense.

And that assumes these are coordinates.

He punched them into his secure laptop and they zoomed in on an area of south-western Germany, the Black Forest. All he could see were trees, the canopy thick. If there was something on the ground, the trees were definitely hiding it.

But the message specifically mentioned Crimson Rush.

There was no way that was a coincidence, and no way anyone could have known about it without insider access. The fact that their internal search networks were tapped was concerning enough, but the fact this Grey Network had been able to act so swiftly, detecting the search, identifying the analyst and the requesting asset, and putting their own asset into play within hours was terrifyingly impressive.

Which meant it had to be taken seriously.

Germany?

If indeed these were coordinates it did make sense. A lot of the old Cold War spies retired to Germany, especially what was once West Germany, many of them having spent decades there before the Berlin Wall fell. It was home to them, America a distant memory for some, a way of life now foreign.

He opened the attachment for the briefing note Leroux had found, the lone mention of Crimson Rush he had so far been able to find. As Kane read the contents his heart rate picked up more than a few beats.

If this is in the hands of terrorists, we're in deep shit.

Using his secure phone he quickly booked a ticket to Moscow, the only destination available out of Grozny, and began to pack, his mission here no longer of any importance. If the intel he had just read was accurate, he had no doubt the nation's entire intelligence apparatus was reprioritizing.

Barr Lenin, Moscow, USSR
February 6, 1982

West sat in the darkest corner he could find, his back to the wall with a clear view of the door. He had used this place before, it making dive bars back home look classy. The windows were filthy, blackened by years of soot and pollution on one side, cigarette smoke and puke on the other. Lights were at a premium, most coated in a heavy filth causing the new ones to glare conspicuously. Fortunately those seemed to be focused over the bar, its wood scarred and chipped by years of abuse, mostly inflicted by Illya, the bartender who had worked the nightshift for as long as West had frequented the place.

Illya never acknowledged knowing West beyond bringing him a bottle of vodka and a glass. No words were exchanged, which was just the way West liked it. As usual he was pretending to be drunk, waiting for his contact to show, *if* he were going to show. West was pretty confident he'd be here, he almost always was, the man an habitual drunk who lived nearby.

Besides, he had slipped a note under the man's door then knocked long enough to hear noises from the other side as someone in the man's family awoke.

If Sergie wanted his payday, he'd be here.

It had been almost half an hour and West had to admit he was beginning to think Sergie had fallen back to sleep when the door opened and the bar's fifth patron entered, shaking the snow off as he scanned the bar. Eye contact was made and Sergie shuffled toward him, no need to fake being drunk, he clearly was.

60

He sat down without a word, motioning for a second glass to be brought. Illya smacked one down on the table, its cleaning pedigree in question, clearly not pleased to see Sergie. He returned to his perch behind the bar without saying a word. West wasn't sure if he had ever heard the man say a word in the decades he had been coming here.

He looked at Sergie.

"Why's he not happy with you?" he asked in English.

"I might have thrown up here last night. I can't remember."

"You really have a problem, my friend."

"I know," said the man, shrugging his shoulders. "It dulls the pain of my miserable existence. I live on the wrong side of an invisible curtain, forced to serve a state of equals while those around me enjoy more equal lives than I, with a bitch of a wife who hates me for it, and two ungrateful brats who constantly remind me I am a failure in a country that doesn't reward success." He drained his glass. "So yes, I have a drinking problem. One of many problems, this one at least bringing me some pleasure at times."

West couldn't argue with the man's logic, nor would he want to. This man's very condition made him vulnerable which made him valuable.

"Perhaps we can help each other," said West, sitting nonchalantly, his voice low, barely audible over the howling wind outside and the scratchy record playing at the bar, Tchaikovsky if he wasn't mistaken.

It's always Tchaikovsky.

"I think I am being watched, my friend. There is a car outside my apartment all the time, and I found a bug in my bedroom."

"Is it still there?"

"Yes."

"Good. Then all they will hear is your wife yelling at you. You never discuss business at home I assume."

Sergie shook his head emphatically.

"Never. I'm not a fool. That bitch would turn me in for a loaf of bread if she knew what I was doing."

"Good. The longer she hates you for your miserable life, the more believable it is that you aren't getting anything on the side." West paused for a moment, leaning in slightly. "What *are* you doing with the money?"

Sergie looked around cautiously then leaned forward, his voice even lower.

"I don't spend it, I keep it hidden somewhere for what you Americans call a 'rainy day'."

"Just how rainy a day are we talking about?"

"The moment I ever see a chance to get out of this country, I will take it."

"What about your family?"

"To hell with them," he said, leaning back then immediately lowering his voice as the bartender glanced in their direction. "They'd leave me to rot if they had a chance, so why shouldn't I?"

West pursed his lips, nodding slowly.

Sergie Tuzik was a perfect asset. A drunk who hated his life and his family and who didn't spend the money he was given in exchange for information. It made him almost above suspicion, but if he were under surveillance, it meant something had happened to put him on the KGB's radar.

Then again it could be paranoia. The KGB might have bugs in every apartment in the concrete grey slab Sergie lived in.

But West knew the KGB. They *were* paranoid, but with good reason. And they wouldn't hesitate to bug an entire building just for one man's apartment if they felt he might be a traitor. Sergie had access to information as part of his job. He had obviously kept his alcoholism out of the office, otherwise they most definitely would have revoked his security clearance and probably sent him to Siberia to dry out. The very fact his information continued to prove solid was why West continued to come back to him, time after time.

Sergie was *his* asset. He doubted the man would dare speak to another agent unless he knew West was dead and no longer available to provide money. A trust existed between the two of them that both would break if needed, this not a comrades-in-arms type bond, merely an acknowledgement between men of the risks both were taking.

"What is it you want this time?" asked Sergie, pushing the vodka glass aside, as if the extra few inches of distance would sober him up.

West paused as the record was flipped, the bar quiet for the first time since Sergie had arrived. The lonely tones resumed and West took a sip of his vodka, still on his first glass.

"We need to know what Crimson Rush is."

Sergie's eyebrows shot up as his eyes, glassy and red, burst into fiery orbs of fear. He shook his head repeatedly, pushing back from the table.

"Not that." He pulled his jacket on. "We cannot see each other again."

Rather than make a scene, West let the terrified man leave and finished his drink. He dropped some rubles on the table along with a sawbuck to ensure he'd be remembered next time and treated in the exact same way. With a nod to the bartender he stepped out into the now heavy snow and plodded after Sergie. He knew the man wouldn't get too far ahead in his condition, and it was essential he talk to him further.

Even if he couldn't catch up, he at least knew two things. One, Sergie knew what Crimson Rush was, and two, it was important enough to terrify the man, a man who had betrayed his country repeatedly by passing extremely sensitive information to the West. For him to be this scared Crimson Rush must be several orders of magnitude more important than anything so far.

Which meant much more money would be needed to grease the man's palms, or if it could be arranged, an extraction to the West and out of Mother Russia.

And if the man's hatred of his family were indeed genuine, then it would be far simpler to accomplish than moving four people including two children.

He could see Sergie ahead, stumbling through the snow, the treads on his boots seemingly bare as West strode confidently forward, his tread designed for just these conditions and now a special order from a custom design-house that any discerning customer could order, thus eliminating them as a CIA identifier.

"Sergie!" he called when he was close enough.

Sergie turned then tried to speed up, only to slip and fall on the ground with a curse. West caught up and helped him to his feet.

"What would it take for you to get me that information?"

Sergie couldn't make eye contact, but he was prepared for the question.

"You need to get me out of the Soviet Union."

"Done."

Sergie's eyebrows shot up.

"And my family."

It was West's turn.

"I thought you hated them."

"I do. But they're my family."

West bit his lip then nodded.

"Okay, I'll see what I can do. But I'll need that intel before anything can happen."

"How long?"

"I'll get a message to my people. Shouldn't be too long."

"How long? Days? Weeks?"

"Tomorrow, but nothing starts until I see that intel."

"I'll get it, but it will be hard."

"Why?"

"If you knew what Crimson Rush was, you'd understand."

"What is it?"

Car headlights pierced the darkness as they turned a corner. Sergie cursed and crossed the street without saying a word. West decided not to follow. He had to get a message to the outside immediately. He continued toward his hotel, the car passing by, the occupants, probably KGB, ignoring him as he stumbled to the ground, his drunken antics not worth a second glance. He fell into a doorway and sat down, quickly removing a small pad and pen, writing out his message in memorized code, folding it in quarters then continuing toward his hotel. He crossed the street and entered a phone booth, the dim bulb inside bathing him in unwelcome light as the door closed. He quickly pulled out the phone book, leaving it open to the government listings, then stuffed the piece of paper behind the phone.

He stepped back into the street and continued for his hotel, the dead-drop message complete requesting the immediate extraction. The phone booth was one of many drops around the city that were constantly monitored by agency staff, most working for the embassy, watching for the open book. Someone would drift in, see what page it was open to, close up the book and surreptitiously pull the paper, palming it. Once retrieved it would be transmitted within an hour.

Responses were never left at the same spot.

As he approached the hotel he froze for a moment then darted into a doorway, poking his head out slightly. What he saw had his heart pounding.

A light was on in his room.

Outside Grozny International Airport, Chechen Republic, Russian Federation
Present Day

Dylan Kane squatted on the outskirts of the airport, his one carryon bag laying in the dust beside him. He surveyed the area spread out below him, the joke of the word "international" in its name obvious. In Chechnya, you could fly anywhere as long as it was Moscow. Light security ringed the fenced in airport, nothing more than when he had first surveyed it upon arrival. His extraction was originally supposed to be over land and across the border into Georgia which at the moment was fairly Western friendly, especially after the Russian invasion during the Olympics.

And they gave them the Winter Olympics!

From Georgia he had many options, not the least of which was a real airport. Alternatively he could arrange an exit via boat, or hike it to Azerbaijan and one of the not-so-secret Israeli or US bases.

But now time was of the essence.

He couldn't waste the time it would take to go overland and sneak across the border. Roads had checkpoints, and here the definition of a road was very loose. It wasn't like hopping on the I-90 and doing sixty for a few hours. In fact, the only road that went south that wasn't a yak trail ended more than sixty miles from the border with Georgia, apparently the two countries never friends, and as Soviet provinces, not strategically important enough to warrant links.

So he had chosen the airport. It was risky, very risky, but he had been through worse. He had paid a local gypsy cab to take him, and in the chit-chat the man had told him in Russian that security had been tightened, authorities looking for some American who had killed a local. Knowing full well they were looking for him, and he obviously wasn't a local, he'd at a minimum be questioned for hours if not days, and if released, might be released into the hands of the Russians, a prospect he didn't savor, the Russia of today far closer to the Soviet Union than most would like to admit.

In fact, it was worse. With the price of oil so high, and the nationalization of the oil companies, the Russian government was swimming with money, and was rearming.

And not only were they rearming, they were recreating the Warsaw Pact, just with different members. Signing non-aggression and mutual defense pacts with their neighbors, including China.

They were resurgent, with overflowing wallets.

Just wait ten years, it will be Cold War II.

Kane had exited the cab early and taken to surveying the airport, debating his options. If he were flying out of here he'd need to get aboard a plane by bypassing security. Getting into the airport would be easy, the perimeter security light, the additional security apparently focused inside the terminal. But any plane he'd get on would take him to Moscow, where he'd have a hell of a time trying to evade their security.

He began to eye the smaller aircraft, a few Cessna sized planes. They'd have the range to get him to Georgia, but not the speed if he were chased down, and with the Russian Stavropol airbase less than two hundred miles from here, he needed speed.

He smiled as he spotted a tiny, bright red plane being fueled far from the terminal. If he could make it there, he just might have a chance. He jumped to his feet and began to jog down a back alley toward the airport. The alley quickly ended, leaving him in the open, the airport ring road directly in front of him. He heard a bell ring behind him and he turned to see a kid on an oversized bike. He flagged him down, and in Chechen offered him twenty US dollars to borrow the bike.

The deal was done in seconds.

Kane pointed to where the bike would be, slung his bag over his shoulder, and began to peddle as fast as he could toward the south side of the airport where the private hangars were, and his possible salvation, as the kid began to run home, waving the green bills over his head.

It didn't take long for Kane to reach his destination, much of it a slight downhill grade, and as he neared, he slowed down to observe security. They were clearly not focused on this side of the airport, the main terminals on the north side. One roaming patrol had passed him without a glance and was now at the far end of the ring road, turning left and out of sight. Other than that he spotted some guards at an access gate and nothing else.

Ditching the bike out of sight of the road, he quickly made his way toward the fence using the brush for cover. At the fence, obviously designed to only keep wildlife and the innocent public out, he untwisted the metal tie holding the chain link to a pole, then pushed the fence aside, shoving his bag under then himself. He replaced the tie, leaving it loose should he need to escape this way, marking the pole by drawing a line in the packed dirt, giving it a darker hue than the surrounding soil that would stay visible enough for the next hour before the sun baked away the moisture.

He continued forward at a crouch, his eyes shifting between the guard post about a half mile away and the hangar with his little red plane now less than a hundred yards ahead.

His heart was pounding in his chest as he neared his goal, not from physical exertion, but from the tension, adrenaline pumping through him. A final glance over his right shoulder showed the guards oblivious to his transgression. He slipped out of sight, his back pressed against the corrugated steel of the makeshift hangar. Catching his breath and calming his racing heart, he reassessed his situation, confirming there were no guards in sight, then edged toward the front corner of the building.

An engine roared to life, causing his heart to skip ahead a few beats as he realized it was the engine of the plane he needed, the refueling obviously finished, and the only way to start the plane needing someone in the cockpit.

He poked his head out and saw the two-seater plane, its prop up to full power, two ground crew stepping back.

Now or never.

Kane burst from his hiding place and onto the tarmac, sprinting unnoticed toward the plane. He rushed past the two ground crew who said nothing at first, probably too startled by what they saw. He jumped on the wing, tossing his bag into the rear seat before the pilot could pull the canopy shut.

The man's eyes bulged as he realized what was happening. He reached up and tried to pull the canopy down but Kane shoved his left arm up and gripped the edge, landing a punch on the man's face before he could react.

The pilot's foot slipped off the brake and the plane jerked forward, quickly gaining momentum as the disoriented pilot had no control. Kane reached in and smacked the pilot's belt release, then grabbed him by the jacket and hauled him from the front seat. The man regained enough of his senses to realize what was happening just as his legs cleared the cockpit. He grabbed onto Kane's arms, desperate to hold on as the ground rushed by.

Kane jerked forward with his upper body, smacking his forehead against the man's nose, effectively knocking him out with the headbutt. He tossed him to the ground, the semi-conscious body rolling several times as Kane jumped in the cockpit, grabbing the controls and guiding the plane toward the runway. As he pulled closed the canopy he buckled himself in as an Aeroflot plane rushed past, massive compared to the tiny Sukhoi Su-29 stunt plane he was now in. With a maximum cruising speed of almost 200 miles per hour, he could reach the border in less than twenty minutes if everything went smooth.

He turned onto the runway and gunned it, shoving the throttle to full. Seconds later he was in the air, banking south toward Georgia. He pulled his phone out of his pocket, punching in his destination of Triblisi then a checkpoint at the border, and stuck it on a mount to his right, the GPS showing his position and required direction.

Forty minutes to Triblisi, nineteen to the border checkpoint.

He found the headset that had been torn off the pilot's head sitting on the floor between his legs. He picked it up and put it on, jacking himself into the comms.

He was greeted with shouts from the tower, ordering him to return.

He ignored it.

Keeping low to avoid any radar, he checked his fuel gauge and confirmed a full tank. He left the throttle at full, not concerned with fuel economy, there more than enough to get him to the border. His only concern now were jets being sent to take him down.

Though his little stunt plane was fast, it couldn't outrace a fighter jet, but it was a small target with incredible maneuverability which might be enough to get him to his goal.

The shouts on the other end of the comm were becoming more threatening so he did a little bobbing and weaving, then activated the comm, singing a Russian drinking song he had been taught a few years ago by a Ukrainian friend. After a few bars he heard a flabbergasted controller announce that the pilot was drunk, at which point Kane dropped back to the deck and cut his signal.

Might buy a couple more minutes of confusion.

He glanced at the GPS.

Sixteen minutes to the border.

The sparse landscape whipped by below, the lone southerly road several miles over his right shoulder. After a few more minutes it suddenly ended in dust, a dirt road continuing for only a few miles then slowly narrowing to nothing, as if it were a forgotten project from before the Chechen wars.

His eyes constantly scanned the horizon, the tiny plane designed for aerial stunts—fast and incredibly maneuverable.

With no radar or other weapons detection systems.

Eleven minutes.

He debated flipping to the left then the right to get a good view of the horizon behind him but decided against it, at these speeds it could cost him a good thirty to sixty seconds of time. His best guess was that at the sixteen minute mark the control tower was still debating what to do, which hopefully meant the airbase hadn't been called. But he gave them at worst two more minutes to contact them and request assistance.

If he assumed there were at least two jets on alert, he would expect them to scramble within tops five minutes, taking less than ten minutes to intercept him, meaning he might actually make it across the border.

But with Stavropol being a training base, most likely at least two of their fighters would be airborne, meaning they'd be as little as eight minutes away at worst.

Nine minutes.

Another scan of the horizon and he still spotted nothing, but he knew his time was running out as his pulse quickened and sweat began to form a trail down his back, the cockpit warming as the tension increased.

Seven minutes.

He strained against the straps holding him in place, his head turned around as far as he could get it, and cursed.

Two dots on the horizon high above him were rapidly closing.

71

I guess the tower called it in a little earlier than I gave them credit for.

He fixed his right hand on the stick, holding the aircraft steady with a slight climb, then placed his elbow on the lip of the canopy, cradling his head in his splayed fingers as he pretended to be passed out.

In less than a minute he heard the challenge from the lead fighter in Russian, demanding he identify himself and turn around.

Kane ignored it, instead continuing his pantomime, his chest heaving, his fake snore filling the cockpit to remind himself of what he was doing. Through his partially open eyes and his fingers, he could see one of the jets, a Sukhoi Su-27, circling him, the roar of their engines drowning out his own prop.

He could imagine the two pilots debating what to do, his ruse hopefully confusing them enough to delay shooting him down, even Russian pilots probably hesitant to shoot down a drunk in a worthless stunt plane of no strategic importance.

His eyes darted toward the GPS display.

Five minutes.

A glance at the controls showed he was a little over fifteen hundred feet off the ground now, there no point to hug the deck now that he had been spotted. The lead pilot yelled his orders again, following it with a "Wake up, you drunk!" in Chechen. He had no doubt that by now the situation had been radioed back to their base and they were awaiting instructions. The question now was how long it would take for their orders to come though, and how grumpy their commander was.

He expected very.

Three minutes.

He had to buy a little more time.

He stretched, both arms out, letting go of the stick with a large yawn, his movements caught by his escort, the pleas to acknowledge the lead's transmission for a moment sounding hopeful.

Kane put his left hand on the stick, gently pushing it into a slow dive, his head now resting on the opposite side of the canopy, his right hand providing the cover as he eyeballed the GPS application.

"Wake up you fool! You're in a dive! You're going to crash!"

The pilot sounded desperate, ignoring protocol, the man apparently genuinely convinced he was dealing with a drunk. Kane watched the altimeter slowly decrease, now at less than a thousand feet. He maintained the steady decline as he watched the seconds count down on his approach to the border, his speed gaining with the descent, precious seconds being gained.

Two minutes.

He was approaching 500 feet, losing about a hundred feet every ten seconds, with that gap slowly decreasing as his airspeed increased. He could see the ground approaching through the canopy to his right.

"Pull up!"

He shifted in his seat, stretching again, then faked a curse, grabbing the stick and pulling up, ending his descent and leveling out at two hundred feet.

"Unidentified pilot! Turn around immediately, or we will be forced to open fire, acknowledge!"

Kane made a show of wiping his eyes clear, gently pulling up on the stick to gain a little altitude for future play if necessary.

One minute.

He looked about and made a squinted eye contact with the lead pilot who was beside him, making hand signals indicating he should answer his comm. The other pilot was nowhere to be seen.

Probably lining up for the shot.

Kane activated the comm, and with his best slurred Russian, asked, "Where am I?"

"Turn around immediately, or we will be forced to open fire!"

Kane looked about in mock confusion, glancing over his shoulder and spotted the other fighter behind him, another Su-27, lined up as he had predicted.

"Who are you?" he asked. "Where am I? What am I doing here?"

"You drunken fool. Turn around immediately or we will open fire."

Zero minutes.

"Am I in Chechnya, or Georgia?"

There was a pause then a muffled curse as his escort peeled away to the left. Kane immediately hit a button on his phone, activating the front facing camera and pushed the holder up so he could see behind him. They were now clearly in Georgian airspace, but Russians didn't care too much about that. Flashes from the guns had him shove the stick down and to the right, the tracers flashing by far too close for his liking. He rolled and as he came out he saw the tracers shifting their line of fire as the pilot adjusted.

Yanking up on the stick, he killed his throttle, his airspeed dropping rapidly as he used the entire bottom surface of the stunt plane to bring him to a near stop.

His attacking jet raced by as Kane pushed forward and shoved the throttle to full again, looking for the lead plane, spotting it just as it settled in behind him.

"This is Major Beridze of the Georgian Air Section to unidentified aircraft. You have crossed the international border and are now in violation of Georgian airspace. State your intentions, otherwise we will engage, over."

Kane grinned as he saw on the horizon four Georgian Sukhoi Su-25 jets racing toward them, and in his camera display, the lead aircraft breaking off, joined by his partner as they retreated back to Russian airspace, most likely not interested in creating an international incident over a drunk.

His new escort settled in on either wing as orders to follow them were broadcast.

Kane gave the lead pilot a thumbs up, his mind already forgetting the last twenty minutes as he planned the next portion of his escape.

He fired off a quick encoded message to Langley requesting the smoothing of feathers for when he landed.

Berlin Hotel (Formerly Savoy), Moscow, USSR
February 6th, 1982

Alex West remained hidden in the doorway, eyeballing the window to his hotel room. The light was on, the curtains closed, one slightly moving with each gust of wind, but other than that, he could see no shadows or movement inside. Turning his attention to his KGB companions, the two men remained in their car, the engine still idling, and no evidence of any urgency from them. In fact, if he didn't know better, he'd say the driver was asleep and the passenger was reading something.

They appeared to be paying no attention to his room.

Then why the hell is the light on?

Then it dawned on him.

When the two KGB men had entered his room to try and catch him, the power had still been down. One of them, out of habit, must have flipped the light switch then forgotten when they left. When the power was restored, after he had already left the room, the light had come on.

Which made his return that much more difficult.

He couldn't use the power outage ruse again, which meant he couldn't enter the building by normal means since he'd be caught on camera. Even a disguise was useless as there was almost definitely a camera in the hallway that would catch him entering his room. His plan had always been to climb to the roof from the back of the hotel, then descend to his room. But with the light on, he would make one hell of a silhouette against the darkened building.

Other than remaining out in the cold for the rest of the night and next day, he could see no other choice. He had to risk it. And if they spotted him, he would either escape or be caught, and hopefully traded after a whole lot of pain.

He stepped out from the doorway and walked toward the rear of the hotel, finding it thankfully deserted. He rushed across the paved delivery area while it was clear then quickly began to climb the drainpipe he had slid down earlier. This one was secure and his adrenaline fueled sense of urgency had him on the roof in minutes. At a crouch he made for the front of the hotel. He could try the loose drain, taking a chance it would hold long enough for him to get to the first landing, or he could try something potentially far more dangerous.

He found the wire that he had hung onto earlier when he had been forced to swing away from the nosy guests. Tugging on it, he satisfied himself it was reasonably secure.

No less than the drainpipe.

A glance at his KGB escort showed nothing had changed. The driver was definitely asleep, the other was reading a newspaper, his view of the hotel blocked by the paper.

They better pray they're not caught like that. Siberia is even colder than Moscow at this time of year.

West decided to damn the torpedoes and go for it. He flipped over the side of the roof, his hands over the ledge holding him in place. Reaching with his right hand, he grabbed the wire, perhaps an inch in diameter, and put his weight on it.

It held.

He let go of the ledge with his left hand and transferred his weight to the wire.

Still good.

He lowered himself as quickly and as steadily as he could, making the first ledge easily, but with the wire fairly tight against the wall, he was forced to take a leap of faith. He lowered himself as much as he could, holding onto the cable with his right hand as close to the thin lip that ringed the building, his toes barely on the edge, his left hand gripping the window frame.

He pushed slightly with his toes, popping off the lip, dropping rapidly. His right hand continued to grip the wire and just as his arm began to stretch, his entire accelerating mass about to yank on the wire, his left hand caught on the lip, swiftly decelerating him and taking much of the weight from the wire.

He hung off the side of the building, gasping. A quick glance over his shoulder showed him still unnoticed by the KGB, and rather than relax to regain his breath, he let go with his left hand and swung to the right slightly, his left hand grasping the wire, as soon as it had a grip his right hand released, dropping several feet to grab on below.

A jerk from above had his heart in his throat as he realized the wire was starting to give. He continued his slide, hand under hand, then felt his feet hit the lip to his floor. Grabbing the window frame and hugging the side of the building, he released the wire as soon as he had his balance. His heart was hammering in his chest at the effort. He quickly slid past the nosy neighbors, this time being careful to not touch their window, then after what seemed an eternity, reached his own window.

He looked down, his watchers still not reacting. Stepping in front of the window, he pushed it aside and stepped inside as quietly as he could. A rapid scan of the room showed it empty, no uninvited guests there to surprise him. The painting was still crooked, his Walkman continued its slumber, and the light blared, highlighting the empty vodka bottle on the floor.

He closed over the window, straightening the curtain, quickly undressed, piling his clothes once again on the chair, then pressed *Stop* on his Walkman, immediately faking waking up.

"What the hell's with the light?" he mumbled, pushing on the mattress so the spring would give a good creak, then stumbled with heavy steps to the switch, turning it off. He returned to the bed, climbing under the covers, his adventures for the night finished.

Within minutes his exhausted self was sound asleep, no need for gadgets to fake the sounds.

1st Special Forces Operational Detachment - Training Facility
Fort Bragg, North Carolina, a.k.a. "The Unit"

Command Master Sergeant Burt "Big Dog" Dawson, BD to his friends, lined up his sights and fired, a hole blown in the head of the paper target gripping an equally two dimensional hostage. He pressed forward, the mockup of a Baghdad neighborhood eerily familiar. He heard the springing of a target to his right, the figure popping up in a window not ten feet away. His body, weapon leading, swung toward the new target as he processed what he was seeing.

He dismissed it, the face of a small boy holding an ice cream, something he wasn't sure was common in Baghdad, not a threat. Gunfire rang out in front of him, the ground torn up by fake rounds as explosions joined in, the hyper-realistic mockup designed to put the fear of God into men while in training so they knew how to cope with it during the real thing.

To Dawson it was nothing, but to raw recruits? He'd seen piss stains and awkward shuffles after some young men exited the arena.

He remembered how scared he had been the first time. You knew it was fake, you knew you couldn't get hurt, but the imagery, the sounds, the explosions, the audio of victims crying out over speakers, of fellow soldiers calling for help, the sound of men going down.

You couldn't help but be scared if you were taking the drill seriously.

But Dawson was no rookie, no battlefield virgin. He had more experience than most in the well-seasoned US Army after over ten years of continuous war.

And his career predated the current excitement.

As head of Delta Team Bravo, some of the highest trained specialists in the world, he had been pretty much everywhere there was a gun and a burning American flag. This simulated urban battlefield at Fort Bragg didn't bother him in the slightest. Fear never entered it, he simply used it to make sure his brain-finger connection was still in synch, it essential the brain came out on top every time otherwise innocent people could die.

An AK-47 touting insurgent appeared from around a corner.

He squeezed, already moving on to the next target.

Suddenly everything went quiet and a siren sounded. He immediately stopped, ejecting his magazine and clearing his weapon, returning it to its holster as the PA sounded.

"Sorry, Sergeant Major, but the Colonel wants to see you immediately. There's a ride waiting for you."

Dawson strode from the simulated city block and toward a Humvee sitting nearby, its driver waiting in the idling vehicle. Dawson jumped in the passenger seat and was ferried to the Delta Force's headquarters, commonly known amongst the men as The Unit. Then again that's what a lot of soldiers in many forces called their own unit's building, the call of "Hon, I'm going to The Unit" familiar to military families the world over.

It was your home away from home, where you worked, trained, socialized and bonded. No matter where you were stationed, everyone hoped to have a unit they called home, where they felt safe and at ease.

And Dawson's unit, tucked out of sight on the massive Fort Bragg installation, was his home away from nothing. Sure he had an apartment that was technically home, but he always preferred to be at The Unit with his buddies, his fellow soldiers, the bond forged under fire tighter than anybody outside of the forces could ever understand.

They studied and trained here, but it was also a central place for the families. Whenever they could they would have barbeques, softball days, car wash days, fake beach days, you name it. There was always something going on here whether it was his team or another; The Unit was the hub of Delta life.

To say he loved it would trivialize his bond.

Love came and went, The Unit was forever. At least for him. He could imagine no other life, and dreaded the day he could no longer keep up with the younger guys. He had been at it a while but figured he had quite a few years left in him barring injury or death.

Death might be better.

At least then he wouldn't be driven nuts by not being able to deploy. Permanent injury? He couldn't imagine what it would be like. There were guys he had served with, and many before his time that had paid the near ultimate sacrifice, now limping around or worse, resigned to a wheelchair for the rest of their days.

You treated them with the respect they deserved, tried to keep involved in their lives for as long as they would have you, the camaraderie helping through the rehabilitation, but eventually you'd stop seeing them as they withdrew from the world of Active Duty they had once known and loved, some successfully transitioning to civilian life, others not.

Death would definitely be better.

He knew he didn't really mean it, but as a single man with no family and no friends outside of The Unit, he had no clue what he'd do if something were to happen.

Move in with sis!

He could imagine how long that would last.

Longer than the French in World War Two, but not much longer.

He climbed from the Humvee and entered the building, striding briskly toward the Colonel's office. Colonel Thomas Clancy was in charge of Delta, and was a man that Dawson trusted implicitly. He knew the Colonel always had their backs, and if there was something they needed to know, he'd make sure they knew it, even if it weren't through official channels.

And the entire "deny knowing you if caught" bit was just that. He would, absolutely, but he'd always be working in the background to get you out.

Colonel Clancy believed in that all important line in the Soldier's Creed "I will never leave a fallen comrade." Even if that meant breaking rules made by politicians to save face.

Clancy's secretary Maggie beamed a smile at Dawson as he walked in. He gave her a wink as she hit the button on the intercom to let the Colonel know he had arrived.

"Yes, sir," she said into the phone, hanging it up. She looked up at Dawson. "He'll see you now, Sergeant Major. Oh, and Sergeant Major?"

Dawson paused, his eyebrows questioning her.

She stood up, rounding her desk, a tissue in hand. She dampened it with a few drops from the water cooler spout and approached him.

"You have a little something on your cheek," she said as she reached up and pulled his head down slightly, wiping his cheek clean with the other hand. She patted it when she was done, letting go of his neck. "Now you're presentable," she said with a smile, immediately spinning and returning to her desk, Dawson noticing her figure for the first time.

And it was damned fine.

He had never considered Maggie eligible before since she was the Colonel's secretary, and had never noticed any vibes from her in the past, but unless his sights were way off, he had just been hit on.

He smiled at her, slightly awkwardly, then, wiping the smile off his face, he entered the Colonel's inner office. Clancy was informal when alone, only putting on the show when the brass or Washington was in town. He waved at a chair in front of his desk while reading something on his computer.

Dawson sat down and waited quietly. A few seconds later Clancy shoved his keyboard away and turned his attention to Dawson.

"Sergeant Major, how's your Russian?"

"A little rusty, but good," he replied in Russian.

Clancy, who Dawson knew didn't speak Russian, simply stared back, his expression hardened. Dawson had known Clancy for years, and knew him to be a man with a wicked sense of humor, quite often jovial, especially when playing Santa at the kids' Christmas party, but when he was serious like this, Dawson knew there was a mission involved, and there was something he wasn't going to like.

"I'll take that to mean 'it's goddamned fantastic, Colonel' and move on." He pushed a file toward Dawson, but kept his finger on it. "The White House called and they need *your* help."

"Mine?"

This piqued Dawson's interest. He was Delta, so he could understand Washington needed an operator, but could see no reason why they would want *him* specifically.

Unless it's related to an old mission.

"Yes, yours. They need you to reach out to Colonel Chernov of the Russian Spetsnaz. We need someone, quietly, to pick up retired Major General Levkin of the *Soviet* Red Army. He was at one time responsible for their entire nuclear arsenal."

Dawson's eyebrows had been crawling up his forehead the entire time Clancy spoke. *Are they kidding?* He had heard some whoppers come out of Washington, but this had to take the cake.

"Why?"

And as Clancy explained, Dawson's eyebrows were forgotten as his chest tightened with the implications of what Crimson Rush could mean.

Clancy paused, looking at Dawson.

"We need to know what this man sold. Convince this Colonel to help us, outside of the chain-of-command if possible, and if they'll agree, take a man of your choice to meet them and interrogate him. Have the rest of the team ready to deploy. This is going to get ugly."

Very ugly.

He pushed the folder the final few inches toward Dawson. Dawson took it, not opening it.

"Good hunting, Sergeant Major. Dismissed."

Dawson came to attention for a split second and left the office, closing the door behind him. Maggie smiled and he nodded, the events of earlier already forgotten as the details of the briefing sank in. He grabbed a room with a secure line and called his second-in-command, Sergeant Major Mike 'Red' Belme.

"Go for Red."

"It's BD. I need you to put the team on standby. And send Niner to The Unit, ready to deploy ASAP."

"Will do. What's up?"

"I'll explain if I'm still here when you get here. If not, see the Colonel. He'll bring you up to speed."

"I'll start making the calls."

Dawson hung up then opened the file Clancy had given him. It was pretty thin. A dossier on the ex-General, little of it since 1990, an equally thin one on Colonel Chernov, a few pages on Dylan Kane's mission, and a single page on Crimson Rush, which proved to be a mere mention of it and the dismissal of it being a threat by intelligence resources over three decades ago.

And now it's about to bite us on the ass.

85

He called the number listed for Colonel Chernov and after several transfers, he was told to wait for a return call. During this wait, where Dawson had decided to reread the file carefully, Niner entered the room.

"Wassup, BD?"

Dawson motioned to a chair on the other side of the table. Carl "Niner" Sung was a Korean-American and one of the funniest men Dawson knew. Even under fire, no matter what the situation, the man would crack a joke to relieve the tension. They weren't all gems, many of them groan worthy, but it helped take the men's minds off how far up shit's creek they might actually be.

"How's your Russian."

"Splendinski."

Dawson cocked an eyebrow.

Niner apparently sensed the seriousness of the situation.

"Sorry, Sergeant Major, I've been told it's perfect. I learned it young in case the Russians decided to pay a visit to my parents' homeland. I kept it up since I figure we're going to war with them at some point during my career."

"Good. We just might be heading there in the next few hours."

Dawson brought Niner up to speed, the severity of the situation leaving all wisecracks unvoiced.

The phone rang.

"Mr. White here."

"Do svidaniya, Sergeant Major. To what do I owe the pleasure?"

Dawson couldn't help but smile. He was quite certain Colonel Chernov was an asshole, but he was his kind of asshole, which made him, at this moment in time, okay in his books.

"*I* need a favor."

"*You?* So not your government?"

86

"*I* need a favor. Let me explain, and I think you'll understand why *I'm* asking."

Dawson spent the next five minutes briefing the Colonel, who remained silent almost the entire time, interjecting with an occasional question.

"And you have his current location?"

"Yes." Dawson read off the coordinates only thirty minutes old. "We will feed you updated coordinates as you need them."

Dawson heard fingers pecking at a keyboard.

"Crimea? You've tasked a satellite?"

"Yes."

"Expensive. You must really want him. And should I do this for you, what is in it for me?"

Dawson smiled.

"*My* gratitude."

There was a pause then the Russian began to laugh.

"Sergeant Major, your gratitude I think could be quite valuable, should I need to call on it in the future." He paused. "I will see what I can do. I suggest you get to Turkey, then we will make arrangements to meet should we be successful."

"Very well. I will contact you shortly with our arrival time."

Dawson ended the call and looked at Niner.

"How's your Turkish?"

"Splendinski."

Berlin Hotel (Formerly Savoy), Moscow, USSR
February 7, 1982

West had another drag of his ice water, swishing it around his mouth then swallowing, the eggs over-salted as usual. It never failed, breakfast at the Berlin Hotel was always a risk. The less fresh their eggs, the more salt the chefs used. Ditto with pretty much everything being served.

It made for a thirsty day.

West sat by the window, looking out at the bright, frigid day as he "enjoyed" his breakfast, included with his stay. He usually skipped it, the quality just not worth it, but today he was starving from last night's adventures, and he knew what lay ahead would be taxing. The sky was a crisp blue, only wisps of clouds spoiling the perfect canvas; the streets were covered in snow, but the odd plow and an army of citizens equipped with shovels were already clearing the roads and walkways with an efficiency born from necessity, relying on the government to actually get the job done foolhardy at best.

A reflection in the window caught his attention and he followed the figure until they sat down at a table to his right, in the far corner of the room. He looked back at his plate, finishing the last bit of over-hard eggs, anything with a runny yoke to be avoided in the Soviet Union. He glanced at the woman who had just sat down, making eye contact with her for a second.

Adelle Bertrand.

Eye contact made and broken with no one else in the room noticing, he returned to finishing his coffee and watching the work outside. He had known Adelle for almost twenty years. She was a French agent for their

CIA equivalent, the DGSE—Direction Générale de la Sécurité Extérieure, or General Directorate for External Security. They had met on one of his first assignments, and he had always had a thing for her, and she for him if their romps were any indication.

It was pure sex, as unabashed as everything was in this business. There was no time for romance, no time for planning futures. There was time for fast, vigorous, primal sex, two people alone in the world looking for a temporary release from the loneliness of the job, and the stress of their daily lives.

He had several women around the world that, when possible, he would meet with. He cared for them enough to treat them well when he was with them, but not enough for them to be used against him.

He hadn't seen Adelle in a few years. They were about the same age, so she would be nearing the end of her career as well, but she had kept her figure, her fantastic looks, and if things hadn't changed in the past few years, she was a dynamo in bed that he could barely keep up with.

Which suited him fine.

With her it was more accurately described as "Wham, bam, thank you, man".

He felt a twinge and tried to push their last encounter out of his mind, it brief but intense in the back seat of a car in Prague.

But in Moscow, the chances of an encounter were slim to none.

That was one of the things he enjoyed about the Berlin Hotel. At any given time there were probably one or more foreign intelligence operatives staying there from any number of countries. Those on deep-cover assignments of course wouldn't be at a place like this, they'd be holed up in some basement or farmhouse out of sight, the KGB not supposed to know they were even in-country. These were the agents smuggled across the border, not flown in on Aeroflot with a fake passport.

His cover was good and the KGB definitely knew who and what he was, which if you were smart made you nervous, but as long as the dance continued, where they would try to catch him in the act, he'd be safe. With the KGB, CIA, MI6 et al, sometimes it was more important to try to figure out what someone was after rather than catch and release them. If they knew he was looking for information on Crimson Rush, then they would know they had a leak in that organization and move to plug it. But if they just picked him up, they'd never know. Catch him in the act, gathering the intel, then they not only stopped their leak, they had a bargaining chip.

He waved the waiter over, signed his bill and slipped a tenner in the bill folder, American dollars like gold in the Soviet Union allowing the bearer to purchase black market goods that could actually make a difference in someone's life. With a casual glance at Adelle, he left the restaurant and ordered a cab from the concierge. Returning to his room he bundled up for the journey as the phone rang to let him know his ride had arrived.

Minutes later he was inside a frozen cab. He slipped the driver ten bucks.

"Crank the heat."

"Yes, sir!" said the man, quickly sliding the selector all the way to the right as he hid the bill closer to his package than West cared to picture, possession of foreign currency illegal. "Where would you like to go?" asked the cabby, his voice much more jovial than the gruff greeting West had received upon entering the cab.

"As close to Red Square as you can get me. I want to do some sightseeing before my meetings."

"Of course, of course," said the man, his accent heavy but his English good. "I will take you to the Resurrection Gates. You'll be so close you can see it. Only a couple of minutes walk."

"That's perfect," said West as they turned on to Teatralnyy Street. West knew the city like the back of his hand, but didn't mind playing tourist from time-to-time if he wasn't in a hurry. Which is why he didn't say anything when the cabby took a more circuitous route to Red Square than was necessary. Then again, it could have been that he knew the massive circular route that ringed the area of the city containing Red Square would be cleared of snow before the other routes.

As they continued to make decent time, West began to wonder if he'd have a chance to feel the heat his ten bucks had paid for, the rate his driver was going assuring arrival at the Gates in minutes. They completed the loop with a turn to the right, the Resurrection Gates in front of them, Red Square beyond that.

"Just let me out anywhere along here," said West, the driver cranking the wheel to the right before the words had finished coming out of West's mouth. West paid the man, slipping him another ten, the man grinning a rotting smile, Moscow's fluorination program obviously still a distant glimmer. "Loop around then wait for me here and I'll give you another of those."

The grin grew.

The cab pulled away as West looked about, taking in the sights as he waited for his escort to make their presence obvious. The black Volga pulled up and stopped not fifty feet away.

Let the games begin.

He strode toward Red Square, around the Resurrection Gates, the cobblestone covered in a dusting of snow, a grid of tiny ridges of the white powder crisscrossing the vast square marking where the hand-pushed shovels had been. He had to admit he loved this place. There was no place in the world, except perhaps the Kremlin, that caused American hearts to leap with a touch of fear when mentioned in the news. Every year during

91

the May Day parades intelligence analysts worldwide would be glued to their screens, analyzing every vehicle that made an appearance, quite often the first glimpse of new equipment the Soviets had managed to cook up under the West's noses, and more often than not, faked equipment simply there to cause analysts at Langley to scratch their heads and wonder why an ICBM had an extra fin.

Krásnaya Plóshchad, as Red Square was known in Russian, was not named after the red flag of communism, but in fact had taken its name from the nearby Saint Basil's Cathedral, the word Krásnaya meaning both 'Red' and 'Beautiful' in Russian. The beautiful cathedral's nickname was passed on to the square, its original name Pozhar, or 'burnt-out place' apparently unappealing to the locals. With 'Beautiful' being an archaic interpretation of Krásnaya, the more modern 'Red' Square was the translation adopted by the locals and the world. But with the Kremlin occupying one side, the headquarters of the second most powerful country in the world hell-bent on world domination, the enemy of democracies everywhere, Red Square became synonymous with the blood soaked coloring of the communist standard, the hammer and sickle adorned crimson flag of the USSR.

West gazed at the spires of Saint Basil's Cathedral as a platoon of goose-stepping soldiers smacked by, undeterred by the snow covered stone. One of his tails was on foot now, the other back in the car, unauthorized vehicle traffic forbidden in Red Square, and a black Volga traveling at walking speed would be rather noticeable.

Which meant he now had a chance.

The car was now at least a radio call behind him. The question was whether or not it was still at the other end of the square, near the Resurrection Gates, or was repositioning for the opposite end of Red Square and his assumed ultimate destination.

West faked a slip on the ice, taking a knee, and with a glance behind him, he saw the black car stopped at the gates, the tailpipe still giving away the engine's idling.

He continued forward, toward the opposite end of the square, his eyes on the colorful spires of Saint Basil's, built almost 500 years ago under orders from Ivan the Terrible. It originally contained eight churches that surrounded a central ninth church, a tenth added a few decades after the initial construction. The colorful spires were meant to resemble the flames of a bonfire and have no parallel in Russian architecture. It is widely considered the most beautiful and unique building ever constructed in the country.

And it was almost destroyed by Stalin. Plans were drawn up to have the church removed to enlarge Red Square, but legend has it that when a scale model was shown to Stalin, and the church was lifted from the model, he immediately cried for it to be put back. Though it was built to be a church, the atheist communists confiscated it in 1928 and to this day it remains a federal property housing a division of the State Historical Museum.

It was beautiful.

West never tired of seeing it, and had to chuckle at how many people back home thought that *it* was actually the Kremlin. Even news reports and supposedly learned magazines would mislabel it. The actual Kremlin was a large palace to his left, surrounded by deep red walls built mostly by Italian masters over fifty years before ground was broken on the cathedral. The sixty-eight acre site was massive, impressive, and thanks to an uninformed Western media, mostly unknown to the average American.

But to people like West, it represented everything he was fighting against. The very walls represented a closed society, the brick a symbol for the separation of the government from its people, those who chose to speak out against this lack of freedom and transparency quickly whisked away to a gulag in Siberia, usually never to be seen again.

A quick glance to his left showed the car gone, it now beginning the trek around the huge Kremlin walls to reposition at the other end.

West smiled to himself, then pulled his sleeve up to look at his watch, holding it high in front of his face so there was little chance of his tail missing it.

"Shit!" he exclaimed out loud before turning back toward the Resurrection Gates at a jog. He passed his tail who had spun around as soon as West had to avoid having his face seen. West looked at his watch again, then shook his head, picking up the pace a little, covering the cobblestoned square quickly, his body protesting as his aging bones felt every abuse the previous night had bestowed.

He didn't dare look back, but he was sure he could hear footfalls behind him. His tail had obviously been ordered to follow on foot as the car tried to catch up, unable to turn around as the mighty traffic loop was one way.

Now the question was whether or not ten dollars was worth a cabby waiting about fifteen minutes. As he passed the Resurrection Gates his heart sank, the cab nowhere in sight.

"Shit!" he muttered as he began to slow. A horn honked and he turned to see a cab rolling to a stop, the driver waving through a rolled down passenger side window.

West waved and jogged to where the vehicle had stopped, climbing in the back.

"Sorry I late, I stuck behind plows."

"No problem, but can you get me to Narodnogo Opolcheniya Street as fast as possible? I have a meeting I'm going to be late for."

The man seemed to hesitate. West handed over the promised tenner and the gas was floored. West casually looked out his window to see his tail shouting into a radio, stomping his feet in anger. West had to wonder if he had just crossed the line. If he had, the KGB would be out to pick him up, meaning his picture would be circulated throughout the city within hours.

He just prayed an extraction could be set up quick enough to get them all out of Moscow and the USSR.

Because Siberia wasn't nice *any* time of year.

CIA Headquarters, Langley, Virginia
Present Day

Chris Leroux rubbed his eyes. He'd kill for a Red Bull right now, the 'wings' it gave you definitely needed. But he had made a promise to Sherrie and he intended to keep it.

There's no way I'm risking a nookie cut-off.

But she was away on an op and he was knocking himself out trying to trace the data packet sent by Aslan Islamov, their Chechen drug lord turned Russian intermediary. So far he had had no success, the packet scrambled and bounced off of dozens of servers randomly, some of the pieces bouncing back, some going into the ether, others successfully reaching destinations on public servers and unsecured home PCs, Malware previously installed by questionable websites, unbeknownst to their owners, then pushing the data to other servers.

Top secret communications using the public's unsecured home PCs.

It was a tactic used by terrorists, criminals, and governments.

Nearly untraceable.

Data would be injected into the network, the thousands or hundreds of thousands of infected computers would poll that network location, pulling any data it might find, then transmit it randomly across the internet and to each other, only one of the destinations the actual destination.

Impossible to detect the needle from the haystack.

His head dropped on his desk and he could feel himself drifting.

She's not here, maybe just one Red Bull?

He smelt something.

His eyes opened, still shielded by his crossed arms his head was resting on. He took a deep breath.

Sherrie!

His head popped up from his desk as he turned. Sherrie was standing in the door of his cubicle, smiling at him.

"Sorry to wake you," she said, stepping toward him and giving him a kiss.

"I wasn't asleep. Ten more seconds though and I would have been."

She sat down in the spare chair, dropping her previously unnoticed carryon bag beside her.

"Did you just come from the airport?"

She nodded.

"I wanted to see you before you got home."

"How'd you know I was here?"

"I called your detail."

He frowned.

"No privacy." He looked at her exhausted form. "You look as tired as I feel."

She nodded, smiling slightly.

"I was playing escort to some female senator. My God can that woman party. I don't think she stopped until four in the morning, then was up again at seven. Non-stop. But she's safely back in Washington."

"Was there a threat?"

"Yeah, but turned out to be nothing, at least for now." She lowered her voice and leaned in. "I can tell you one thing, they're scared about something."

"What makes you say that?"

"Whispered conversations, worried looks. Nobody came out and said anything that I overheard, but I think it's Crimson Rush."

"Wouldn't surprise me. We're at DEFCON Four and Director Morrison had me provide him the dossier on that Delta Sergeant Major you worked with during the New Orleans crisis." He lowered his voice even further. "I think they're picking up the ex-Soviet General."

Narodnogo Opolcheniya Street, Moscow, USSR
February 7, 1982

West sat on a bench, enjoying the view, sipping a god-awful cup of coffee. It was a welcome respite from the cold, regardless of its questionable origins. Hundreds of uniformed young men, and an equal number of old, streamed up and down the street and in and out of Military Unit 35576, or as it was known to the few in the know, the Soviet Army Academy. And to even fewer? The Military-Diplomatic Academy of the Soviet Army. It was the equivalent to The Farm where spies or operators were trained for the clandestine service. Most likely it would or already had produced the agent that would kill him some day.

And it was where his good buddy Sergie worked.

As part of the training they worked with actual agents. Sergie was counter-intelligence with the highest security clearance outside of the high command. And even then, need-to-know extended to the underlings. West had no doubt Crimson Rush was ultra-top secret, and Sergie's reaction at the mere mention of it proved he knew what it was, or at least its importance.

A man sat down beside him, opening a broadsheet, ruffling its pages, his own coffee sitting beside him. West ignored him, sipping his bitter brew, feeling the rush of warmth surge through his core, the harsh Soviet cold halting it from travelling any farther, his extremities still quite frigid.

"It's all arranged," said the man as he flipped a page. "Extraction for one plus four, tonight, twenty-one-hundred hours. Location is on page twelve, Echo-Six encryption protocol."

The man folded his paper, stood up and dropped it on the bench, merging into the heavy pedestrian traffic.

It was bold, it was brazen, and it made perfect sense. The Soviets would never expect two CIA agents to meet ten feet from the walls of their spy school, which meant it wasn't carefully watched. Why should they? There were thousands of trained troops here, with hundreds on the street at any time. It was one of the more busy military installations in the city.

Which made it perfect.

The best cover is no cover, in the open, where they least expect you, and are least likely to be looking.

Meetings like this happened all the time in front of important government installations, the arrogance of the KGB, who did the exact same thing in the West, forcing the assumption it could never happen here.

West hadn't acknowledged the man the entire time, instead he had continued his casual observation of the pedestrian traffic, carefully watching, without obviously watching, a side entrance to the Academy where he knew Sergie would be exiting at the end of his work day.

A figure emerged from the gate, stepping out to the curb and stomping his feet several times, his alcoholic body already feeling the cold. West drained his turpentine and rose, picking up the paper and dropping the cup into a nearby garbage can.

Sergie's path would take him in the opposite direction, past at least one seedy bar, then home to his 'loving' family on any normal evening. West just wondered if Sergie considered this a normal evening. After all, he was supposed to have stolen the Crimson Rush intel and be prepping to leave the country at any given moment.

Ten minutes of walking and Sergie was rubbing his hands all over himself, trying to keep warm. He stopped in front of a bar, eyeballing the entrance, then like a good alcoholic, entered.

West followed him in, taking a seat at a corner table and ordering a coffee and a house-plate, which normally consisted of crusty bread, some type of sausage, and if he were lucky, real butter, but most likely some type of lard spread.

He flipped his paper to page twelve and looked for the fifth paragraph, the "Echo" paragraph, 'E' being the fifth letter in the alphabet. He skipped to the sixth sentence after that. He then added his own unique assigned increment, which happened to be seven. The seventh word started with a Cyrillic 'R'. As part of each mission he was given a set of three locations to memorize that were safe houses. He was never to go to them unless it was prearranged, and that prearrangement involved telling him which one to go to. Today, 'R' meant he was to go to the second address on his list, which made sense based upon his extremely detailed knowledge of the city. It was less than five minutes from Sergie's apartment on foot, and if he wasn't mistaken—which he was sure he wasn't—it was a warehouse of some sort, which usually meant many possible egress points.

He refolded the paper as his order arrived. Taking a sip of his coffee, he sighed in appreciation at the dramatically higher quality than the previous attempt he had been drinking. He quickly finished his food, one eye on Sergie in the back corner downing several shots of vodka as he warmed up.

Alcohol is a coolant, you idiot.

Sergie finished his drinks and rose, tossing some Rubles on the table. West scarfed the last of his meal down, letting Sergie leave ahead of him, his path known. He downed the rest of the not-too-bad coffee, placed a few bills under the glass then left. Sergie was at the end of the street with a none-too-subtle tail car following him, stopping at the side of the road then moving forward every hundred feet.

West kept pace with the tail car until Sergie turned off the main road, cutting toward his apartment. West turned down a parallel street and broke out into a jog, covering the distance to the next street quickly, then turning left to catch up to his target. As he reached the street Sergie would be on, he slowed down, catching his breath, his lungs expelling warmed air that immediately froze in the frigid conditions, a constant reminder of where and when he was.

He crossed the street as Sergie arrived, oblivious to the fact he had two tails. West kept his pace, slightly faster than Sergie's as the tail car rounded the corner.

"Don't look back," he said as he approached Sergie. "You have what I want?"

"Da," whispered Sergie, suddenly tensing up.

"Relax or you'll get us both killed," admonished West. Sergie regained his easy stride, his shoulders once again slumping in the defeat that was his life. "Have everyone ready in the lobby for eight-forty-five tonight. Don't bring anything except your cash. Tell your family that it's a surprise you've been saving up for, and that they'll find out when they get there. Understood?"

"Da," whispered Sergie.

"You will use the rear exit and turn right. Keep walking until I meet you. You will greet me as a friend named Boris. We will joke about the surprise, but not reveal it. The hints will be that it is a pet dog."

"My family has always wanted a dog."

"I know, you told me last time I was here. That is the surprise, but we can't tell them, we must keep them excited so if you're seen, it won't look suspicious."

"Okay."

"Good, I will see you tonight, eight-forty-five. Don't be late."

West continued walking past Sergie, then turned left, away from Sergie's destination and away from his tail's watchful eyes. There was no doubt now that Sergie was under surveillance, which meant they suspected him of something.

West just hoped they didn't spring their trap tonight.

Sochi, Black Sea, Russia
Present Day

Colonel Kolya Chernov sat at a plastic table in the corner of a small patio, one of many lining Sochi's Ordzhonikidze Street, sipping his coffee. At another table sat his target, former Major General Levkin, he too enjoying a coffee in the early morning sun, the temperature slightly brisk but tolerable. An unknown man was at the table with the General, chatting animatedly about how he supported Putin's moves to curtail gay rights, and how he respected Ahmadinejad for taking the issue head-on in New York City several years ago.

"*They* don't have the problem," said the man, "they solved it by killing them off. Now you don't have the genetic mutation that causes it. We need to do the same!"

The General said nothing, merely nodding his head, several of his security detail seeming to distance themselves slightly from the table.

Chernov put his coffee down, his blood boiling over something he hadn't given a second thought to until Putin passed the new laws to placate the hard right that was his base. Chernov believed in equality for all and didn't care what you did in the privacy of your bedroom. And that was *key* for him. He hated public displays of affection, regardless of sexual orientation. A peck on the cheek was fine, even a small kiss of greeting or thanks. But tongue down the throat displays should be saved for when no one could see you.

Kids today!

He swiped his finger across the display of his iPad, the camera image from the heavily modified TrackingPoint gun mounted on the adjacent roof swinging. The weapon had been introduced with much fanfare recently, a nearly fully automated weapon that would allow novices to make shots previously possible only by marksmen. As soon as it had been released the Russians had secured several copies and modified it extensively, something he was certain every military in the world, and terrorist organization, was now doing.

He had been fortunate enough to be provided with two working prototypes only weeks before that made his mission, completely off the books, possible. The weapon had been modified to now be mounted to a tripod with motors that could be controlled by the Linux based software it contained, the iPad acting as a remote control.

It also was able, with an additional wide-angle camera, to track multiple targets, rather than the single target the unmodified weapon could follow.

He selected the last of the guards with the weapon mounted across the street, then activated the program with a ten second countdown, flipping to the control screen of the second weapon, activating its own five second countdown.

Placing the iPad in his bag sitting on the chair beside him, he reached into his jacket, faking a scratch should any of the security detail be alert enough to catch it. An engine started down the street and a black SUV began to roll forward, its driver his trusted second-in-command, Major Maxim Somov, one of only two men he risked taking on the mission, his scratch a signal that all hell was about to break loose.

Half a dozen cracks echoed through the square, the entire incident taking less than five seconds, six bodies crumpling to the ground as Chernov jumped from his table, putting a bullet in the homophobe, then injecting Levkin with a sedative as he pulled him to his feet. Before it fully took effect, the aged man was shoved into the back of the SUV and seconds later they were out of the square, a gathering crowd left to wonder what had just happened.

And they would be left wondering; the two automated weapons already being collected by his third man and returned to Moscow, nobody the wiser they had been used.

Sergie Tuzik Residence, Moscow, USSR
February 7, 1982

Sergie could feel the shaking in his hands as his body demanded more alcohol, the withdrawal painful, but tolerable. Every day at his job he endured it, drinking on the job frowned upon even in the vodka loving republic. Especially for intelligence officers.

He sat in his chair and watched yet another rerun of the Seventeen Moments of Spring—part four if he remembered correctly—on their tiny black and white television, glancing at his watch for the hundredth time since he'd been home. While his wife had prepared dinner and the children did their homework, he had retrieved his cash from its various hiding places and gathered all their IDs should they be stopped on the street. He had dropped a hint at dinner of a surprise tonight, and the kids had grilled him but he had refused to say anything except that it was something they all had wanted, and that they would all be incredibly surprised and happy when they saw it.

Even his cold-hearted bitch of a wife had seemed excited, her hand actually touching his for a brief moment, squeezing it as if there might still be some love there.

He closed his eyes, tuning out the television, picturing his wife Katarina when she was younger. They had been happy. Deliriously happy. But that was youth. No responsibilities, no realization of what the world was really like. Grand ideas, grand visions, grand naiveté.

They had married in their mid-twenties, held off having kids for a few years while he established his career and they used his meager salary to

107

create a home out of their state issued apartment. Then two kids in rapid succession, and then the bliss turned into misery, Katarina not taking well to motherhood.

That's when he had begun drinking.

He was Russian so he had been drinking from a young age, but rarely to excess. Drinking was thought of differently here than in the West. As long as it didn't affect your job, your contribution to the State, then nobody cared.

And it hadn't. His career was a success, a Lieutenant Colonel by forty, with prospects of a promotion in the near future. He was good at his job, dedicated, and enjoyed the rewards that went with his higher position—a slightly bigger apartment if available, and one vacation per year in the Crimea. Soon he'd be eligible for a vacation in Cuba. He couldn't even imagine what that must be like.

But soon he wouldn't have to. Once he was safely in the United States, he would disappear and move south, to Florida or California, and never experience the cold again.

I hate the cold.

He looked at his watch.

8:35.

He stood up and turned the television off.

"It's surprise time!" he yelled, his voice genuinely jovial as he pictured a beach umbrella with he and his wife perched under it, enjoying the sound of the surf, the kids playing in the crashing waves.

Could we be happy again?

"Just what is this surprise?" demanded his wife from the kitchen, her tone all bitch.

Maybe not.

"Just get dressed, we're going out. We have to be there in ten minutes."

"Ten minutes! Are you crazy? At this time of night? I'm not going anywhere."

"Please, Katarina, I beg you, don't ruin this for the kids. I promise you that you'll love the surprise."

She frowned at him and tossed her tea towel on the counter, stomping down to their bedroom. The kids, who usually had no respect for him, were already at the door dressing for the frigid outdoors. He went to the bathroom, locking the door, and began stuffing his cash into his socks, underwear, and an unsuspicious amount in his wallet to 'pay' for the surprise.

With their identity papers secure in one pocket, he went to the front door and shoved his boots on, lacing them tightly, then putting on his jacket, hat and gloves as his wife joined them, still not pleased.

He pointed at the boys' feet.

"Make sure your boots are tied tight. You might have to do some running for your surprise."

The boys immediately dropped, exchanging excited glances, redoing their laces so tightly circulation might have been affected.

"If you think I'm doing any running tonight, you're kidding yourself."

"Yeah yeah," he muttered, glancing at his watch.

8:42.

"Let's go!" he said, slapping his gloved hands together. They all exited and the boys excitedly rushed down the six flights of stairs, his wife slowing them down with her lackadaisical attitude, constantly bitching.

Maybe I should leave her behind.

He felt a pit in his stomach at the thought.

Let's just get to America, and all of our troubles will be over.

It was 8:44 when they finally went out the back exit. Sergie took the lead, setting a brisk pace that the boys eagerly followed, Katarina falling behind as she continued to whine.

At the next street corner West stepped out of the darkness, hailing Sergie jovially in fluent, unaccented Russian.

"Sergie, my friend! Are you ready for your big surprise?" asked the man, shaking Sergie's hand as they exchanged kisses on both cheeks. "And I see your sons are all excited for their surprise, eh?" They both nodded vigorously, smiles spread from cheek to cheek. "And this must be the beautiful Katarina you are always telling me about," said West as Sergie's wife finally caught up. She seemed to almost blush, casting a surprised glance at him as West greeted her with a kiss of the gloved hand. "Very pleased to meet you," he said. He held his hand out, indicating they should all proceed. "We must hurry. The surprise won't like being kept waiting!"

West set the pace, and this time everyone, including Katarina, kept up. Several streets were covered and within less than ten minutes they walked up to a warehouse. A side door was lit by a lone bulb. West walked up to it and knocked in a one-two-one pattern followed by a pause, then two more taps. He winked at the boys who were thrilled with the mystery of it all.

The door opened and West urged them all inside. The boys went first, then Katarina, herself seeming to now be fully engrossed in the adventure, then Sergie, and finally West, who closed the door behind them.

The room flooded with light as a man immediately approached them, a van in the center of the large room, all its doors wide open, roaring to life.

West immediately turned to Sergie.

"Intel?"

Sergie reached into his mouth and found the string tied to a rear molar. He pulled on it, gagging as the small container at the other end pulled through his esophagus and popped into his mouth. He spit it out, along

110

with a none-too-small amount of vomit. He yanked the string off his tooth then handed the dripping mass to West. West didn't seem fazed at all, he simply took it and wiped it off with a handkerchief.

West pointed at the van.

"Everyone inside, quickly," he said as he opened the canister, removing the microfilm.

"What is going on here?" demanded Katarina.

"We're going on a trip," replied Sergie as he herded his family toward the van, the man moving to the door of the warehouse. He glanced at West who was already examining the microfilm with a magnifying glass.

"Where?"

"To America."

Her jaw dropped then she suddenly sprung into his arms, hugging him hard and giving him his first genuine kiss in years. She let him go and immediately climbed into the van, urging her children to be quiet and listen to the men.

"We've got company!" called the man at the door.

"Let's go, now!" ordered the driver.

The man at the door ran over to the passenger side, slamming the rear door shut, then to the opposite side of the warehouse, opening a garage door as West strode over to the van.

He shook Sergie's hand.

"Good luck."

"You're not coming with us?"

"No, I'm going to stay behind and buy you time. You just worry about your family now. You're part of the Underground Railroad. You'll be safe, but it will be a difficult journey. Listen to them, they know what they're doing."

Sergie nodded and climbed in the back seat, West slamming the door shut behind him. The van rolled forward, toward the open door, the other man jumping in the passenger side, the vehicle roaring from the garage as soon as his feet were clear of the floor. Sergie waved at West as the American closed the garage door behind them, the children and Katarina joining in.

West returned the wave, then disappeared from sight.

And Sergie wondered if he would ever see the man again.

Thirteen miles from Turkish coast, Black Sea
Present Day

Command Sergeant Major Burt "Big Dog" Dawson scanned the horizon with his binoculars, spotting dozens of craft of varying sizes in all directions. The Black Sea was busy with commercial, military and pleasure craft, and it was early morning, primetime for traffic on the world's sixteenth largest body of water. He looked at his watch again.

Five minutes late.

He shouldn't really be concerned. Five minutes wasn't outside the window of leeway he had given the operation. Colonel Chernov had signaled coordinates when they had arrived a few hours before after over twelve hours of travel on commercial carriers as Mr. White and Mr. Green of the State Department.

And now we're sitting in the middle of the damned sea.

Dawson had to admit he was impressed when the secure message had arrived. Chernov was fast, and if successful, it would be the second time he had come through for Dawson in only months. He shuddered to think what Chernov might one day ask for. Dealing with the Soviets—scratch that—Russians, was difficult at the best of times. And in recent years their increasingly belligerent government seemed to suggest they were heading back to the days of the Soviet Union, with an ignorant populace cheering it on due to a lack of progress on the economic front that only the naïve could possibly think would be improved by a return to communism.

But Dawson didn't for a minute think that was Putin's intent. Communism doesn't work, at least not Soviet style communism. Chinese style—at least that of the past ten to twenty years—seemed to be working

113

for them as a country, just not a people. Dawson was hopeful that at some point the Chinese middleclass would be so large with wallets so full that they would demand and receive their freedom, and a country with a powerful economy would join the democracies of the world.

When the Soviet Union had collapsed, a corrupt, bankrupt basket case had been handed over to the people, and it had never really flourished. Frustrations had led to the "election" of Putin, a former KGB spy, who didn't tolerate dissent, and changed the rules to fit his needs, essentially making himself leader for life until someone had the courage to put an end to it.

Dawson feared the Russian people wouldn't have the courage to stand up to him in time, and by the time they did, all the hard won freedoms they were slowly losing would be gone, and his death would only hasten the next dictator such as ex-Major General Levkin, who would take things even further.

It was a slippery slope as his own country was learning. The knee-jerk reactions after 9/11 seemed perfectly sane at the time. Why wouldn't you give your security apparatus more power to prevent further attacks? Why wouldn't you invade countries that were a clear and present danger to your own? And now his country had been at war longer than even World War II, was nearly bankrupt, and had been caught with its pants down, spying on pretty much everyone on the planet, including its allies and own innocent citizens.

And they wanted even more power.

And the government seemed prepared to give it to them, one side calling it patriotism, the other using it as a bargaining chip to get other things rammed through that they wanted. Both were equally guilty of shredding the constitution and steering the country toward economic and democratic ruin.

The entire damned world needs a wakeup call.

He wondered if Crimson Rush might be a reminder to those who had forgotten that almost fifty years of the Cold War had brought the world to the brink several times. If it did go public, or worse, succeeded, perhaps the world could be taught a lesson that history shouldn't be forgotten, lest it be repeated.

An expensive lesson.

"Check it out, BD."

Niner pointed slightly to the port side. Dawson turned and spotted a sixty footer heading toward them at full speed, and as it approached, he recognized Chernov at the helm. The engine powered down as the new arrival turned and moments later both boats were lashed together.

Chernov waved, Dawson returning it after jumping aboard, then another man Dawson didn't know pushed an elderly man he immediately recognized as former Soviet Major General Levkin, bound and gagged, toward the front of the boat, shoving him to his knees. It appeared he had taken quite a beating.

The man eyed Dawson with suspicion, but no fear.

"Did he tell you anything?"

"Very little," frowned Chernov. "I have confirmed however that he has indeed sold the codes for Crimson Rush to the Chechen Islamov, but that Islamov was only a middleman."

"Who was the receiver?"

"He wouldn't tell us."

Dawson motioned for the gag to be removed and the second man yanked it from Levkin's mouth.

"I've read your dossier, General. Seems you'd like to see a return to the old ways, to the old Soviet Union."

The man said nothing.

We don't have time for this.

"Listen, nuclear codes have been sold to somebody and they intend to detonate those weapons for whatever purpose. I don't care about your involvement. I just want to stop it. We're talking potentially millions of lives here."

The man again said nothing.

Dawson shook his head, pulling his weapon and aiming it at the man.

"Are you going to be of use to me, or not?"

Levkin glared.

"Very well."

Dawson shot him in the left thigh.

Levkin cried out in pain, tumbling forward onto his face. Chernov shook his head, smiling, as he pulled the man back to his knees.

"Like I said, I read your dossier. You have a wife, three sons and two daughters, and fourteen grandchildren. That's a big family." Dawson squatted in front of the man, pushing his gun under Levkin's chin, shoving it up so they were eye-to-eye. "If a single weapon detonates on American soil, I'm going to personally kill every single living member of your family, starting with your sons. What was your eldest son's name? Yuri?" There was a flicker from the man—almost imperceptible, but there to see by the trained eye. "He lives in St. Petersburg if I'm not mistaken. My team will take out him, his wife, and their children—your grandchildren."

Dawson shook his head, removing the gun from the man's chin.

"I know it's a horrible thing, but when you kill thousands of my countrymen, and perhaps millions, we will retaliate. We levelled Afghanistan for 9/11. Do you think we'll hesitate to remove all traces of the family responsible for this attack? There's no country to point at. If you had hoped to trigger a war with Russia, it won't work. We know it isn't the Russian government involved, it's just you." Dawson stood up. "So, what's it going to be?"

Levkin looked up at Dawson, his eyes burning with hatred.

"If you touch my family—"

"You'll what? Bomb my country?" Dawson flicked his weapon, dismissing the statement. "We've already covered that." He squatted back down. "Get this through your skull, General. I don't care about your family. I don't want to touch your family, and I won't touch your family, if you tell me what I want to know."

"What *do* you want to know?"

"Who the codes were sold to."

"I have no idea. All I know is they were sold on condition they be used within two weeks."

"How many codes did you sell?"

"All of them."

"And how many is that?"

"Slightly over one thousand."

Dawson felt his chest tighten as he exchanged a glance with Chernov who, standing behind the General, could express his "holy shit!" expression.

"And how many are still active?"

"That I don't know. Enough, I am certain."

"And where are they located?"

"Again, I don't know. But you do."

Dawson's eyebrows shot up.

"What do you mean?"

"You stole the list, with locations, in 1982."

"Explain."

"One of your spies stole the list and we were never able to recover it. Your own intelligence apparatus has all the answers you need, and has had it for over thirty years."

Levkin began to chuckle as Dawson was unable to keep the surprise from appearing on his face, even if only for a split second. The chuckle became a roaring laugh and Dawson was about to kick the man in the bleeding thigh to shut him up when Niner interrupted from the prow of their smaller boat.

"BD, something's up!"

He pointed to the north and Dawson peered into the distance, his hand shading his eyes, but could see nothing.

"What is it?"

"Looks like two helicopters coming our way."

"Type?"

"Looks like two Mi-24 Hinds."

The laughter stopped and Dawson looked down at their prisoner.

"And now you pay for what you have done," smiled Levkin.

"Did you check him for a tracking device?" asked Dawson as he flipped over the railing and back onto their boat, Niner untying them.

"Of course," replied Chernov, stripping out of his clothes and donning scuba gear along with his partner. "It must have been a delayed activation beacon."

"Activated when he or one of his men didn't check in after a certain interval," said Dawson, nodding in agreement. He pointed at Levkin as Niner started the engine. "He's all yours, we got what we needed. Thanks again, Colonel." He gave the Russian a casual salute as Niner pushed the engine to full power, banking away from the larger boat and heading back toward Turkish soil to the south.

Dawson looked back to see Chernov kick Levkin overboard, then the two Russian Spetsnaz members rolling over the side and into the water, disappearing seconds later, Levkin struggling against his bonds as he began to sink. Dawson could see the two Russian Hind helicopters clearly now, both racing toward the beacon that had obviously been activated.

"Give it everything this old tub's got!" he yelled at Niner, knowing it was already being done, his words more directed at the old tub herself. He was quite certain these helicopters racing toward them were *not* under Russian military control, most likely mercenary or corrupt military.

Which meant they wouldn't hesitate to fire upon a vessel in Turkish waters.

The gunships' noses pulled up as their pilots killed their speed, two men dropping from each gunship's cabin into the cold water below in search of their drowning leader. The lead gunship's weapons pods, bristling with ordnance, flashed momentarily in the sun, and Dawson had memories of seeing them for the first time while watching Rambo 2.

They were much more terrifying in person.

The bullets in their Glocks would simply bounce off the armor, and unlike Sly, neither of them had arrows with explosive heads.

If they were engaged, they were dead.

The helicopters circled the boat, waiting, then suddenly the surface of the water was broken, the rescue team, their charge in the grip of one of the men, bursting from the water. They swam to Chernov's abandoned boat, and as soon as Levkin was on board, Dawson saw the two gunships slowly turn toward them. Dawson quickly entered a message into his secure phone and hit Send as the helicopters banked, their noses dipping as they picked up speed, heading directly toward them.

"Here they come!" he yelled over the roar of the engine and the crashing of the waves against the prow as the boat skipped along, entirely too slowly.

He joined Niner at the helm then spotted several flares strapped to the side. Grabbing the flare gun, he loaded a cartridge.

"The mujahedeen wouldn't have needed Stingers if flares worked, BD," said Niner as he glanced at the flare gun.

"Any better ideas?"

"Go back in time and remind our Russian friend that he should scan for radio signals at regular intervals?"

"Fire up the flux capacitor."

"There's no way this thing is getting to eighty-eight miles per hour," yelled Niner as one of the helicopters roared overhead, banking so that it ended up facing them, blocking their path. "Okay, now what?"

Dawson glanced at the second helicopter, it keeping pace on their starboard side, none of its weapons trained on them except what was probably a fifty caliber manned by someone dressed head to toe in black, the side door open. The gun was pointed at the water rather than at them, which to Dawson meant the lead gunship, blocking their path, was the one who was going to engage them.

"Secure the wheel," ordered Dawson.

Niner grabbed two ropes on either side of the wheel and hooked them over two of the spokes then joined Dawson near the rear of the boat. Dawson looked ahead. The Hind gunship hovered in front of them, the distance rapidly closing.

"If they open fire, or we hit, jump," he said to Niner, counting down the seconds in his head before impact. A missile dropped off the right weapons pod. "Jump!" he yelled and Niner bailed over the side as Dawson spun, firing the flare gun at the gunship to his right. The flare launched, racing toward the open side of the gunship as Dawson dove over the side, their boat erupting into a ball of flame as his body pierced the water.

The action above turned into a dull roar as he swam away from their craft, a glance over his shoulder showing it now a smoldering mess, flames licking the surface of the water directly overhead, debris beginning to rain down on him as he continued to try and put some distance between him and the boat.

As he swam his lungs burned in protest and he began to kick toward the surface. His face broke the water and with a gasp he pushed out the stale air from his lungs and sucked in a fresh breath. To his left the boat was no more, what remained slowly sinking as the gunship that had fired advanced toward its victim, but to his right he heard the whining of an engine and his head spun as he heard a splash. He caught a glimpse of someone dropping into the water about a hundred feet away, the helicopter banking hard to the right, smoke billowing from the open door, a red glow emanating from within as his aim had obviously been true.

To his dismay however the helicopter didn't plunge into the sea, the pilot not panicking like in the movies, instead regaining control and hovering in position until the flare burned itself out. The roar of the lead gunship's main guns caused him to spin toward the wreckage. Little spurts of water shot up from the surface as the shells pierced the choppy sea and Dawson's thoughts immediately turned to Niner. He scanned the area but couldn't see him. He looked farther back, the boat having travelled some distance after Niner had bailed, and breathed a sigh of relief as he saw his friend about two hundred feet back. It was just for a moment as he took a breath then dropped below the surface again.

Which is a damned good idea.

Dawson filled his lungs then dropped below the waves, slowly swimming forward, toward Turkey, the coast now only a couple of miles distant. The swim without the gunships would be fairly easy, but with them circling overhead, it would be almost impossible. Their only hope was for the gunships to be engaged by Turkish forces.

He popped up and sucked in another breath just as the lead gunship banked directly toward him.

Shit!

He bent forward and began kicking hard, trying to gain as much depth as possible, when the first rounds sliced through the water ahead of him. The streaks of vacuum caused by the red hot shells as they instantly boiled the water in their paths tore apart the water ahead of him, their speed trimmed dramatically by the water but not enough to prevent them from tearing him apart.

Suddenly the shots stopped and he began to push for the surface, his lungs screaming in protest, desperate for air. He breached the water with a gasp in time to see the lead chopper pushing forward as it tried to gain speed, the other gunship, smoke still coming from inside, banking for home to his right.

He looked back to see Niner treading water behind him, pointing to his right. Dawson looked over his other shoulder and saw a Turkish frigate slicing through the water, almost on top of their position as it opened fire, two missiles leaving their pods and streaking across the sea, barely above the surface, then slamming into their targets, both fleeing gunships erupting into massive explosions, the shockwave roaring across the water as their weapons and fuels tore at everything around them, moments later plunging into the cold waters, nothing but smoldering wrecks remaining on the surface along with quickly dissipating clouds of black and grey smoke where they had flown only moments before.

Dawson waved at the ship as it slowed near their positions, two rescue craft launching within minutes. As he was pulled aboard the dinghy by several Turkish sailors, he breathed a sigh of relief, searching the horizon for the boat Colonel Chernov had brought, and Major General Levkin's rescuers had taken him to, but found nothing but a mix of dots on the horizon, the General obviously now in the safety of Russian waters.

A seasoned naval lieutenant commander pulled Dawson upright from the bottom of the boat.

"Are you Mr. White?"

Dawson nodded.

"I am Lieutenant Commander Balik and I have a message from Mr. Grey."

Grey was Colonel Clancy's code name for situations like this.

"What's that?" asked Dawson as he wiped the water from his face.

"You have some explaining to do."

Litschental Road, Black Forest, Germany
Present Day

Dylan Kane's neck, back and ass were killing him. Not necessarily in that order. After a ridiculous number of hours waiting in various airports he had finally arrived in Frankfurt. Eventually clearing customs, he had picked up a car prearranged by Langley with a care package locked in the trunk that Kane had waited until outside of Frankfurt to open.

Glock 22, suppressor, a few mags and new comm gear, his old stuff destroyed intentionally before landing in Georgia—he couldn't risk being caught with it.

The GPS in the dash was indicating he was almost at his destination, if the destination even existed. They were still assuming the numbers were coordinates, yet had no evidence anything was actually at the presumed location.

One thing that had Kane partially convinced he was at least in the right country was the fact he had picked up a tail at the airport. Somebody knew he was in Germany, and they had followed him almost all the way to Munich before he lost them, switching rentals in case the original was bugged. He then crossed southern Germany toward the Black Forest, or Schwartzwald as the German's called it, tail free.

It had doubled the length of his trip, but at least he knew he was alone.

As he drove along the quiet, winding road, the trees thick on either side, an area opened to his right revealing a gasthaus. His stomach rumbled as he resisted the urge to pull in, his foot now off the accelerator, slowing the car, nearing the entrance to the parking lot with a smattering of vehicles.

One caught his eye, it matching the make, model, year and color of his tail he had lost in Munich. It sat parked, facing the road, a grey haired man sitting behind the wheel, staring straight at him.

The man waved.

What the hell is going on?

Kane lifted a few fingers off the steering wheel in acknowledgement, gently pressing on the accelerator, his appetite gone, both sides now knowing each had been made.

But who the hell is the other side? Grey hair? Grey Network?

Kane felt slightly uneasy. It was clear these people were well connected and very good at their jobs, it obvious they weren't concerned about being spotted by him. But who the hell were they? And why were they following him without any concern about being seen? It ran contrary to pretty much every op he had been on. You almost never wanted to be seen.

Unless you're trying to herd someone somewhere.

The thought had his heart racing a bit. This was the only road into the area where the GPS coordinates were located, so the man had taken a chance he'd be coming from the north-east. And that assumed there wasn't someone else sitting at the other end of the road watching for him.

No matter what, they had him where they wanted him, and they knew he knew.

But why?

This entire mission had bothered him since the beginning. Coordinates handed over by a stranger to his friend, with inside knowledge on what was now the largest counter-intelligence operation since after 9/11.

The only difference this time was they knew something was up, and had a chance to prevent it.

And prevent it they must, the repercussions potentially devastating.

A thought popped into his mind, suggesting a possible alternative to why this Grey Network might be following him.

Protection.

His eyebrows shot up at that idea as he drove deeper into the forest. If that were the case, he appreciated it, but would rather a Delta Team than some septuagenarians.

His rearview mirror showed clear, there obviously no need to follow him now. Various lanes were cut into the forest leading to houses, cottages and campgrounds, and according to his GPS he was only a few hundred meters away from the coordinates, which meant a turn was due. The map showed the coordinates to his right and a small dirt road, overgrown with brush on either side, made for an uninviting turn.

He cranked the wheel and turned into the lane, the leaves and branches of the brush scraping at the paint job on either side. He bumped along for about fifty feet, the tree roots crisscrossing the lane giving the suspension a workout. The brush thinned, the lane widening slightly, then a cleared area opened in front of him, sunlight pouring in, revealing a small half-timber home, the dark wood beams and white stucco clashing beautifully, large flower boxes spilling over the windowsills and railings of the inviting porch.

As he continued the final few feet, he parked under a large fir tree, once again cast into shadows from the branches overhead. Which was when he noticed the small house was built in the center of half a dozen large Norway Spruces, their lower branches trimmed, the upper branches blocking any overhead view of the house, the cleared area where the sun was shining showing no signs of human life.

If Kane had to guess, life did exist there except during satellite flybys, the schedule of which he was certain the tenant knew.

An array of satellite dishes suggested modern communications and electricity, so if the tenant was off the grid, he wasn't completely off.

A Volvo, late model, was parked inside a nearby shed, it too under the shadow cast by the treed canopy overhead, suggesting its owner was at home. Kane walked across the bed of needles, a mix of deep orange and brown, thick from many seasons of shedding. He didn't bother putting his hand on his weapon let alone drawing it. There was no way his arrival was missed, and if he were indeed in danger, he would have been taken out by now.

He knocked on the door.

"Come in!"

English.

Definitely expected.

Kane opened the door and stepped inside. It took a moment for his eyes to adjust. To his right was a cramped living area, several chairs facing a wall with an impressive plasma display, every other wall filled with bookshelves lined with an array of tomes or knickknacks, some of which he immediately recognized from the Cold War era. Hats, badges, guns, cameras, microfilm readers. A veritable treasure chest of history most spy museums would kill for.

It was clear to Kane that once inside this home, guests were meant to know this man's craft, which meant uninvited guests either never made it in, or never made it out.

To the left was a kitchen where sounds of someone busying themselves could be heard, and ahead of him appeared to be the door to a bedroom, another to a bathroom.

It was small by North American standards, but in Europe, more than acceptable for a single male.

"Take a seat, I'll be there in a minute," said the voice from the kitchen.

Kane entered the living area and selected a chair with a good view of the front door, window and kitchen. To his left was a small table with a lamp, turned off, what looked like a first edition copy of David Copperfield, and a pewter frame with a picture of a very attractive woman in perhaps her forties. There was no evidence of a woman's touch anywhere, no pictures of family, but this was obviously his host's usual chair, and she therefore of some importance to him.

Moments later a man, easily in his seventies, exited the kitchen carrying a tea service, the tray and its contents shaking unapologetically as the obviously spry man strode with confidence and strength toward the center of the room where he placed the tray on a table, then wiped his hands on an apron he wore.

He extended his hand.

"Dylan Kane I presume?"

Kane nodded, rising and shaking the man's hand.

"Please, sit," said the man, waving off Kane's politeness. "How do you like your tea?"

Kane was tempted to inform the man of his hatred for all hot beverages, but decided to bite his tongue and play along.

"Two milks, two sugars."

The man smiled, preparing the tea, then handing a cup and saucer over. As he prepared his own, Kane noticed that the service was for three.

He kept silent.

The old man sat down and sipped.

"Ahh, that's better. I'm so happy you arrived when you did, otherwise I would have had to delay tea."

The man's accent was clearly American, the tea shtick seeming a little out of place.

Kane still didn't say anything.

The man looked at him, resting his tea on his lap.

"You have questions."

Kane nodded.

"Many."

"Where would you like to start?"

"How about your name?"

The man smiled, his head bouncing slightly.

"Alex West. Pleased to meet you."

Safe House 'R', Moscow, USSR
February 7, 1982

West closed the garage door behind the departing van then hid the microfilm canister atop a rafter joint, jumping back down as he heard someone try the door. With the microfilm hidden, and unlikely to be found without an exhaustive search, he was clean for the moment, however how he would be able to explain away his presence here was another thing entirely.

Alex West, Canadian tractor salesman, had evaded his KGB "escort" this morning, had not returned to his hotel, and had not kept his scheduled meeting this afternoon with the Soviet Ministry of Agriculture and Food. He had however called them and postponed the meeting until tomorrow, claiming food poisoning from his questionable breakfast. He had hung up before they could ask where he was, nursing his condition.

It was possible his cover could be maintained.

But he still couldn't explain his presence here.

His task now was to try and delay any search from beginning for Sergie and his family. He only needed five minutes, the second stop on the Underground Railroad never more than five minutes from the first. During those precious five minutes the first man in the passenger seat would be gathering all their ID and other identifiable items, giving them their new identities, then explaining what would happen at the next stop. And at that next stop they would swap vehicles in under a minute, the first vehicle leaving in the opposite direction, ensuring they hadn't been followed. If any tail was detected, there were bail points all along the route where the driver could escape on foot down a path too narrow for vehicles to follow, where another vehicle would be waiting at the other end to swoop them away.

In all the years of operating the Underground Railway, not a single CIA operative had ever been caught on the first leg of the trip, or the decoy. It was so meticulously planned and practiced, almost every eventuality was planned for. And West knew that if the second part of the route was begun successfully, there was almost no chance of the family being caught.

Any number of routes could be used that would take them across the country to various points. Checkpoints were never avoided, the human cargo always well hidden in secret compartments. End points could be in Poland where they'd depart by ship, sympathetic Solidarity labor union members providing assistance, East Berlin, where transit into the West was easier than the Soviet's wished, Turkey through the mountains, or any other number of border countries through unguarded, deserted terrain. Even submarines and small planes were used.

It didn't matter how, the route, though rarely used, functioned well.

And West had absolutely no clue where stage two started, or where the railroad ended.

Sergie and his family were most likely safe, and he was about to have his cover blown.

There was a knock at the door, the rattling having stopped.

KGB doesn't knock. At least not gently.

He stepped over to the door and unlocked it, deciding he might as well take a chance. Opening the door his jaw nearly dropped, the last person he expected to see stepping inside quickly, closing the door.

It was Adelle Bertrand, his consort and French spy.

"What the hell are you doing here?" he asked, looking out the small window in the door.

"Trying to save your bottom, mon chéri."

131

"Is there anybody out there?" he asked, looking at her.

"They just raided your friend's apartment and have begun a sweep of the area."

"How did you find me?"

"I've been following you all day, since the hotel this morning."

"Impossible!"

"And yet here I am."

West couldn't argue with that logic.

"Any idea if my cover is blown?"

"A colleague has informed me that your room at the hotel was searched, then ordered made up again to hide the fact they were there. It may still be intact."

"If we arrived together, it just may save us."

Adelle frowned.

"And risk blowing my cover?"

"And yet you are here."

She smiled, patting his cheek.

"What is so important that I should do this? You know as soon as we are seen together, we will be forever linked, and if they know either of us are what we are, they will assume the other is too."

West cocked an eyebrow, dropping his chin slightly, staring at her.

"Do you honestly think, after all these years, they don't know exactly who we are?"

She grinned.

"A girl can always hope." She looked about. "So, what is the big secret?"

West retrieved the microfilm and handed it to her along with a Swiss Army knife, magnifying glass extended.

She quickly began to look over the intel, gasping on several occasions, stopping before the end, there just too much information to read now.

"Has this been deployed?" she asked as she handed everything back to him.

"Near the end there is deployment information including dates and locations."

"Where?"

"All over the United States, Europe, the world."

"This could change the balance of power!"

West nodded.

"Absolutely. And we need to get this intel back to our side so they can stop this."

"If they even think you have it, there's no way you're getting on an aircraft tomorrow and flying home."

West thought for a moment then looked at Adelle.

"But if you had it…"

"Then they would search you, but find nothing."

"I would need assurances that you would pass the microfilm on to my government."

"Of course. After I have made a copy for the French government."

"Of course," smiled West, returning the microfilm to its container and handing it to her. "How will you get it out?"

"We have a drop near here. I will go there now, then return to my hotel. And what will you do?"

"I was supposed to evac with them, but when the lookout saw you, I decided to stay in case you were KGB so I could buy them time."

"So it is my fault you are stuck here?"

She seemed genuinely crestfallen, and West stepped closer, placing a hand on her cheek.

"No, it's not your fault. I should have gone with them regardless. And besides, you were trying to help. I could never fault you for that."

She looked up at him, smiling.

He leaned in and kissed her, gently at first, then as his hand moved from her cheek to the back of her head, his fingers intertwining in her hair, she pushed herself against him, her arms wrapping around him, her hands sliding under his open jacket, gripping at his shoulders as the kiss smoldered, the frenzy building as years of pent-up frustration began to release. He felt movement below, and so did she, breaking the kiss, her fingers pulling on his hair, separating them for a moment.

"Do we have time?" she asked, breathlessly, then dove back in, devouring his mouth before an answer could be given, her hands reaching for his belt buckle.

West couldn't have said 'no' if he wanted to.

Seconds later his pants were around his ankles along with his briefs, the chill of the warehouse on his now exposed self brief as Adelle dropped to her knees and made him remember why he could never resist her. He enjoyed her ministrations, removing his jacket and tossing it on the floor. He dropped to his knees, pushing her onto the jacket as she removed her own pants.

He grinned at the lack of panties.

"Were you expecting this?" he asked as he lay on top of her, kissing her now exposed chest, his lips and tongue exploring territory it hadn't enjoyed in years.

"One always has hope," she gasped. She grabbed his exposed buttocks and pulled him inside, crying out as he did so. "Hurry! We may only have minutes."

West smiled, kissing her as he obeyed her orders, the frenzied danger of it all, the adrenaline rushing through both their systems, more than making up for any lack of foreplay, had them both gasping in ecstasy within minutes.

West lay on top of Adelle for a few seconds, his lips kissing her bare shoulder, catching his breath. She tapped him on his back.

"We better hurry," she whispered. He pushed himself up on his elbows, and kissed her one more time, a kiss returned with a passion that threatened to reawaken flagging things.

She noticed and broke the kiss.

"Get off me you bad boy!" she laughed, pushing him away.

He rose and quickly dressed, she doing the same, he ogling her incredible body the entire time. She buttoned up her blouse and he groaned. She grinned.

Pulling her jacket back on and zipping it up, she planted a quick kiss on him then rushed for the rear door.

"Until we meet again, mon chéri!"

She was gone before he could reply. He picked up his jacket from the floor and held it to his nose, taking in her scent, then put it on, the cold now making itself felt.

He checked the front door and saw a lone car approaching, but no evidence they were being watched. Leaving through the back door he saw the footprints of his French vixen go to the right. An irresistible urge told him to follow her, to see if there was some way they could reunite for the night, then the more logical side of him drove him forward on the mission of making certain she was safe.

He quickly followed the footprints before they became lost in the new falling snow. They were heading back toward the hotel, but then took a turn away.

The drop must be close.

He looked ahead and saw a figure in the dark step out of an apartment building and continue away from him. There was no doubt it was her.

The drop must be in the apartment.

135

Which meant the hard-won intelligence should be safely out of the country tomorrow in a French diplomatic pouch, then hopefully into his government's hands shortly thereafter so they could find and disarm the already deployed Crimson Rush before it could be used by the Soviets.

She turned a corner and strode out of sight. West quickened his pace slightly, his mission to ensure the safe delivery of the intel to the drop off now completed, his mind instead racing to figure a way for them to spend some more time together.

But he knew it was impossible.

He slowed himself, checking his libido, chastising himself for jeopardizing the mission for the sake of another roll in the hay—a spectacular roll, mind you. Shifting his thoughts to his return to the hotel, he pulled out his wallet and removed a piece of cardboard from the billfold lining. He popped it in his mouth, beginning to chew it, and within moments he could feel his stomach start to churn as the ipecac it had been soaked in began to release and do its damage.

A scream ahead had him spitting the cardboard into a snow bank as he began to run to the end of the street. He skidded to a halt in time to see Adelle being shoved into the back of a black Volga by two men, clearly KGB. She looked out the back window as the doors slammed shut, the light inside cutting out but not before he could see her shaking her head, signaling him to do nothing.

He turned around, stepping back into the shadows when he heard a match flare. Spinning around, he saw the face of his old rival, Viktor Zorkin, one of the KGB's better agents, their clashes legendary amongst themselves. West was about to pop him in the nose when Zorkin shook his head, raising his weapon into view.

"Uh-uh," said Zorkin, taking a drag on his cigarette then blowing it in West's face.

American brand.

"Shall we go quietly?"

"We both know you have nothing on me," said West.

Zorkin smiled, flicking his Makarov pistol.

West, hands raised slightly, stepped back and began to walk toward the warehouse.

"This time things are different, my friend. We have photos of you with Lt. Colonel Sergie Tuzik, meeting on several separate occasions that we know of. And now he and his family have disappeared after he stole some very valuable intelligence from us."

"Search me, Viktor. I don't have anything of the sort on me."

"Of course you don't. But you will tell me where you hid it before the night is through."

"I think you know better than that."

Zorkin chuckled.

"Oh, I know you won't break. But your friend? I don't think you could stand to watch her being tortured."

West's heart began to race. *Adelle!* This was exactly why you couldn't form attachments for a woman in this business. It meant leverage.

And they had it.

He hadn't admitted it until tonight, and he was pretty certain Adelle hadn't either, but there was something there, some spark that went beyond just sex.

There were genuine feelings there.

And he cursed himself for it.

"Who?" he asked, playing dumb.

"Adelle Bertrand. French spy. Very sexy."

"Sorry, I have no idea what you're talking about."

137

"You may play dumb, but it won't help you or her. We know about the two of you." Zorkin sighed. "I'm sorry, Alex, but you screwed up. They have leverage on you now, and there's nothing that can be done about it."

West knew Zorkin was right, and he was at a loss as to what to do other than appeal to the man's humanity, which he knew existed.

West stopped, turning to face his adversary.

"Please, Viktor, she has nothing to do with this."

Zorkin stopped, tossing his cigarette butt into the snow.

"We both know that isn't true."

West decided to take a different tact.

"Do you even know what this is all about?"

Zorkin gave no indication of whether he knew or not, simply replying, "It doesn't matter."

"But it does. All of what we have done in the past, those things, those missions, they didn't matter, not like this. This tips the balance of power too much."

"Which means we will be victorious."

"No, it means your leaders might just get foolish enough to think the same thing, and start a war that they may very well win, but not before the world is turned into a nuclear wasteland, the hammer and sickle fluttering in the cold wind of a nuclear winter."

Zorkin said nothing, merely flicking his weapon for West to move on.

West stood his ground.

"Have you heard of Crimson Rush?"

Zorkin shook his head.

"Don't do this, Alex. You're embarrassing yourself. You never struck me as the type to plead for your life."

West shook his head, lowering his voice.

"I'm not. And I'm not pleading for hers. I'm pleading for theirs," he said, pointing at the apartment block across the street, "and those like them back home. I think you need to know what Crimson Rush is before you continue down this path."

"I have no interest—"

West interrupted him, giving him the briefest of descriptions.

Zorkin's eyebrows shot up, his weapon dropping slightly before he regained his composure, raising it again.

"And you have proof?"

West had already anticipated this question and had decided against trying to retrieve the microfilm. Even if it meant his and Adelle's lives, it was more important for that intel to make it out of the Soviet Union.

"You have my word. And the fact you are here."

Zorkin pursed his lips, the gun lowering slightly.

"Go on."

"Why are you here?"

"Huh?"

"Why are you here? You've never picked me up before."

"You evaded your tail and skipped your scheduled meeting."

"And they assigned *you*?"

Zorkin paused for a moment, as if searching for an answer. He fished another cigarette from his pocket, lighting it.

"I'd offer you one, but I know you don't smoke."

West smiled slightly.

"Thanks for remembering me."

Zorkin jabbed the air with his cigarette.

"You do have a point there. I was due to go on a mission but was pulled to track you down."

"How'd you find me?"

"It was easy once I saw Adelle was staying at your hotel."

West felt himself flush and was thankful the light on the street was dim at best.

"So you followed her?"

"Da. A much better assignment, I assure you," he said with a wry smile, "but then again you already know that, receiving a demonstration of her feminine wiles tonight."

Now he outright blushed.

"You weren't—"

"Watching?" asked Zorkin with a wink. "What kind of man do you take me for?"

West's head bobbed as a smile spread across his face.

"Exactly the type that would watch at the window."

Zorkin laughed, taking another drag on his cigarette.

"So what are we going to do about this?"

"You need to let that intel get out."

Zorkin looked over at the building where Adelle had done her drop only minutes before. A pit formed in West's stomach as he suddenly realized that Zorkin knew exactly where it was since he had been tailing Adelle.

"There is some merit in that idea," Zorkin finally said, turning back to West. "I agree, if it is what you say it is—"

"It is."

"—then it will upset the balance, and there are those who would take advantage of that in the Politburo. I agree this can't be allowed."

"So what do we do?"

"I bring you in and tell them that I saw you burn the microfilm before I could stop you."

"And Sergie and his family?"

"They are already out of our reach."

"And Adelle?"

"Unfortunately there is nothing I can do for her. She is already in the hands of my colleagues, who will have already begun interrogating her." Zorkin threw the cigarette at the ground, as if in disgust. "Women should not be in this business. It is too easy for us men to abuse them in ways we would never do to each other."

West felt bile fill his mouth as a mental image of Adelle being raped repeatedly filled his mind.

"Do you think they'll do that?"

"There are many good men in the KGB," replied Zorkin. "Most, in fact. We are patriots that love our country. But there are too many that are drunk on the power their position gives them who would definitely do such a thing if given the chance."

"Let's hope good men have her now."

Zorkin shook his head.

"That, I cannot say."

"What now?"

Zorkin raised his weapon again.

"You come with me, and I try to keep you alive."

Alex West Residence, Black Forest, Germany
Present Day

Dylan Kane took a polite sip of his tea as the old man's name played through his head, coming up blank.

"Biscuits!" exclaimed his host, jumping from his chair and rushing back to the kitchen. "Mustn't forget the biscuits," muttered the voice, Kane beginning to feel like Luke Skywalker with Yoda preparing dinner. If he found himself whining about meeting a CIA master he'd slit his own throat.

West returned, a tray filled with cookies, tea biscuits, crumpets and other assorted treats proudly held out in front. Placing them on the table next to the tea service, he returned to his seat, it too with a good view of the front door and window. The old man looked slightly uncomfortable in it, as if Kane had taken his favorite chair.

"They're all homemade, I assure you," said West, motioning toward the tray. "Please, try something."

Kane was starving, his stomach rumbling at the array of food in front of him. He selected a tea biscuit, splitting it in two, a burst of steam escaping, these clearly having come out of the oven recently. Kane had to assume this West was a former spy. It made him wonder of his own future. Would he too be living like a hermit, off the grid, baking treats and drinking tea?

No effin' way.

He had always expected to be six feet under or vaporized, an anonymous star added to the Memorial Wall at Langley, mourned by few if any. He just hoped it wasn't something stupid. If he were to go out, he wanted to be going out serving his country, doing something useful, bettered by a better man, not dying because he goofed.

He bit into the tea biscuit and nearly died.

"This is fantastic!" he exclaimed, genuinely surprised at the man's culinary skills.

West beamed with pride, himself selecting a crumpet and buttering it.

"I'm pleased you like it. And also pleased you trusted me enough to taste something before I did."

Kane chewed through his chuckle, swallowing as he held up a finger indicating a response was to come. His mouth clear, he said, "I figured you'd poison or drug the tea. Much simpler."

"True, but you hate hot drinks. Maybe I couldn't be sure you'd actually drink it, or enough."

Kane's eyebrows jumped at the statement.

"Now how the hell do you know I don't like hot drinks?"

West laughed.

"You just told me."

"Uh huh."

"Deductive reasoning. You've barely touched your tea, you were uncertain even what to ask me to put in it, and every sip has been accompanied by a painful expression. Not to mention that at every rest-stop along the way here you never bought coffee, you bought Coke Light or some other caffeinated soft drink as opposed to the traditional large cup of coffee most road warriors use to stay alert."

"So that was your man following me?"

West nodded.

"When did you make him?"

"Pulling out of the airport."

"That quickly?"

Kane nodded.

"A couple of too eager lane changes. I think he's a little rusty."

West laughed.

"He'll be devastated to hear that, I'm sure. In his day he was one of the best."

Kane put his plate down, eyeing another tea biscuit, but deciding against it.

"What's this all about?" he asked. "Why am I here?"

"Patience, young man, patience. This is the moment for tea, for pleasantries."

"And when can we expect your other guest to arrive?"

West smiled.

"Any moment now, if I still know him."

"Who is he?"

"An old rival, an old friend."

The sound of a car driving over pine needles caused the old man to pop up from his chair. He stepped over to an old roll top desk and pulled a gun from the top drawer, checking to make sure a round was chambered and the safety was off.

"Why do you need that?" asked Kane as West returned to his chair.

"I'm not sure how good a friend he is."

West Berlin, West Germany
February 12, 1982

Alex West sipped a cup of glorious Western coffee. Sometimes he wondered if NATO just dropped good coffee all over the Warsaw Pact if they'd surrender just to have access. It would definitely demonstrate the West's superiority.

"Where is this microfilm now?" asked Control.

"The French should have it. Didn't they pass it on?"

"No."

Goddamned French.

They called themselves part of NATO, but never really bought into it fully, their government being one step away from communist. If they had Poland on their eastern border rather than Germany, they'd have probably joined the commies.

"Press them on it. I know the drop was made, and that it was allowed to go through."

"A drop made by a French agent who has not been seen since."

"No, she was captured by the Soviets just before they picked me up."

"And you claim despite them knowing what you were up to, the drop was allowed to proceed."

"Yes. Viktor Zorkin is a patriot, but he's not insane. Once he heard what Crimson Rush was, he agreed with me that it had to be stopped."

"A top Soviet agent agreed with you that his country shouldn't have an advantage over yours."

"Yes."

"It sounds to me as if this entire mission went astray because you hooked up with an old flame."

"Bullshit!" West held up his hand, halting any response. "I'm sorry, but I'm tired. Haven't you debriefed Sergie Tuzik yet? He can confirm that the intel was delivered into my hands and what was on it."

"He's refusing to cooperate until he's on a beach in Florida with a government pension."

"Then put him on the goddamned beach!"

"The Soviets have asked for him back, claiming he is a high-level bureaucrat that was abducted by you."

Bullshit!

At least this time West kept his anger bottled.

"Listen to me. Why would I make this up?"

"Nobody is accusing you of that."

"Huh?"

There was a pause, then the usually cold voice softened slightly.

"Alex, I believe you. I believe everything you have said. But do you really think it's plausible? Think about it. The first word we received about Crimson Rush was almost two weeks ago, and that middleman is dead. Hole plugged. Sergie, a hole in their security for years, is now plugged. You and a French agent have been captured and neutralized—your careers are effectively over. Isn't it more likely that Crimson Rush was invented to draw people out so they could identify the leaks?"

West felt his chest tighten and his pulse quicken. His stomach began to flip as he realized everything Control was saying was completely plausible.

"But what about Zorkin? Why would he cooperate?"

"Perhaps he wasn't in on the plan."

"But why was he here?"

"To save you."

146

West's eyebrows popped.

"Huh?"

"Viktor Zorkin walked into one of our offices and gave himself up, told us about your status, and gave us the contact information to initiate an exchange."

"What?!"

"He let himself be captured so he could save you."

West sank back in his chair, no longer certain of anything.

Alex West Residence, Black Forest, Germany
Present Day

Kane remained seated but reached around his back to remove the Glock he had tucked into his belt. His host, Alex West, sat in his chair calmly, gun resting on the arm, lightly gripped in his right hand, aimed at the door.

Footsteps on the pine needles could be heard through the partially opened window, then finally the sound of shoes on the wood porch. There was a knock, three crisp raps.

"Come in!" called West, rising to greet their visitor. Kane didn't rise, instead he shifted his weapon slightly, aiming it at the door, waist height.

The doorknob turned and the door was pushed open slightly. Kane could see a tall figure but no details, the door with eastern exposure, the sun well on its way to setting in the west. The door opened some more and a foot made an appearance, and finally the entire body, the light inside revealing an elderly man with a large nose and overgrown ears, his hair a brilliant silver, his cheeks flush with energy.

He looked at Kane and nodded, then turned to West, pointing at the gun.

"Is that for me?" he asked in near perfect English, a hint of a Russian accent in the background that most wouldn't detect, but Kane had been trained to.

"Do I need it?" asked West.

"If you did, I wouldn't have come. I would have sent some old friends instead."

West laughed, placing the gun beside the tray of biscuits then extending his arms. "Viktor!"

The new arrival, apparently named Viktor, broke out into a wide smile, his own arms extending. The two men embraced warmly, thumping each other on the back until finally they both pushed away and simply stared for a few seconds, each sizing the other up as if they hadn't seen each other in years.

"Forgive my manners," said West finally, motioning toward Kane. Kane rose, tucking his weapon back into his belt. "This is Dylan Kane, CIA Special Agent Dylan Kane."

"Viktor Zorkin," said the man, extending his hand. Kane shook it, surprised by the strength of the grip, returning it slightly so the man would realize that Kane knew exactly what the man was doing, and wouldn't tolerate any bullshit, septuagenarian or not. Zorkin smiled, easing his grip slightly. "Good. Very good. Never allow a man's perceived weakness to lower your guard. Just because I am old does not mean I am not a threat."

Kane released the man's hand with a nod and a slight smile.

"Never be under the false assumption I wouldn't kill you where you stand, regardless of your age."

Zorkin began to laugh, his head tilting back as the volume increased. Suddenly it turned into a hacking cough and he covered his mouth, reaching into his jacket as he searched for a seat. Kane stepped aside to offer him his when Zorkin's hand emerged from his pocket with a small Beretta gripped tightly, pointed at Kane's belly.

"What was that you were saying?" asked Zorkin, still coughing. "Never let yourself be distracted by another's discomfort."

Kane cleared his throat and motioned with his eyes for Zorkin to look down. Zorkin did and again began to laugh as he saw Kane's Glock already pointing at Zorkin's testicles. Zorkin stepped back, shoving his gun in his pocket and retrieving an inhaler as he dropped into West's chair. He shook the small device then took several puffs, his cough quickly subsiding. He looked at West and pointed at Kane.

"I like him!" he said, his voice still raspy. "He's not like many of them today I hear about. He might actually survive to our age."

West nodded as he poured tea for the new arrival. Handing it to a grateful Zorkin, he sat down in the third least favorable chair for covering your back, and resumed his own cup.

"I see you got my message," he said as he placed his cup on its saucer, balanced on his knee.

"Of course, why else would I be here?"

"I wasn't sure you'd come."

"What has it been? Thirty years?"

"And then some. The last time I saw you was at Checkpoint Charlie, the night of the exchange." West took another sip, Kane and Zorkin doing the same. Kane winced to which West jumped to his feet. "I'm so sorry," he said as he rushed into the kitchen. "We were interrupted and I forgot." Kane and Zorkin exchanged glances and Kane shrugged. Moments later West reappeared with a tall glass of soda and ice. "I forgot you hate tea!"

"You hate tea!" exclaimed Zorkin. "And you expect to be a spy?"

Kane took the glass with a smiled thank you, and took a sip of the ice cold brew, immediately recognizing the Coke Light taste.

"Thanks," he said to West, then turned to Zorkin. "I've managed so far. When I'm undercover I hide my dislike better."

"I hope so," said the old man, reaching forward and refilling his own cup, waving West off. "Sit old man, I can do it myself."

West chuckled and leaned back in his chair, taking a bite of a crumpet he had just buttered.

"I never saw you again after the exchange, what happened?"

"I was promoted."

"Ooh, sorry to hear that. Same thing happened to me."

Kane listened to the exchange, trying to size both men up. They were obviously friends of a sort, both spies, and with talk of an exchange at Checkpoint Charlie, they were obviously rivals, with Zorkin most likely former KGB and West CIA.

Their exchange continued for a few minutes, Kane remaining silent, merely sipping his diet soft drink, when finally the reminisces became more relevant, or at least Kane hoped they did.

"So why am I here?" asked Zorkin.

"I think you know why."

Zorkin nodded.

"Crimson Rush."

CIA Headquarters, Langley, Virginia

Chris Leroux had nearly sprinted the entire way from his cubicle to his boss' office, the Chief's aide waving him in. Leif Morrison, National Clandestine Service Chief for the CIA, sat behind his desk and looked up as Leroux entered, panting slightly. Though naturally slim, he had never really been one for exercise, but was blessed with good genes allowing him to eat pretty much whatever he wanted. But after recent events, he had realized he needed to get into shape, the ability to run for your life sometimes meaning it might be slightly prolonged.

Hence the treadmill at the Agency gym whenever he had a chance, and his only slight panting now. Three months ago he'd be gasping for air, the filling of his lungs imitating a barking seal.

Morrison pointed to a chair and Leroux hit it, pulling out his newly arrived Blackberry Z30, its larger display and secure network making it ideal for him to take notes with and still use as a phone.

"We just received an update from Delta," began Morrison.

Holy shit they're fast!

"Our contacts picked up Levkin and interrogated him with no success. Delta had a little more. It turns out it was detonation codes for the Crimson Rush weapons, and that there may be as many as one thousand deployed. Before his rescue"—Leroux's eyebrows shot up—"Levkin refused to provide any additional information, except to say that our own operatives stole all the information we needed, including locations, over thirty years ago."

"Holy shit!" exclaimed Leroux, immediately wincing. "Sorry, sir, I didn't mean—"

Morrison waved his hand, cutting him off.

"I said far worse when I heard." He leaned forward. "We've searched our own databases and found only the single reference to it, essentially dismissing it as a counterintelligence operation. Now we know it's most likely real, and apparently we've known for three decades exactly where it was deployed."

"Most likely, sir?"

"Assuming this isn't some bullshit hoax."

"Oh," said Leroux, biting his lip. "Do you think it is?"

Morrison shook his head.

"Not for a second."

Leroux wasn't sure how he felt about that. Part of him was happy they weren't wasting their time, a bigger part wished they were, the devastation that could be wrought horrendous.

"Are we sure Levkin was telling the truth?" asked Leroux. "I mean about us having the intel?"

"I'm not sure. If we have it, it's been buried somewhere. Our best lead is to track down the original agent who filed the Crimson Rush report and ask him."

"I'll get right on it."

"And get this latest intel to Kane. I have a funny feeling his little side trip to Germany might just pay off."

Leroux's eyebrows shot up.

"I wasn't aware you were, well, aware."

Morrison stared at Leroux for a moment, Leroux beginning to shrink into the chair.

"Do you really think I don't know everything that goes on around here? Or at the malls in our fine town?" He motioned for Leroux to leave. "Now track down our former agent. He just might have the answers we're looking for."

Leroux jumped, not saying a word as he fled the office, Morrison already picking up his phone.

God I hope he doesn't know what Sherrie and I do in private!

Leroux ran back to his desk in time to see the DEFCON indicator switch from the green Four to the brighter yellow of the number Three, which if he remembered his briefings, meant the Air Force was prepping to mobilize within fifteen minutes.

But who the hell are we going to war with?

Messina Residence, Phoenix, Arizona

Rick Messina rinsed the shampoo out of his hair as his wife called to him from the bedroom, her message lost to the suds and water. As he ran his hair through the water, he thought about how this was probably the last real shower he'd have for a week. They were minutes away from heading to the River Island State Park near the Parker Dam on the Colorado River for a week of camping with the kids. They had all been looking forward to this trip for months, it booked ages ago.

Camping was how he had met his wife Angela twelve years ago while in college. They were both in Yosemite with different groups of friends, had hit it off and married a year later. Both avid campers, they went out almost every weekend when they were younger, but now, with careers, kids and his decision to join the weekend warrior brigade—the Arizona National Guard—free time was at a premium.

Which was why this weekend away was so important to them all.

A hand shoved aside the shower curtain and a phone appeared.

"It's for you."

He tossed his head back, slicking his hair with two hands then wiping his face as he took the phone, mouthing 'who is it?' to his wife, who shook her head, signaling she was pissed with her 'talk to the hand' pose.

Uh oh.

"This is Rick."

"Lieutenant Messina, this is an emergency activation. You are to report to your duty station within sixty minutes. This is a mandatory call-up, and is not an exercise. Understood?"

"Umm, yes. What's this about?"

155

"You'll be briefed when you arrive. Can you confirm you'll be on station within sixty minutes?"

"Yes, I'll be there."

The call ended with a dial tone. He looked out into the bathroom to find it deserted. Bending over he placed the phone on the floor then finished rinsing, climbing out and toweling off quickly as he headed into the bedroom to find his wife furiously brushing her hair.

"You can't go, can you," she said, her tone indicating she already knew the answer.

"It's a call-up. I have to go."

"You should never have joined!"

"You don't mean that."

"Yes I do!"

"You know why I joined. I have a duty to give back, even if in just some small way."

"We have kids—"

"Who might be saved one day by a guardsman, just like I was."

Messina flashed back to that night as a child when Hurricane Andrew was hammering the coastline of Florida and his parents had foolishly decided to tough it out. They had paid with their lives, and if it weren't for some young corporal in the National Guard who had spotted him clinging to a piece of their destroyed house, he would be dead. Instead, he had been pulled out of the water and hoisted into a helicopter.

He had sworn he would join, to pay it forward, but had come up with excuse after excuse. The first excuse was college, then new wife, then starting a career, then children, then saving for a house, then nothing—just apathy. When Katrina had hit New Orleans, and he watched the devastation unfold on CNN, he turned to Angela and said, "I'm signing up. Tomorrow."

And she had supported him at the time, knowing it was something he had always wanted. Unfortunately the next day his grandfather had died, and all thoughts of the National Guard drifted away until Hurricane Sandy hit.

He signed up the next day.

It had only been a little bit over a year since he joined. He had done his duty, losing minimal time from the family, and never had it interfered with any of their plans.

Until today.

He came up behind Angela and put his hands on her shoulders, squeezing them gently.

"I'm sorry, babe, you know I didn't want this to happen."

Her shoulders slumped and she leaned back against him, her anger deflated.

"I know, it's just we were all so looking forward to this. We haven't gone camping all year."

He turned her around to face him, sitting on the bed and pulling her toward him. He looked up at her and smiled.

"Why don't you guys go on your own?" he said. "This thing might only last a day, then I'll come join you."

"We can't go without you!"

"Why not? You know what you're doing, probably better than me—"

"That's for sure."

"—and the kids know what they're doing. The three of you go, and I'll join you when I'm done."

Angela brightened at the suggestion, wrapping her arms around him and pushing him back on the bed, straddling him.

"You better get there quick, mister, before I meet somebody else."

He felt her hips grind and a stirring that if he wasn't careful might lead to something else. She planted a kiss on him that stoked the fire down below that even if he wanted to he couldn't resist. He flipped her over, glancing to make sure the bedroom door was closed.

"We have to be fast."

"I can be fast," she said in a hoarse whisper as she pulled her panties off.

"I mean lightning fast."

"Like when we first met?"

He feigned a hurt expression.

"Hey, you said it didn't matter."

She grabbed his neck and pulled him tight against her.

"And I meant it. Now shut up and make love to me, soldier."

Messina followed her orders, glancing at the alarm clock on the nightstand, doing the math in his head to figure out if there was any chance he'd actually make it on time.

No problem.

Alex West Residence, Black Forest, Germany

Kane read the flash message that had just come in over his secure phone, maintaining control of his facial muscles despite the urge for eyebrows to pop and a jaw to drop. Instead he returned the phone to his pocket and looked back at the two elderly men sitting in front of him.

"How about we start with exactly what Crimson Rush is?" he asked the room.

"Well, first how about I explain what it isn't," began Zorkin.

"Isn't?"

"Isn't," repeated Zorkin. "What it isn't is a weapon."

"Huh?" This time eyebrows and jaw muscles lost control. "Then what the hell are we running all over the place for?" exclaimed Kane.

"You misunderstand. *Crimson Rush* isn't a weapon. It's a battle plan that uses a specific type of weapon."

Kane's lips pursed as he sucked in a deep breath.

A battle plan?

He liked the sound of that even less.

"Explain."

"In the sixties our scientists figured out how to shrink a nuclear weapon down to the size of a large crate. This miniaturization continued and by the early eighties the RA-155 was created. It was a fully functional nuclear bomb that weighed about thirty kilos—"

"That's less than seventy pounds for us Yanks," interjected West.

"—and could be carried in a backpack or suitcase."

"I've heard of those," said Kane. "I thought it was bunk."

"That's what you were meant to believe. A disinformation campaign was begun and your side was made to think it was simply a false flag put out to catch moles inside the Soviet Union. Your side responded with a message through private channels that if the weapon were real, and were to be found on US or NATO soil, detonated or otherwise, it would be considered an act of war and would demand a nuclear response."

Kane looked at West for confirmation, and the man nodded, a frown creasing his clouded face, as if old memories were flooding back.

"I'm sensing a 'but'," said Kane.

"There always is it seems. In the early eighties things were pretty turbulent in the Soviet Union, and the upper echelons were beginning to realize that we would inevitably lose the war due to simple economics. Some in the Kremlin wanted to prevent this at all costs, therefore they developed the RA-155 program, and once it was ready, immediately deployed it, and didn't stop deploying it until the warning from your government."

"How many were deployed?"

"That I don't know. In all the years I have been searching I have never been able to find details on deployment, except to say that over one thousand of these low yield weapons were manufactured."

Kane leaned forward in his chair, his heart skipping a beat.

"Just how powerful are these things?"

"Not very when compared to a conventional warhead. They were mostly half a kiloton to two kilotons. Enough to completely contaminate about ten square kilometers. Anybody in the blast radius would be instantly killed just as in a regular nuclear detonation. About half of the population would die immediately or soon thereafter out to about a kilometer in all directions. Then the radiation would spread out to about ten square kilometers, and then be carried with the prevailing winds, contaminating anything in its path."

"So if this were set off in a city…" Kane began.

"Thousands would die immediately, tens of thousands within days, and many more over the coming years. Not to mention birth defects, cancer, and a whole host of problems for decades to come."

"And that's just one bomb," said West, rubbing his forehead.

"And you said there were a thousand of these made."

"Yes, but about half at least weren't deployed."

"How do you know that?" asked West.

"They're stored in two secret warehouses, ready for use if needed."

West put his tea aside as he leaned forward.

"You're kidding me! You mean they're not on the record?"

Zorkin shook his head.

"No, if they were, then we'd have to account for *all* of them, and that's not possible. It would have led to an international incident that might have completely derailed peace talks."

"Because we could never have peace and nuclear disarmament when possibly hundreds of Soviet nuclear devices were already pre-positioned at their targets," said Kane, almost breathlessly, his head slowly shaking back and forth in shock. "This is incredible! It completely changes the balance of power!"

Zorkin nodded.

"I agree. Which is why we're here, isn't it?"

"What do you mean?" asked Kane.

"We're the only ones who know Crimson Rush is real," said West, "and we're offering our help."

Kane turned to Zorkin.

"RA-155 is the weapon, but what is Crimson Rush. You said it was a battle plan?"

"Yes. The idea was to pre-position as many of these weapons as possible at key locations such as military bases, power stations, government buildings—essentially anywhere there was a strategic asset that might aid in the war effort. The intention was that on the eve of war, we would begin massive exercises in the North Atlantic and Pacific, as well as air and land exercises in Eastern Europe near the borders. The majority of the suitcase bombs would be detonated all at once just as a coordinated attack into Western Europe would begin. Your forces would be unable to respond, your communications and supply lines destroyed, along with a significant portion of your land and air forces. We would conquer Europe within a few weeks, all the while threatening further nuclear devastation on America should she respond. We would detonate another suitcase bomb or two just to prove we could still do it."

West squeezed the bridge of his nose.

"So we would refuse to use nukes, the supply chain from North America would be broken, and Europe would fall."

"And the United States would be significantly weakened, and no longer a threat. And with all of Europe's resources and industrial capacity, we could quickly move to isolate and eventually take the US mainland."

Kane doubted that last part, a couple of hundred million guns in the hands of civilians ready to thwart any invasion, but the fall of Europe could absolutely have happened.

"Okay, that's history," he said. "What we know now is that the codes have been sold to parties unknown, and that they intend to detonate the weapons. To what end, we don't know. What we need to know is where they are, and how to deactivate them, or, who has the codes, and how do we stop them before they're used."

"All good questions and all without answers at the moment," agreed West. "Or more accurately, all without answers *now*."

"What do you mean?"

"I stole all of the information with respect to technical details and deployment locations over thirty years ago. That intel disappeared."

"How?"

"We were betrayed is the most likely explanation."

Kane looked at Zorkin then back at West.

"By who?"

"By the French."

Goddamned French!

"How?"

"I passed the intel on to one of their agents as I was about to be picked up. She successfully delivered it to one of their drop locations, and as far as we know, it was picked up and delivered to France. From there we have no idea where it went, and any inquiries made were met with denials."

"Perhaps the French agent lied to you? Didn't make the drop?"

"No, she made the drop," replied Zorkin. "I saw her do it."

"As did I," added West.

Kane looked at Zorkin.

"So I guess you were the one about to pick him up?"

Zorkin nodded.

"But when he explained to me what Crimson Rush was I realized it had to be stopped, and that the best way to stop it was to let the intel fall into enemy hands. Unfortunately it either never made it out of the USSR, or the French decided to keep it for themselves."

"Which with the way politics were back then, I could absolutely see," said West. "You could never really trust the French."

"Still can't," muttered Kane. "Any ideas how we can find this intel?"

163

"I suggest we call in an expert," said Zorkin.

West's eyes opened slightly wider.

"And just who would you suggest?"

"An old friend," said Zorkin, rising and going to the front door. He opened it and waved, both Kane and West exchanging confused glances as a car door opened then closed, footsteps crossing the bed of needles then the wood porch.

A woman's steps.

Kane saw her first, a rather striking elderly woman, perhaps a few years younger than her counterparts, but with a dignity that no young woman could pull off. He glanced at West to get a sense of whether or not he knew who this woman was, but there was no doubt. West's eyes were glass, his smile broad as his lips trembled. He pushed himself from his chair and nearly stumbled toward the woman, his hands outstretched.

Hers rose to meet his, and as their fingers intertwined, his voice finally trembled the words he was so desperate to say.

"Adelle! I thought I'd never see you again!"

CIA Headquarters, Langley, Virginia

Chris Leroux pushed back from his keyboard, frustrated. He had hit a dead end in trying to trace the transmission sent by Islamov. They all had, the murky underworld of malware having lost the message in the ether, a disproportionate number of techs having been assigned the task of finding the receiver.

All to no avail so far.

The proverbial haystack wasn't actually a good comparison anymore. It was searching for a specific needle in a stack of needles. No one profile stood out from any other, meaning there was no way to distinguish, and with tens of thousands of infected machines, it would take an army to round up their owners for questioning to see who had actually opened the file that was transmitted.

Ding!

He had an idea.

His fingers began to fly over the keyboard, launching his scripting software and within minutes he began designing his own chunk of malware to piggy back on the one hiding their receiver. As the script quickly grew, he remembered how much he loved to code, something he didn't get much of an opportunity to do anymore now that he was a full-fledged senior analyst. He felt exhilarated with the idea of actually *doing* something rather than just reading or creating searches. This was real, actual spy work that would be unleashed on the world, that could do some good.

Which meant he better get it approved before he launched it.

A throat cleared at his cubicle entrance and his head spun to see Sherrie standing there, a smile on her face.

"How long have you been there?"

"Long enough to see that smile on your face grow so wide it was making me jealous."

He wiped the smile off his face, but it quickly reappeared, he too excited to keep it hidden.

Sherrie sat down and looked at the screen.

"Whatcha doin'?"

"Writing some code."

"That will do?"

He leaned forward, lowering his voice.

"I had an idea," he began.

"Of course you did," said Sherrie with a smile. "You're the smartest guy here."

"You're biased," he replied, then continued. "We've been trying to trace the data packet to its intended target, but there's no way, there's just too many people who received the packet due to the malware installed on their computers."

"This is the Chechen transmission?"

Leroux nodded.

"Sorry, yeah, I guess I've just been so tied up in this I assumed you knew."

"Go on."

"Sorry, so anyway, I just realized that there's no way to figure out who the transmission went to since it went to tens of thousands of people if not more. *But*, only the person who *knew* the transmission was being sent would know to *open* the data packet when it landed on their machine as part of the malware's normal update cycle."

Sherrie's eyes opened wide as she realized what Leroux was saying.

"You mean tens of thousands had it downloaded, but only the guy who knew it would be arriving would open it."

"Exactly."

"And can you find out who opened the file?"

"I think so. I'm going to push an update to the malware software, and every infected machine that is logged onto the Internet, or that eventually logs on, will automatically download the update. The update will check to see if the machine has opened the data packet that was transmitted, then send the IP address back to me. Assuming the receiver hasn't disconnected from the Internet or removed the malware from their machine, we just might find them."

Sherrie rose from her chair and placed a kiss on his forehead.

"My genius!" she whispered, then stood up straight. "I'll leave you to finish your work. I'm about to get a briefing on Crimson Rush." She pointed at the keyboard. "If the rumors are true, we're probably a prime target, so you better hurry."

Leroux nodded and watched her sway out of his office, then returned to his keyboard. He resumed coding then suddenly stopped as her words sank in.

We're probably a prime target.

His heart leapt into his throat and he began typing even faster.

Alex West Residence, Black Forest, Germany

Kane had risen out of respect for the elderly woman's arrival, but hadn't said anything as she and West embraced, tears streaking both their faces, Zorkin standing by silently, a huge smile on his face as even his heart seemed to be cracking slightly.

Kane glanced at the photograph sitting on the table beside his chair then back at the new arrival. The resemblance was striking, and the affection obvious, leaving no doubt they were one and the same person. The reaction however, and the age difference between the two photographs of at least thirty years, made him wonder how long it had been since they had seen each other.

The embrace finally broken, West turned toward Kane, his arm extended to present this woman to him.

"Special Agent Dylan Kane, CIA, this is Adelle Bertrand, formerly of the Direction Générale de la Sécurité Extérieure."

Kane smiled, taking Adelle's hand in his and gently squeezing as he gave her a slight bow.

"French Intelligence. A pleasure."

Adelle smiled then took the seat West had been sitting in, relegating their host to the worst seat in the house, the only one with its back to the door. He looked clearly uncomfortable, but ignored it for the moment, instead serving tea, with two lumps of sugar, handing it to Adelle with a smile.

The man knows how she takes her tea.

Kane took a sip of his soda.

"How long has it been?" asked Zorkin. "Thirty years?"

"Over thirty," replied Adelle, putting down her tea. "Thirty long years."

"I only saw her one more time after the night you had her picked up."

"But it did last several months," smiled Adelle with a wink. "Several long, wonderful months."

West blushed causing Kane to smile, exchanging a glance with Zorkin who seemed delighted by the entire exchange.

"I never understood why you two didn't stay together," commented Zorkin, clearly not concerned with addressing the elephant in the room. "I always expected you two to settle down and disappear."

"Our countries had different plans," replied West, his face gloomy. "The CIA reassigned me after that, gave me a desk job, and basically isolated me to Langley."

"DGSE did essentially the same to me, then other…things, shall we say, took over my life."

"Life seems to always be the thing that gets in the way of everything, including true love," said Zorkin with a sigh. "It's criminal what happened to you two."

"It was criminal what we did," replied West. "We were both lucky to not go to jail. Three months AWOL? In those days? After what had just happened?" West shook his head. "We're damned lucky we weren't tossed into some prison cell somewhere."

"Indeed," agreed Adelle. "We were very lucky." Her voice was subdued, almost as if she were unconvinced of what she was saying. She took a deep breath, then looked at Zorkin. "Will someone bring me up to date on the latest developments?"

Zorkin motioned toward Kane.

"How about we let the kid fill us in?"

Kane gave a half-smile, putting his drink down and pulling out his secure phone to reference if needed.

"This is where we stand. Major General Levkin sold the detonation codes for the Crimson Rush devices to a Chechen drug lord, who was playing middleman for person or persons unknown. The email with the codes went into the ether that is the Internet, but we've got our best people on it, trying to trace it. We know there are as many as one thousand devices, but have no way of knowing how many are still active, or where they are, except that apparently half are in storage in Russia. I've just received an update that an off the books op resulted in Levkin's capture and interrogation, confirming what we suspected. The little piece we didn't have was that apparently we've had the locations for over thirty years, but no one seems to know where this intel is. The last person known to possess it was you, Miss Bertrand."

Adelle nodded, frowning.

"It was the first time I can recall being ashamed of my country. When I returned to DGSE after our—what shall I call it—hiatus?—they at first denied the microfilm had ever left Moscow, but eventually I found out that was a lie, and that it had indeed made it out, but was never passed on to the Americans. Instead, they used it to track down and defuse any of the weapons on French soil, then shelved it in hopes it could be used as leverage in future negotiations with the Americans or Soviets. I was nearly sick when I found out."

"How did you find out?" asked West.

"I held the Director at gunpoint in an underground parking garage and forced him to tell me. That's when I was put on administrative leave for a while."

"I'm surprised you weren't arrested."

"I acquired some compromising photos of the Director before I confronted him. The only reason I was put on leave was because there was a witness. They chalked it up to hormones and stress. I spent three months

170

in a state 'spa' then returned to work, reassigned to a desk with my security clearance all but gone."

"I'm sorry to hear that," said West. "I lost my clearance level too which meant admin duties from then on. I kept questioning Crimson Rush but was stonewalled at every turn, and eventually told it was classified and if I mentioned it again, I'd go to prison for the rest of my life for violating national security."

"So it was a cover up?" asked Kane.

"Sort of," said West. "My guess is our side never wanted to admit that such a device could exist, because it would terrify the public. The Soviets never wanted to admit to their existence so they could use them if they had to, then when the thaw began, they were too scared to admit to the truth."

"And the French?"

"Back then they were never really on our side," said West, with a quick, "Sorry" and a shoulder shrug to Adelle.

Adelle batted her hand in the air as if it were nothing.

"All I knew was I was always spying for and on the side of France. Most of the time I had no clue whose side France was on."

Zorkin and West had a hearty laugh at that statement, Adelle finally joining in with a giggle. Kane smiled, but was in a hurry to move things along, time literally ticking away.

"Is there any way to find that intel?" he asked, ending the frivolity.

Adelle covered her mouth for a second, composing herself, then looked at Kane.

"I believe I may have a way."

"Explain."

"My daughter followed in my footsteps—"

"You have a daughter!" exclaimed West, the look on his face something between joy and heartbreak, the poor bastard happy for his old flame, but devastated that she had moved on without him, and judging by the ages in question, quite quickly onward.

"Yes, I do," she said quickly, avoiding eye contact with West, evidently not wanting to witness the pain she had just caused. She continued to meet Kane's eyes. "My daughter works in intelligence. She's an agent, with the highest clearance. As soon as I received your message"—she looked at Zorkin—"I contacted her. She will be pre-positioned by tonight at the main data archive containing all of DGSE's old files. She will get us in and logged into one of the terminals. The rest is up to us."

"Us?" said Kane. "Forgive me, but I think it's best if I go in alone with your daughter.

"You'll need our help," said West. "We know what to look for."

"You can brief me on the way," replied Kane. "With all due respect, no matter how sharp your minds obviously still are, even you have to admit you're in no shape physically to go out on an op."

Zorkin leapt to his feet, his head jerking from left to right, his arm up and cocked at the elbow.

"I'll arm wrestle you, right here, right now, you insolent little bastard! I'll show you how strong this feeble old man is."

Kane remained seated, keeping a straight face as the man continued to look for a flat, clear surface to lay down his challenge. West shook his head, smiling.

"Sit down, you old fool, you know he's right."

"Bullshit!"

"We all know you're in fine shape for a man your age. In fact, you're probably in great shape for a man twenty years your junior," soothed West.

"Damn right!"

"But think about that, Viktor. That's fifty-five."

Zorkin spun and glared at West, then dropped his arm, his hands shifting to his hips as he began to laugh, then cough. He fished the inhaler from his pocket and took several puffs, then sat down. He pointed at Kane.

"When this is done, we arm wrestle."

Kane nodded, allowing a slight smile.

"I will try to call in some help just in case, but worst case scenario is me and your daughter go in alone. You three can cover our escape if you'd like."

"Absolutely!" barked Zorkin, who then looked at his two companions a little sheepishly. "Sorry, I don't mean to speak for you all."

"There's no way you're keeping me out of this," said West. "After all, this is my party, and you are the invitees."

"And it is my daughter who is risking her career, so I too am of course 'in' as you Americans say."

"Then we should leave immediately," said Kane. "Can we get air transportation from here?"

Adelle nodded as she rose, the rest of the room following.

"I've already had it arranged. We will be in position in less than three hours."

Kane nodded, impressed with the initiative his new team was showing.

His new team of four with a combined age of over 250.

Papago Army Aviation Support Facility, Phoenix, Arizona

Lieutenant Rick Messina ran as fast as he could, his damned car having broken down two miles short of the parking lot. His legs were on fire as were his lungs, the unexpected two mile run with duffel bag exhausting. As he burst into the assembly hall he discovered everyone was already there and his chest tightened as they turned to look at him. He rushed into place at the head of his platoon, relieving his second-in-command.

The commanding officer, Lt. Colonel Ford, stood at the head of the group of several hundred men, his jaw squared and his dark, piercing eyes glaring at Messina.

"Nice of you to finally join us, Lieutenant."

"Sorry, sir, I had car trouble, sir."

"Excuses are for school girls on prom night, Lieutenant! No matter the excuse, somebody got screwed. Either she got screwed, her boyfriend got screwed out of a promised roll in the hay, or her father got screwed out of a good night's sleep. And if you had been here on time, you'd realize how screwed we'd all be right now if everyone didn't realize that sixty minutes isn't sixty-five minutes!"

"Sorry, sir," mumbled Messina. He hated being yelled at, and it was one of the hardest things he was trying to learn how to deal with in the Guard. Not only was he getting yelled at from time to time, but he had to yell from time to time. It seemed all orders had to be barked or screamed, otherwise apparently they wouldn't be obeyed.

Lt. Colonel Ford pointed at Lt. Kirk Darcy, Messina's second in command and good friend.

"Brief our prom queen on the situation! We roll in five! Dismissed!"

The parade came to attention then the colonel marched toward his mobile command center.

"Parade, dismissed!" yelled a lone voice and the men broke, rushing toward a series of transports pulling up outside. Darcy dismissed their men, sending them to one of the trucks, then turned to Messina.

"Christ, Rick, where the hell have you been?"

Messina flushed.

"With Angela, you know, saying goodbye."

"My God, Rick, of all the days you should have kept it in your pants!"

"Hey, I would have been here on time if it weren't for the goddamned car breaking down."

"I thought you had a brand new SUV?"

"I do, but Angela's taking that to the campground with the kids."

"She's still going?"

"Yeah, I told her to."

"That might be for the best."

"Why, what's going on?" asked Messina as the two of them headed for their assigned transport.

"We've got a major situation. Apparently there might be a nuke hidden somewhere in the area."

"What?" Messina felt his knees weaken slightly. "Are you screwing with me?"

"No, I'm serious. Each platoon is being assigned radiation detection equipment and a list of high priority targets. We're to sweep them completely and move on to the next site."

"How sure are they about this?"

Darcy shrugged his shoulders then stopped, grabbing Messina by the shirt and bringing him to a halt.

"Listen," said Darcy, lowering his voice. "I was on the horn with my brother earlier this morning, and he said we were already, at DEFCON Three. Something serious is going on."

"Holy shit!" gasped Messina. His thoughts immediately went to his wife and kids.

I've got to get them out of the city!

"Aren't they going to evacuate?"

Darcy shook his head.

"No, they don't want to start a panic."

"That's insane! Are we allowed to at least tell *our* families?"

Darcy shook his head as he climbed in the back of the truck. Messina jumped on the back lift and looked at his men.

"I've just been briefed and I know how messed up this situation sounds. Our jobs are clear. We search our assigned targets, and we search them well. No screwing around and doing a half-assed job. Lives are at risk. Lives of our own families and friends, so we don't want to miss anything. We'll do the job right, then move on to the next one. Questions?"

Silence.

"Good." He pointed at the gear sitting in the middle of the truck, turning to Darcy. "Lieutenant, make sure the gear is broken out and distributed for when we arrive. I'll be up front."

"Yes, sir!" said Darcy as Messina jumped down. He heard orders being barked as he walked to the passenger side door, fishing his cellphone out. He quickly fired a text message to his wife.

Get to campground ASAP! Will explain later.

CIA Headquarters, Langley, Virginia

"Are you sure it will work?"

Chris Leroux shook his head, wishing he could provide his boss with another answer, but he couldn't. There was no way to know if this would work. All he knew was that the code *should* work, then any number of variables had to hold true, not the least of which being the perpetrator had to have not turned off his computer.

"No."

"No?"

"No. But it *could* work, and that's better than the nothing we've got now."

Leif Morrison leaned back in his chair and chewed on his cheek for a moment, his jaw bobbing up and down as Leroux watched the man think. It didn't take long as Morrison popped back upright quickly, swiping his mouse and clearing the screen saver that had kicked in.

"What do you need?"

"An ops center?" asked Leroux, hesitatingly. He had never actually asked for one before, it never being necessary.

"Done."

Leroux felt his pulse quicken.

"And someone to command."

"This is your idea, your op. You're in command."

Leroux could feel the room start to spin and he gripped the arms of the chair tightly, his fingernails digging into the leather.

Focus!

He picked a spot and stared, the room slowly coming back into focus as sweat beaded on his forehead. The room stopped and he realized the spot he had picked to focus on was his boss' head.

He quickly looked away.

"Me?"

"You don't think you can handle it?"

"Not for a second."

"So you *can* handle it."

"No, I mean I can't."

Morrison laughed.

"Chris, you'll never get ahead in life being honest." Morrison rose and Leroux began to when he was waved off. Morrison rounded his desk then leaned back with his hips, perching on the front of the old antique. He leaned toward Leroux. "Chris, *I* think you're ready. Don't worry about your age, don't worry about experience. The men and women in that room are professionals, and are used to dealing with all manner of people from first timers to old timers. All they care about is that you are in command, and they'll follow your orders. If you have any questions, just ask. There is always an experienced coordinator assigned to the room. They'll help you."

Leroux didn't feel any better, but he nodded.

"If you say so, sir."

"I *do* say so." Morrison stood up and returned to his chair. "When can you be ready?"

"Now, sir, assuming the code has been reviewed and no problems were found."

"Very well, I'll have it set up for you."

Leroux nodded, standing up and heading for the door.

"Good luck, Mr. Leroux. You'll do great."

Leroux turned and gave a nervous, unconvinced nod to his boss, then stepped out into the reception area, closing the door behind him. He squeezed his eyes shut and pressed his back against the door, his knees weak and shaking.

This is insane! Me, running an Op Center?

A throat cleared.

He opened his eyes and saw Morrison's assistant looking at him from her desk.

"Are you okay, Chris?"

He shook his head.

"No," he said, pushing away from the door and retrieving a handkerchief from his pocket. "But I will be when I'm forty," he added, wiping his forehead dry.

Maybe by then I'll have grown some balls.

He pursed his lips at her knowing smile, then marched from the outer office and back to his desk, all the while his fingernails digging into his palms. He dropped into his chair, praying that they had found something wrong with his code that would nix the entire operation, but instead found glowing reviews from the three other techs he had sent it to for review.

Damned competence.

He fired a message to Morrison that he was ready, then a text message to Sherrie.

If you've got a minute, come see me.

A message immediately popped back from Morrison indicating Op Center 3 was tasked to him, then a text from Sherrie arrived.

In meeting, 30 mins?

His thumbs flew over his Blackberry.

I'm running an op in OC3. I think I'm going to die!

He downloaded his code to a memory stick and locked his computer, thanking God and Sherrie for not being on Red Bull right now. His heart would have probably stopped after it raced past 200 beats a minute. As it stood, he was probably approaching 180. He took a deep breath then a drink of water, closing his eyes and trying to picture something that made him happy.

Right now all he could picture was high school, sitting at Dylan Kane's dining room table and helping him with his math. He had to admit he was surprised it wasn't something with Sherrie that had popped into his head while seeking that safe place, but as he thought about it, every moment since he'd met her he had been on edge. It wasn't her fault that he required a guard detail, it was just that he had been under tremendous pressure accompanied by too many bouts of pure terror since they had been together.

With Kane, in their youth, he had always felt safe when his older friend had been around.

Kane, I wish you were here.

He pushed himself from his chair as the phone vibrated.

Good luck! I'm so proud of you!

Leroux grunted.

You wouldn't be if you knew how desperately I wish I was wearing Depends right now.

Instead he just sent *Thanks.*

As he headed for Ops Center 3 he took deep, steady breaths that seemed to increase with frequency the nearer he got, to the point where he was almost hyperventilating. He dodged into a bathroom that was thankfully empty and turned on the cold water at one of the sinks, splashing it on his face as he tried to calm down.

A toilet flushed and he nearly shit his pants.

The door to one of the stalls opened and a man stepped out he recognized from another section—Donovan Eppes. He had at least ten years on Leroux, and was someone he had always envied in the confidence department.

"Hey Chris, what brings you to this end of the building?"

Leroux grabbed a paper towel and dried his face.

"I'm running an op in OC3," he said, not believing the words as they came out of his mouth.

"First time?" asked Eppes as he washed his hands.

"Yeah."

"Man, I remember my first time," said Eppes as he lathered his hands with soap. "I was so effin' terrified I almost shit myself. Before I even got to Ops I vomited three times. I remember the controller I was leaning over gave me some Tic Tacs because I was killing her with the smell." Eppes laughed and turned off the taps. "But I did it, it was a success, and the next time was a million times easier." He dried his hands and tossed the paper into the garbage can. "You'll do fine. You never would have been assigned command if they didn't think you were capable of taking it."

Leroux smiled, his head bobbing slightly as they walked out of the bathroom together.

"Mistakes happen," muttered Leroux.

Eppes laughed. "They do, but that's why we have an office in Alaska!" He laughed even harder.

"You're not helping."

Eppes slapped Leroux on the back.

"Don't worry about it, Chris. I'm just trying to loosen you up. You're going to do great."

Eppes retreated down the corridor Leroux had just come from as Leroux resumed his rush for Ops Center 3, surprisingly a little calmer than he had been, Eppes' pep talk actually doing its job.

If Eppes was scared, then it's okay for me to be scared.

He breathed a little easier and as he turned the corner, two guards stood on either side of the door marked OC3/Restricted Access. He swiped his card then placed his right hand on the scanner.

"Thank you, Mr. Leroux, you may proceed," said the guard manning the scanner. The other one opened the door.

"Thanks," said Leroux, stepping through and into the Operations Center.

And all of his anxieties came rushing back.

There were a dozen terminals, about half manned, along with a dozen large screens laid out in a curved grid fashion at the front of the room. The entire room was jet black, the ceiling and walls covered in sound dampening materials and devices to reduce any echo should the room begin to get loud. At the back of the room, slightly higher than the rest, were two stations, one occupied by a woman he recognized, the sign etched on the front of her station indicating her position—Ops Center Coordinator.

She looked at him and smiled.

"Mr. Leroux, I'm Shirley Dimka, OC Coordinator. How may we assist you?"

The room was staring at him now and his palms started to flow sweat freely from the pores. *They're not staring at you, they're waiting for you!* He took a deep breath and focused on Dimka.

"Nice to meet you," he forced out with a nervous smile. He put his hands on a safety rail that rimmed the platform the two command stations sat on and looked down into the pit, but actually at the back wall, the light dim enough he hoped no one would notice. He raised his voice slightly, praying it didn't shake too much. "My name is Chris Leroux, I'm a senior analyst here. I'm sure you're all aware of the Crimson Rush situation. Our intel tells us we have up to one thousand of these devices on American and allied soil, and the activation codes have been sold. Our job today is to try and find who received the transmission containing those codes." He reached into his pocket and retrieved the USB key containing his program. "I've written a program that we will insert into the malware's update website—for lack of a better term—that will modify the malware running on infected computers the next time they are connected to the Internet. This program will then check the user's computer to see if they accessed the file containing the codes that was downloaded to their PC. In theory, only the intended recipient would know about the file's existence, so they should be the only ones to access it."

A hand popped up from the pit.

"What about virus scanners or some other routine? Couldn't we be dealing with millions of accesses?"

Leroux shook his head.

"No. First, if they had a virus scanner, they most likely wouldn't have the malware in the first place, and second, I've accounted for that. A virus scanner, or other type of active scanner, would touch the file immediately upon arrival. The code compares the creation date of the file on the hard drive, and the last touch timestamp, and if they are within three seconds of each other, flags it as a false positive. I'm hopeful we should have a very small number of positive hits to sort through when we're done."

The man nodded as if satisfied with the answer, and Leroux suddenly found himself feeling a lot better. His voice was strong, his hands weren't leaking anymore, and his breathing had steadied.

Large and in charge!

"Any other questions?"

"How long will it take?"

Leroux shook his head.

"That's the tough one. We might need to run the program for hours, days or even weeks, and may never get the answer we're looking for if the perpetrator has shutdown. What we're hoping for here is that the malware program is used for secret transmissions within the organization, assuming there is one, which means they will have left their computers infected, and connected. If they have, we should find them in the list of positives. If they haven't, then we'll never find them. It's a gamble, but it's all we've got."

Heads bobbed around the room, and Leroux turned to Dimka. He handed her the USB key.

"Is this the code?"

He nodded.

"Upload instructions are on the USB in the 'read me' file."

Dimka looked down into the pit.

"Conway."

The one who had asked about the virus scanners jumped up and grabbed the USB key. As he began to read the contents, Leroux stepped over to Dimka's desk and bent over.

"Is it okay if I check to make sure he does it right?" he whispered.

"It's fine and they expect you to. Just remember they're professionals who do this every day, so you don't need to micromanage. At this stage however, since you wrote it, and since this is the most important part, definitely feel free to double-check."

Leroux smiled, then as casually as he could manage, he rounded the platform, stepped down to the main level and approached Conway's station. Conway already had the instructions opened in a window on one of his screens, and was following them on another with a second tech double-checking each step before they executed them.

Conway looked up at Leroux then back at his screen.

"Everything is smooth so far, sir."

Sir! It sounded so strange coming from people at least his age. He wondered if they felt weird saying it.

"Excellent."

Excellent? Are you kidding me? Please don't follow it up with "Good work" or something lame like that!

He remained silent, watching each step being executed. Conway hit several keys, then hit a button and one of the large screens came to life showing a macroscopic depiction of the Internet, a massive number of lines, almost hub and spoke like in appearance, spread across the globe, the heaviest concentrations in North America, Europe and the Asian Pacific rim with the borders of densely connected countries like South Korea and Japan almost impossible to distinguish behind the lines indicating Internet linkages.

Conway executed several more instructions and then another display went live with several statuses shown.

Malware Status: Uploading.
Number of Downloads: 0
Number of Positives: 0

"Final instruction uploaded, sir."

"Great, now we wait," said Leroux, returning to the platform and standing at his station.

"Why don't you take a seat," suggested Dimka. "This could take a while."

Leroux smiled at her appreciatively, and sat down. He moved the mouse and the three displays arced in front of him, recessed into the station so he

185

could easily see over them and into the pit where the analysts were working, came to life.

"Malware update has been successfully uploaded," came Conway's voice from below. It was low and he could barely hear him. He looked at his desk and noticed the headset sitting there. He put it on and Dimka slid over with her chair. She pointed at a red button on the station. "Press that to talk. Let it go when you're done otherwise they'll hear everything you say," she said with a wink.

He nodded and adjusted the headset to be comfortable, then looked at the large screen showing the status. Conway's voice echoed the status update as it appeared.

"Test malware update successful."

Leroux pressed the red button, leaning forward, forgetting for a moment that the microphone was attached to the headset and immediately in front of his mouth, no matter where he turned.

"We should begin to see activity any moment now as logged in computers pull down the update. Depending upon the size of the infection, this could be very slow"—suddenly the *Number of downloads* count started to spin rapidly—"or it could be very quick."

Leroux had a hard time hiding the excitement as the counter spun and the screen showing Internet traffic suddenly burst into color, the white lines of earlier rapidly being replaced by a rainbow of colors, shooting out across the globe as the downloads were traced back to their infected computers.

He realized his finger was still on the button, and decided an explanation might be in order.

"The yellow lines indicate requests for the malware update, the green indicate that the update was successful and that the detonation code file had not been accessed on that machine, and red lines, should they appear, are machines that have accessed the file and need to be investigated."

He removed his finger from the button and leaned back, staring at the *Number of Positives* indicator stubbornly stuck at zero. He looked back at the rapidly updating map and smiled.

It's like I'm in War Games!

As the download indicator flipped past ten thousand, he felt his chest slowly tightening as the *Positives* indicator continued to refuse to budge.

What if this doesn't work?

Then another thought occurred to him.

What if it works, but it's too late?

Outside Nawa-I-Barakzayi, Afghanistan
Seven years ago

Dylan Kane lay on the cold hard ground, his position well hidden from the insurgents below. He had been holed up in the ruins of what was once the humble home of a farmer, it now abandoned for years in the middle of almost nowhere, the family either having fled, or more likely dead. That was Afghanistan today, that was Afghanistan before we came, and that was Afghanistan for the past thousand years.

Brutal, bloody, and completely unprepared for democracy.

This was the Stone Age.

But his views on his government's orders were irrelevant. He worked for his country, he followed his orders unless he felt them illegal. And in the CIA, that was a fine line, with many of his missions illegal in the view of many.

Today he was targeting Baseer Khan, third in command of al Qaeda and one of bin Laden's most trusted men. Intel had put him in the area, and word on the dirt path was that his sister was getting married in the village that lay only a mile from his current position, and that wedding was today.

Kane had been sent in advance to confirm, and two F-22 Raptors were in the air at all times since, awaiting his signal.

Suddenly a thirty foot wide spider appeared in front of him and he shoved himself away from his weapon, reaching for his knife instinctively knowing he couldn't make a shot. As he drew the blade his conscious mind kicked in and he began to laugh as he saw the camel spider scurry over the barrel of his M-24 Sniper's Weapon System, it having appeared in his scope as something out of Eight Legged Freaks or Starship Troopers.

He shook his head with a smile, put his boot to the creature lest it decide to check out his bits and pieces, and returned to his position, his racing heart calming down.

I hate spiders.

A three vehicle convoy was racing into the town and he took a bead on the middle vehicle, cursing at the lost opportunity to take them out before their arrival. They came to a halt in the town square and armed guards swarmed out of the lead and trailing vehicles, the front doors of the middle vehicle opening as the area was scanned. The square quickly filled with curious onlookers, the sign of guns not a reason to flee in these parts.

This was solid Taliban ground, no matter what the brass would have the public believe. This war was unwinnable for there was no enemy territory to take. Loyalties went to the highest or most brutal bidder, and Afghanistan's only hope of freedom from the yoke of Taliban oppression were the warlords. Restore the warlords, arm them, and let them deal with the Taliban.

And don't expect democracy with equal rights for all.

Afghanistan was decades if not centuries away from that.

Improve their economy with trade and modern communications if they wanted it, then flood them with Western culture through movies and music and the Internet, and let people see there was another way. Eventually Westernized pockets, most likely in the cities, would begin to evolve, and gradually spread. But forcing it on an unwilling, ignorant, illiterate population like was being tried?

It was a recipe for complete and utter failure.

The rear doors of the middle SUV were pulled open and Kane smiled as two figures stepped out, the one on the passenger side Baseer Khan himself. Kane activated his comm.

"Castle-Keep, this is Sierra Four, come in, over."

"Sierra Four, this is Castle-Keep, we read you, over."

"Castle-Keep, I have eyes on primary target, relaying coordinates now, over."

He lased the target with his laser target designator and transmitted the GPS coordinates.

"Sierra Four, we have the coordinates, dispatching Package Echo Two to your position now, ETA sixty seconds, advise when ready, over."

"Roger that, out."

Kane followed Baseer Khan through the scope as he shook hands, surrounded by dozens of people who greeted him like a hero. And that was part of the problem in Afghanistan. There was no TV, no radios, no Internet, no newspapers. Ninety plus percent of the population couldn't read and didn't have electricity. Their news was delivered by word of mouth, and they believed whoever they trusted, which were not people sent from the new central government in Kabul or foreign soldiers talking through translators.

It was the people they had grown up with.

Did they care about 9/11?

They'd never heard of it, calendars meaningless.

The Twin Towers?

They couldn't even fathom buildings so high, so even if they heard the story, they wouldn't believe it.

Thousands of innocents dead?

That was daily life in Afghanistan. Why cry over it?

That foreigners were here to free them from their oppressors?

What? Like the Soviets? Throughout Afghanistan's history foreigners had invaded their soil for various reasons, from Alexander the Great to Genghis Khan, from the British Empire to the Soviet Union. Now it was the United States and its allies. To the average Afghani there was no distinction, all they knew was the current batch of invaders weren't locals, and had to be repelled.

Which meant a hero's welcome for those who tried.

Kane radioed in the strike confirmation as he continued to lase the target. Khan made a hand motion and his guards quickly cleared a path as he approached the rather large house—by rural Afghani standards—several adults greeting him outside, then ushering him inside. The crowd in the square dissipated and Kane lased the house, the package that was about to be delivered more than capable of taking care of the mud and stone to get to the juicy al Qaeda center. Khan's guards surrounded the house, keeping any who would approach at bay, which was fine by Kane since it would keep collateral damage to a minimum.

"Raptor One, Sierra Four. Target is hot, deliver package, I say again, deliver package, over."

"Sierra Four, Raptor One. Package away, ETA ten seconds, over."

"Roger that, Raptor One."

Kane kept the bead trained on the center of the home at the edge of town, the green light bouncing in his sights, but steady enough for the Maverick missile to home in on during its final approach.

Something caught Kane's eye just at the edge of his sight and he fought the instinct to adjust his position so he could see what it was. He didn't dare move since the missile was only seconds away. Suddenly a large group of kids raced toward the house and past the guards.

"Raptor One, Sierra Four! Abort! Abort! Abort!" he yelled, shifting the laser target designator to the right and away from the house, but it was too late. To his horror he heard the missile streak in and the horrendous explosion as the house was obliterated.

"Oh God no! Oh God please no!" he cried, shoving his weapon aside as he tried to jump up, but something was holding him down. He struggled

191

against whatever it was, but he couldn't see it, he could only feel it. He felt the sting of tears on his dry skin as he continued to shout for the mission abort, but it was no use. Even from his position he could hear the cries and wails of those that had survived, and the relatives of those who hadn't.

And it was his fault.

If it wasn't for the spider, if it wasn't for his moment of panic, he could have lased the convoy and had the target eliminated before he even entered the town, but instead, he had been foolish, giving in to a childhood fear, and now countless children were dead because of it.

Because of him.

"Dylan!" came the shouts over the comm still plugged in his ear. Whatever had him was shaking him and he struggled against them, determined to escape their clutches and help those who had survived. "Dylan! Wake up!"

Suddenly he opened his eyes and found himself lying on a couch, someone shaking him by the shoulders that he didn't at first recognize. He shoved them off, sitting upright as the room suddenly snapped into focus, and where he was, and when he was, flooded back. West, Zorkin and the French woman Adelle were all staring at him, looks of concern on their faces. Another woman, younger, stood in the background. Gorgeous with short dark hair, she stared at him, her expression a mystery, but he could tell he was being judged, and the rapidly fading nightmare told him she hadn't just seen him at his best.

The nightmare that just wouldn't go away.

"I'm okay," he said as the others backed off and he swung himself to a seated position, wiping his sweat drenched forehead with the back of his hand. "Just a dream."

West sat across from him.

"I have one similar."

192

"As do I," said Zorkin, handing Kane a glass of water.

"And I," added Adelle. "You can't have worked in this business as long as we have without something you regret, something you can't put behind you."

West reached out and took Adelle's hand, giving it a gentle squeeze.

The expression on the young woman's face was crystal clear this time.

Hands off, old man!

"I assume you're Adelle's daughter?" asked Kane, standing.

She nodded.

"Sorry, where are my manners?" exclaimed Adelle as she rushed to her daughter's side. "She arrived just as you began to have your nightmare." She stood beside her daughter, the resemblance remarkable, and took her by both of her shoulders. "Gentlemen, I'd like to present to you my daughter, Alexis Bertrand."

Eyebrows popped in the room, including Kane's, as suddenly what should have been obvious from the get-go finally became obvious. He glanced at Zorkin who had just noticed it too. The only person who seemed to be oblivious, was West.

Alexis was clearly Alex West's daughter.

Alexis smiled politely to the room as Adelle introduced everyone, leaving West until last.

"And this is Mr. West."

West leaned forward and shook Alexis' hand.

"Call me Alex."

Alexis nodded, she too apparently unaware of the fact she had just shook her father's hand. Kane looked at Adelle and she gave him a quick 'don't say a word' look that he nodded slightly to. He glanced at Zorkin who had caught the look and adjusted his shocked expression accordingly.

The room spun as a shave and a haircut knock was tapped out on the door of their hotel room. West started for the door when Kane jumped to his feet, readying his weapon.

"I'll get it, cover me," he said as he passed West. He looked through the peephole and smiled, opening the door and waving West off. Two familiar faces entered the room and quickly closed the door behind them.

"Everyone, this is Mr. White and Mr. Green, friends of mine that are here to help."

Burt Dawson shook Kane's hand, as did Niner as they entered the now cramped hotel room, dropping large duffel bags near the entrance. Introductions were made and everyone perched wherever they could as Alexis rolled out a map of the complex they were about to hit.

"This is the Charles de Gaulle National Intelligence Archive. Since it is an archive, and not an active office, on any given day there are not a lot of personnel, and those that are there are merely clerks, not trained in self-defense. Security is light from a manned standpoint, with electronic measures being relied upon. Since I have clearance, entry should be easy. We'll use my pass to gain entry into the building, overcome any opposition with *non*-lethal force, break into the archive itself, retrieve the microfilm, and depart the way we came in."

Kane cleared his throat.

"When the break-in is discovered, won't they track you down in about ten minutes?"

"Absolutely. Which is why when this is over, you will tie me up and beat me so that it looks like I was forced to cooperate. I'll eventually be cleared, and if not, at worst I'll be assigned to a desk which is most of my life these days regardless. France is still very chauvinistic when it comes to putting their women in danger."

"This is true," agreed Adelle. "Besides, this is a crisis situation. Whatever the consequences, we must get our hands on the microfilm and locate those bombs before they can be used."

Dawson leaned over the plans.

"They won't let the four of us in without ID," he said, pointing at the front gate.

"No. I have an official delivery van with no windows in the back. I'll tell them it's just a delivery."

"And they won't search?"

"No, they never do unless it's a heightened security alert."

"How do we know there isn't?" asked Niner.

"I would have been contacted."

"Okay, let's get this show on the road," said Kane as he began to gather his gear. "How far is it from here?"

"Ten minutes. It should only take ten minutes inside, ten back. If all goes to plan, we will return here in thirty to forty minutes," replied Alexis. She turned to her mother. "Be ready to copy and transmit the microfilm as soon as we arrive."

Adelle nodded, motioning toward a box in the corner.

"We'll have everything set up for when you return."

"Good," said Kane, grabbing the bag with his gear. "Let's go."

Adelle gave her daughter a hug and a kiss on the forehead.

"Mom!" protested Adelle quietly. Kane and the others chose to ignore the maternal concern, all just glad their own mothers weren't there to send them off on a mission in front of "the guys".

Kane could just imagine the ribbing Niner would give.

Mooney Park, Memphis, Tennessee

Tony Black pushed his daughter Clarice on the swing, her squeals of delight filling his heart with joy as he laughed along with his wife, Sandy, who pushed their other daughter Jamie beside them. The sky was blue, barely a wisp of a cloud overhead, the sun shining down on them just enough to be warm, but not hot.

It's a perfect day in every way.

Tony couldn't remember the last time they had all been able to get to the park on a weekday. The kids were off for some teacher development day and he had wisely booked the day off well in advance. Sandy had lost her job three years ago and after two years of searching unsuccessfully for something in her field, they had agreed to make some adjustments to their lifestyle, downsizing and dropping to one used car so they could live off just his salary.

Sandy had become a stay-at-home mom.

And she loved it.

At least that's what she told him. He hoped she did, and judging by the smile on her face, he was certain she did—at least at this moment.

"How about we get something to eat?" she suggested, and the cries of agreement from the little ones had the gentle pushes from mom and dad halted, the kids quickly slowing down as their feet were shoved into the ground. Seconds later Sandy had a blanket spread out over the grass, underneath a large tree, the type of which he had no clue except that it had long leaves and was shady—weeping willow?—and a perfect location to look out over the rolling park and the city surrounding it.

"This was a great idea," he said as he took a sip from his Dr. Pepper. Sandy grinned and handed him a paper plate loaded with fried chicken, potato salad and coleslaw. KFC flashed through his mind as he stared at the plate, but he knew better. Sandy had rediscovered her love of cooking and everything they ate now was homemade, unless they treated themselves to an evening out on the town.

And the Friday night pizza night with the kids; pizza just had to be ordered in and served out of a box to be good.

He took a bite of a chicken leg and moaned as he chewed.

"This is so good, hon," he said, covering his still full mouth. "You're the best!"

She flashed a smile as she wiped Jamie's mouth of some mayonnaise. He winked at her then returned his attention to his plate, shoveling a mouthful of coleslaw into his pie hole, suddenly wondering if there was pie for desert. As he chewed, he looked at the view, thanking the Lord they were blessed to live in a smaller city rather than some monster that could only dream of a setting like this. He slowly turned his head from shoulder to shoulder, scanning the horizon, and about the only eyesore he could spot was the rail yards, and even that didn't seem so bad from here.

Suddenly there was a brilliant flash of light from the rail yards. Jamie cried out, as if in pain, her hands letting go of her plate as she covered her eyes. He looked to his left where the flash had come from and gasped as he saw a massive fireball erupting into the air, clawing its way toward the sky. The ground began to rumble, Jamie continued to cry, saying something about her eyes, and Clarice simply whimpered as Sandy tried to soothe them both.

Tony pushed himself to his knees, facing the blast when he noticed the bottom portion was expanding rapidly and it was then that he realized it was not only expanding outward to the left and right of his field of vision, but toward them as well.

Oh my God!

As the blast wave raced forward, across the park, engulfing everything in its path, screams began to break out all around them. He turned to Sandy and saw the horror on her face as she too realized what was happening. He jumped for the kids, grabbing them and pulling them toward him as he hit the ground, his back to the explosion, his torso a human shield for his children, Sandy grabbing onto him, their eyes meeting, his heart breaking as he saw hers fill with tears, the rapidly growing mushroom cloud behind him reflected in the glassiness.

"I love you!" he yelled over the roar, but before she could reply, he felt a blast of wind hit them. He squeezed his eyes shut as the kids screamed, then he cried out in excruciating pain as the heat hit him, his clothes bursting into flame, the skin of his back instantly melting, the intense pain enveloping him, the screams of fear from his family turning into those of pain, as his last thoughts were of how he had failed to protect them, of how sorry he was he hadn't spent more days like this with them, and of how he prayed there was a Heaven where he would see them all again, soon, because there was no way he wanted to live another moment.

And the screams stopped, the wind calmed, the heat dissipated, and the skies cleared, leaving nothing but a mushroom cloud in the air, a charred park, and a dark carbon outline of what was once a loving family in its final embrace.

Charles de Gaulle National Intelligence Archive, Longjumeau, France

Kane sat with his back against the front of the rear compartment of the delivery van, Dawson against the side panel to his right, Niner to the left. By Kane's watch they were only a few minutes from the front gate. Assuming Alexis was right and they wouldn't be searched, gaining initial entry should be a cakewalk. But from his experience, things never went entirely to plan, and he had the impression that this woman, though perhaps older than him by a few years, didn't have much experience in field ops.

"So, what do you think?" asked Dawson as he inspected his weapon and Taser. "Can we trust her?"

Kane nodded.

"I think we can trust her to not betray us. I'm not so sure we can trust her to be correct in her assumptions that this will be a clean in and out. If the French get wind of what's happening with Crimson Rush, they're liable to increase security countrywide, especially where the microfilm is being stored."

"That assumes they even know about the microfilm," said Niner as he holstered his Glock. "Maybe even they've forgotten about it."

Kane shrugged.

"Possibly, but I wouldn't count on it. That's prime blackmail material for any type of negotiations with the Russians. I doubt they've forgotten about it."

"It makes me wonder if it's even here," said Dawson. "Wouldn't they hide it away somewhere special if it's that important?"

Kane shifted, trying to get comfortable on the hard metal floor of the van.

"They don't need to. Nobody knows about it outside of probably a handful of people, most of them retired. There's probably a note when a new president gets briefed referring to it, and that's about it. Time and arrogance would have them archive it just like anything else from that era."

Three knocks against the panel separating the driver compartment and the rear indicated they were approaching the gate. All three men became quiet, each pulling their Taser in the event something did go wrong.

The vehicle made a turn to the right then slowed, eventually coming to a stop. Muffled voices could be heard through the panel, then the vehicle began to roll forward again. If the map was correct, they had only a few hundred feet to go before they would pull into the shipping area. It was 11pm with only a skeleton crew expected to be on site.

The van came to a stop and the engine shut off. The panel between the cabin and the rear slid open.

"From this point on I am your prisoner. Remember there are cameras everywhere."

Kane pointed his gun at Alexis through the panel.

"Understood," he said with a wink as they all raised their balaclavas.

Dawson and Niner exited the van through the rear doors and rounded to the front then Kane joined them, Dawson now covering Alexis with his weapon as she climbed out.

"Which way?" asked Kane, more for the benefit of the cameras, flicking his weapon at her.

Alexis lead them to a nearby door, swiping her pass and pulling it open. They stepped inside and found a surprised security guard sitting behind a desk. Kane strode forward, Taser at his side, slightly behind him, and as the guard stood up, his jaw dropped when Kane whipped the Taser into sight and squeezed, the probe bursting from the weapon and embedding itself in the man's chest, the 50,000 volts surging into his body, incapacitating him instantly.

Niner quickly zip tied the man's hands and feet, then taped his mouth shut as the rest continued forward, Alexis still playing the prisoner. Two flights of stairs, three security doors and no personnel in the hallways, and they were at the main computer lab where archival requests were processed by clerks working a grueling thirty-five hour work week, socialism run amok in the old republic.

"There will probably be one or two clerks beyond this door," whispered Alexis, her head down.

Dawson held his weapon to her head for show, saying, "Open it!"

Alexis swiped her pass. Niner yanked open the door and Kane rushed in, sweeping the room from right to left, firing his Taser on the first target he found, a young man sitting at his desk playing World of Warcraft on taxpayer time. He heard the snap then sizzle of Niner's Taser taking out the next target to his left and the playacted protests of Alexis as Dawson shoved her in the room.

Kane checked the rest of the room after ejecting the probe from the Taser while Niner bound the two analysts. Kane stepped over to his target's computer and with a few keystrokes had sold all of his avatar's possessions for one gold coin and typed an apology to the taxpayers as other logged in users cheered and jeered.

Niner grinned at him as he yanked the final zip tie tight, Alexis already at a terminal logging in and executing the search. Dawson kept his weapon on her for show as Kane and Niner watched the doors at either end of the room.

"Got it!" announced Alexis. "I've sent the retrieval request. It should be ready when we get down there."

Kane didn't bother asking what she meant, instead checking the door then opening it a sliver, looking for any wandering security as she continued to type.

None.

"I've killed the cameras. Let's go."

Alexis led the way at gunpoint and minutes later they entered a massive warehouse with shelves towering to the ceiling in neat rows for as far as the eye could see. Rails ran up and down each row with machines, now idle, resting at the head of each aisle, awaiting instructions. In the distance the sound of one of the machines could be heard, then a conveyer belt roared to life. Alexis pointed to the far end.

"Here it comes!"

"What the hell is this place?" asked Niner.

"It's an automated warehouse. Everything is coded and stored in a specific aisle, shelf and location, coded by size. The computer tells where the retrieval machine will find the item, and what size it is, and it will deploy the appropriate tool to retrieve it, then place it on the conveyor belt. At this end a human takes the item and has it delivered to the requesting party. It's all quite ingenious."

"Amazon has something similar I think," said Kane.

"I was thinking this was all going to be digitized and we'd just be retrieving a file," said Niner. "Don't get me wrong, I'm impressed with the Transformers getting us our tiny microfilm, but still, I thought if you're this hi-tech, then why not go all the way?"

Alexis chuckled, then remembered she might still be on camera and tried to phrase her response to fit in case the tapes were reviewed.

"You Americans are so arrogant. There is an ongoing digitization project and over half this warehouse has been converted so far. This particular item however hasn't been yet."

A small box arrived, ending the conversation.

"Open it," said Dawson as they all leaned in. Alexis cut the seal on the box with a box cutter sitting nearby and opened it. Inside was an envelope with a microfilm container.

"Should we make sure it's what we're looking for? Just in case?" asked Niner.

The reply to his question was the sounding of an alarm and flashing red lights on the walls around them.

"We've been discovered!" hissed Alexis.

CIA Headquarters, Langley, Virginia

National Clandestine Service Chief Leif Morrison listened to the latest update provided by the Joint Chiefs from one of the many secure conference rooms, the talking heads displayed on a grid of monitors on the far wall. He and several of the CIA's top brass sat around a table taking in the latest briefings and providing their own intel. At this moment the hottest leads were both CIA based—Chris Leroux's computer trace generating the most excitement and hope around the virtual table.

But Morrison knew it was a long shot. There were a lot of things that had to go right for there to be a hit. And what if there were dozens or hundreds of false positives? They didn't have a lot of time to waste chasing down possibly hundreds of dead ends.

Unfortunately it was their only hope at the moment for tracking down who now had their hands on potentially hundreds of nuclear triggers throughout the country.

"And the French operation?" asked the Secretary of Defense.

"It's underway as we speak. We should know any time now."

The Secretary of State cleared his throat.

"I was speaking to the French ambassador less than fifteen minutes ago and I've made it clear to the French how disappointed we are that they kept this piece of intelligence from us, and how we expect—"

"You did what?" erupted Morrison.

There was stunned silence in the room and over the speakers as the words the Secretary of State had just said sank in with the others.

"I merely expressed—"

"You told the French that we were aware that they had the microfilm?"

"Not in so many words. In diplomacy you usually dance around an issue, letting the other side—"

Morrison was certain his blood pressure would have his doctor rushing him to an ER as he felt himself flush with burning rage.

"I don't give a damn what words you used! You just told the French that we are aware they possess something that at this very moment I have a team trying to retrieve! Just what the hell do you think the French are going to do?!"

It was as if a switch was flipped and the idiot at the other end suddenly clued into his stupidity, his face paling and his jaw dropping.

"I'm sorry—"

"Mr. President, if you'll excuse me, I need to warn our team that the mission has been compromised."

"Very well," said the President, the tone of his voice indicating to everyone his own incredulity at what he had just heard.

Morrison pushed up from his seat when every phone in the room and over the videoconference began to vibrate or ring. He grabbed the phone off his hip and read the message.

Nuclear detonation confirmed in Memphis, TN.

"Jesus Christ," he whispered as he dropped back into his chair. "Mr. President—"

"I know. Meeting adjourned. We will reconvene in one hour."

Morrison looked about the room at the others, some looking as green as he felt.

I think I'm going to be sick.

As he sat there for a moment collecting his thoughts and searching for his fortitude, he suddenly remembered what the idiot had done, and fired a message off to operations to have Kane notified of the security breach. And to not mention the detonation until the mission was completed.

205

The last thing they need is another distraction.

Operations Center 3, CIA Headquarters, Langley, Virginia

Chris Leroux's eyes were beginning to glaze over as the adrenaline fueled excitement of watching his plan unfold for all to see on the huge screens of Operations Center 3 began to wane. He blinked rapidly, moistening his drying eyes and watched the ticker pass one hundred thousand devices contacted. It was a staggering number and showed no sign of slowing, the malware obviously well distributed.

He had often wondered if there should be a law that prevented morons from connecting to the Internet. Perhaps morons was too harsh a term. Uneducated? Uninformed? It would only be too easy to do so. Simply make Internet Service Providers responsible for making certain their customers all had up to date anti-virus software, and that it was actually being used. The operating system companies could easily add something to their software that would show when the last scan had been performed, and that their anti-virus software was intact, functioning, and properly updated. This could be polled during a login to the Internet, and the ISP could then reject the connection to anyone not properly protected, redirecting them instead to any number of anti-virus manufacturers, including those with free offerings.

Simple. Cheap. And it would save billions in lost revenues and millions of man hours wasted in trying to fix infected machines. Would it stop everything? Of course not, but it would stop most.

But then some would say forcing people to use software that scans everything on your computer and everything coming into and going out of your Internet connection would be a violation of your privacy, and a violation of the fundamental principles of the Internet—free access for all with no government interference.

This of course ignored the fact that access was rarely free, and the Internet had been invented by government, specifically the US military's DARPA wing.

"Say again?"

It was OC3 Coordinator Dimka that broke his train of thought. He looked over at her and the expression on her face had his heart racing.

"Yes, sir, right away."

She pressed several buttons on her station and the two screens showing his program running suddenly were joined by news broadcasts from around the world, CNN, Fox, NBC, CBS, ABC, BBC, CBC and others popped onto the screen, all showing the same thing, or just switching over their programming. CNN's broadcast was put through the speaker as the doors behind them flew open, Director Morrison and several other CIA brass rushing into the room.

Morrison pointed at Leroux.

"Any success yet?"

"No, sir, not yet," he replied, his eyes darting between Morrison and the horror on the screens, his shoulders collapsing as all muscle control seemed to leave his body. "We're too late, aren't we?"

"It's never too late to catch whoever is responsible. What do you need to keep your operation going?"

Leroux turned to Dimka whose eyes had glassed over from the images on the screens surrounding them.

"Just one tech? Conway?" he suggested.

She nodded.

"Yes, that's all that's needed until we find something," she agreed.

"Good. Conway, you continue what you're doing!" ordered Morrison, pointing at the tech Leroux had been working with. "The rest of you I want monitoring local broadcasts, pulling—"

Morrison stopped when all of the broadcasts began to switch over to something new. The CNN audio was still being fed through the speakers for everyone to hear.

"—*just delivered to our studios via email. We will broadcast it now in its entirety, without comment.*"

The talking head disappeared, replaced by the image of a man, or rather a person, their details obscured in the shadows, a banner in the background a familiar green with half crescent and something written in Arabic.

The English was unaccented, the voice altered electronically. It was deep, the bass rolling through the floor and up Leroux's spine. It was terrifying in its depth, and in the evil that was its message.

"*By now you are aware of the power we hold over your nation. For too long America has been the uninvited policeman of the world. For too long America has shed the blood of innocents to spread its ideals throughout the world. For too long the American plague has spread its culture where it is not welcomed, nor wanted. It is time for America to leave the world to unfold on its own, without interference.*"

Everyone in the room was silent, but the fear and the tension was palpable. Leroux wondered what the public at home would feel if they knew what everyone here knew—that this was just the beginning. That there could be a thousand more targets like Memphis, and that millions could die as a nation's infrastructure was destroyed.

"*Today's detonation is merely a demonstration of our power. Your government has known for some time the power at our disposal, but has decided not to inform you—*"

"The President's not going to like that one," muttered Morrison.

"*—of the danger you now face. We are in control of over one thousand devices, already pre-positioned throughout the United States and its allies. And as we have already shown, we are not afraid to exercise this power. Our demands are simple, and easily met. Our demands are easily summed up with this one statement: America, go home. We demand the immediate withdrawal of all American land forces from Iraq,*"

209

Afghanistan, and any other country they find themselves in today, invited or uninvited. This includes Europe, Japan, South Korea, and others where you believe you are welcome, but in fact are not. We demand all combat air forces grounded today. We demand all naval forces involved in any hostile acts including blockades and sanction enforcements withdrawn. Those involved in humanitarian actions are welcome to continue their much appreciated activities as long as they immediately pull out when no longer required or when requested to do so. We demand that plans be announced for the immediate drawdown and eventual withdrawal of all forces from foreign soils to be completed within one year. We also demand that all foreign military aid be immediately halted. This includes direct funding of military purchases, loans for military purchases, and so called military advisors who ostensibly train other countries' soldiers for proxy wars.

"Let us make this perfectly clear. One year from today, the only American soldier whose boots are not on American soil, is an American soldier who is either on a humanitarian mission, on a naval vessel on a mission of mercy, or is on vacation with his family. If we do not see evidence of our demands being met, each day we will detonate another device and more innocent Americans will die. We ask the people of America to save themselves and insist their leaders meet our demands rather than make bold proclamations of justice for those responsible, and defiance in the face of inevitable defeat.

"For too long American military might has been used to push its values and goods on an unwilling world. Today, this ends. Today, the world rises up and rids itself of the yoke of oppression foisted upon us by your country and its selfish ideals. Today, the world is free for the first time in sixty years, free to make its own mistakes, free to enjoy its own successes. Today, the world rejoices, as the last super power retreats within its own borders, with the threat of destruction to keep it contained.

"Today, America trembles at our *might, as we have been forced to tremble before hers."*

The screen went black, then the talking heads reappeared, their words mere murmurs in the background as Leroux gripped his workstation, the implications of what he had just heard sinking in.

Is the American dream dead?

"We've got one!" came Conway's voice over the headset and at first Leroux wasn't sure what he meant, having to repeat the words several times in his head until their meaning finally sank in. He jumped from his chair and looked at the display now flashing amongst the news broadcasts.

Number of Positives: 1

Résidence Hôtelière de la Cerisaie, Longjumeau, France

Alex West hated waiting, doing nothing. He wondered if Control in the old days had felt the same. Never in on the action, only getting occasional reports if possible, then either finding out at the end whether a mission had been successful or not, or sometimes, in the worst case scenario, never hearing at all—an agent captured and never heard from again.

There were enough of those over the years, the Memorial Wall at Langley a testament to that. He had fully expected he would have become one of those lonely stars on the wall, but after the Crimson Rush mission, and his being benched, he hadn't had a risky day since.

Life had become a boring routine.

Then retirement!

He had never thought he'd see the day. The days. The long, boring days. He occupied his time as best he could with reading, writing his memoirs that no one would ever be able to read, and tending his garden. He had almost no friends. He had never married, never dated, had never been with a woman since his three months with Adelle.

And he had never stopped loving her.

He had to admit he was hurt when he found out she had a daughter. She had moved on, replaced him when he couldn't do the same. It had him wondering if it had meant as much to her as it had to him. He looked over at her, standing by the window, looking down at the street below, her fingers tapping a rhythm out onto her lips, something she always did when she was nervous.

He was happy for her with respect to her having a daughter. Alexis was beautiful, and there was obviously love and respect between them. He had never wanted kids, never expecting to live long enough to see them through to adulthood, and when he had voiced that to her during their hiatus from their jobs, she had agreed.

Spies aren't meant to be parents.

They were her words, not his, but he agreed with them. But seeing Adelle and Alexis together, and how proud she was of her daughter, opened a pit of regret in his stomach that was gnawing at him, and had been since the younger generation had left to save the world.

"I miss the old days," he sighed.

Zorkin, sipping on a club soda, nodded.

"I too, my friend. Life had a purpose. Now…" Zorkin's voice drifted.

"Now it's not life, it's existence," finished West.

Adelle turned from the window.

"Nonsense. There's still plenty we can do to contribute. Look at what we have accomplished here in just the past two days. You, Alex, had the forethought to have any intelligence searches for Crimson Rush flagged so you would be notified. You also were instrumental in putting together the Grey Network. How many times has it helped out this generation, whether they knew they were being helped or not? You pulled us together from across the globe, creating a team that is already in action, following a plan we put together. No, Alex, we may be old, but we're still living. I for one am alive, and I will continue to live, even after I die, through our daughter. And so will you. She's our legacy, she's the reason we continue to live today, and continue to help protect the world from the messes created during our day. She's—"

"*Our* daughter?"

West felt his chest tighten, his heart begin to race, as he looked at Adelle, his jaw sagging toward his chest, his eyes searching hers to see if he had misheard her, to see if she had misspoken.

Adelle smiled and sat down beside him on the couch, taking his hands in hers.

"*Our* daughter."

West wasn't certain what his reaction should be, but he knew what it was. Tears filled his eyes, spilling down his cheeks as he took Adelle in his arms and hugged her, the thrill and excitement and joy of having something he never knew he had wanted, unleashed. He tried to stop the tears, to fortify himself against the emotions pouring out of him, he of a generation that tried to keep tears at bay, but he couldn't help it.

"Are you happy?" asked Adelle, her voice a whisper in his ear.

"C-can't you tell?" he asked, laughing as he gently pushed her away. He looked over at Zorkin who continued to sip his club soda, apparently unmoved by the entire display. "Did *you* know?"

Zorkin shook his head.

"Everyone knew! Only you and Alexis—*A-lex-is!*—seem to be the only two in the dark! You call yourself a spy? She has your damned nose, the poor girl!"

West wiped his face dry with a handkerchief as there was a shout from the room next door, then someone yelling to turn on the television.

The three friends exchanged glances, then Zorkin reached for the remote control and pressed the power button. He selected local television from the hotel menu then flipped through the channels until hitting a news channel.

And once again West felt his chest tighten for entirely different reasons, the scene displayed one of utter devastation.

"We're too late!"

Charles de Gaulle National Intelligence Archive, Longjumeau, France

Alexis led the way as Kane, Dawson and Niner followed, their footfalls heavy through the corridors as they raced for the exit and their van. There was no way to know what was going on except that most likely one of their trussed up "victims" had been discovered, or one had escaped and set off the alarm. Whatever the cause, it didn't matter.

They needed to get out of here before reinforcements arrived.

"Nobody dies," said Kane as they reached the entrance that had led them into the building. "These are our allies, we're the aggressors here. Non-lethal force only."

Kane looked out the window and saw several of the guards, their weapons raised, aiming in various directions, apparently confused as to what to do.

"Who's going to tell them?" asked Niner as he double-checked his gear.

Alexis turned to Niner.

"Can you 'geek up' as you Americans might say?"

Niner's eyebrows shot up as his head dipped.

"Huh?"

"You're Asian. You look intellectual. Our stereotype would have you working late and likely to work somewhere like this."

Niner glanced at Dawson with a grin indicating he wasn't offended.

"Political correctness hasn't reached France yet, I see."

"What did you have in mind?" asked Dawson.

"The two of us go out there pretending we're employees fleeing you, then take them out."

Now Kane's eyebrows shot up.

"Two against four?"

"I'll take the three on the left if you think it necessary," said Alexis with a smile. "It's our only chance of getting out of here before reinforcements arrive."

"Expected response time?"

"Less than ten minutes."

Dawson nodded in agreement.

"Go ahead, Beeker."

Niner was already stripping out of his gear, leaving himself wearing black military issue boots, black pants that could be mistaken for dress pants in the dark, and a black t-shirt. He tucked his and Kane's Tasers in his pants, behind his back, then looked at Dawson.

"Don't you dare have my nickname changed to Beeker. I'll kill you where you stand."

Kane and Dawson laughed as Alexis inspected him.

"Too bad we don't have a pair of glasses for you," she said, then grabbed the door, opening it to the outside. She rushed through the door, Niner following, Alexis crying out for help in French, Niner smartly staying mute, simply flailing his arms and looking behind him as if fearing pursuit.

Dawson grabbed Niner's gear, Kane picking up Alexis', as they watched through the doors. The four guards immediately trained their weapons on the two "clerks", soon lowering them as she waved her ID in the air, pointing at the door. As they approached two Tasers fired, taking two of the men out of the action, Niner kicking his remaining opponent's weapon aside then incapacitating him with a quick blow to the nose. Alexis hoofed hers in the balls then kneed the man in the head as he doubled forward.

It was over in seconds, Kane and Dawson racing out the door toward the writhing group, quickly zip tying their hands and feet. Sirens wailed to the west and they all spun to watch two police vehicles rush around the corner, screeching to a halt at the front gate, more sirens in the distance.

Shit!

Four miles from Charles de Gaulle National Intelligence Archive, Longjumeau, France

Alex West lay on the pavement, writhing in agony, his left hand grabbing his hip as Zorkin tried to bend over and help him, and Adelle stood at the edge of the street waiting for a passerby to help. The roar of engines and shifting gears had them all looking down the road at a small convoy of six police vehicles approaching quickly.

Adelle stepped out onto the road, waving at the convoy, the lead vehicle swerving to avoid her, the others following suit. West looked up in pain at the first vehicle, the passenger on a radio, looking at him. As the vehicles raced by, Adelle yelling for help in French, Zorkin glaring at the bastards for ignoring their plight, West continued to cry out in pain.

The rear vehicle hammered on its brakes, the two men in the front of the transport vehicle jumping out.

"What's wrong here?" asked the passenger as he approached West.

"He slipped. I think he broke his hip," said Adelle as the two officers approached. West moaned again, this one louder than any before, and turned his back to them.

"He needs an ambulance," said the young driver. "I'll call you one."

"How about we just take *your* vehicle," said Zorkin, matter-of-factly, as West rolled back toward the men, his Glock pointed directly at them, Zorkin and Adelle already with their weapons out.

"Hey, what's going on here? I thought he was injured?" exclaimed the driver.

"They're robbing us, you moron," said the older officer as West scrambled to his feet, a little less efficiently than he might have hoped.

"What's in the back?" asked Adelle.

The older officer shook his head.

"Nothing, we were supposed to pick up some prisoners and transport them."

West leaned into the cabin of the truck and saw an access panel to the rear. He slid it aside, revealing an empty transport area.

"Here's what's going to happen," said Adelle with a smile. "First, you're going to strip."

"What?"

"Strip. Down to your briefs. All of you."

West's eyebrows popped.

"Huh?"

"All of you. Take off your clothes. You two"—she motioned to West and Zorkin—"put on their uniforms."

Nobody moved.

"Quickly!"

All four men jumped slightly at her bark then began stripping. West and Zorkin eyed each other, Zorkin apparently none-too-thrilled with the idea of exposing himself either. West had tried to keep in shape, but gravity inevitably had taken its toll, and Zorkin looked like he might have an extra little padding on him since their last encounter.

West sighed and kicked off his shoes, dropping his pants and stepping out of them as he unbuttoned his shirt, he and Zorkin huddled as close to the truck as possible. Fortunately traffic was almost non-existent at this time of night on this road, so there was no one to question what the hell was going on. Adelle grabbed the clothes of the driver who fortunately seemed to match West's body type, and handed them to him. She ran a finger down his chest to his stomach, a little too soft for his liking.

"You kept yourself in shape," she smiled. "That's good."

219

He felt himself blush as he took the clothes and hurriedly put them on. Adelle handed the passenger's uniform to Zorkin, who pulled the shirt on.

"Are you kidding me?" he asked. West turned as he finished with the last button on his perfectly fitting shirt and laughed. Zorkin had the much shorter man's shirt on, the sleeves half way to his elbows, the first button of his shirt screaming for relief.

"No choice," smiled Adelle. "We have to work with what we've got."

West climbed into the provided pants then put his shoes back on, not willing to put the man's boots on in case he had to do some running, and ill fitted shoes wouldn't do.

"How do I look?" he asked, Adelle turning to inspect him.

"Like a brave officer ready to make the streets safe," she said, patting his cheek. She motioned at the two prisoners. "Now secure them in the back."

West zip tied their wrists and ankles with ties from their own utility belts, gagged them with handkerchiefs, then pushed them into the back. Adelle had her phone out, sending a message as Zorkin finally finished putting on his uniform.

"This is ridiculous," he complained once again.

West looked over and snorted.

Zorkin's pants were four inches too short and each button was like the span of a suspension bridge between the two sides, his stomach and chest exposed in varying degrees all the way up.

Adelle shoved her cellphone in her pocket then opened the door to the cab, looking inside. She reemerged with a jacket and tossed it at Zorkin.

"Try this."

Zorkin pulled it on and smiled, it obviously belonging to the driver. He zipped up the near perfect fit, and looked down at himself.

"Now as long as I don't need to get out, we'll be okay."

Adelle climbed into the back of the truck.

220

"Let's hurry. You know how to get there?"

"Yes."

"Good, then here's the plan."

Provost Drive, Newburgh, New York

Agent Sherrie White's heart pounded as she watched from the sidelines, CIA strictly observing on this take down. Throughout the country every law enforcement officer had been mobilized, including the National Guard, and military forces across the world were on the highest alert they had been since 9/11.

To think this is already far worse!

She shuddered at the thought. The detonation in Memphis had been devastating. Casualty reports were starting to pour in, hundreds believed vaporized, the train yard completely obliterated. Memphis was an important rail transportation hub, even more so today than it had been during the Cold War, and its loss would have major economic ramifications. The last briefing she had received before being assigned to this op indicated a yield of under a kiloton, with a radiation cloud that had quickly dissipated. Rescue efforts were already well underway, along with aerial dispersal of anti-radiation foam from water bombers and helicopters.

It was a rapid reaction only made possible by the fact the entire country had been put on alert earlier, the reason unbeknownst to the public.

But the quick response, and equally rapid address to the nation by the President had done little to calm the panic now spreading across the country. Hoarding had already begun with grocery stores and pharmacies stripped bare within hours of the terrorist broadcast. Looting and rioting had been reported in some of the major cities, residents stocking up on essentials like flat panel televisions and iPads.

It disgusted her.

Looters should be shot on sight, no questions asked.

It was one thing to steal supplies, that was understandable—you were trying to save yourself and your family. It was another to take advantage of the situation and try to upgrade your miserable existence.

Sherrie's eyes flicked between the CNN broadcast on one monitor, and the feeds from the head-mounted cameras of the tactical team moving in on the house identified by her boyfriend as the only computer in the country to have opened the transmitted file.

He's a genius!

She loved him. Of that there was no doubt. Why, she wasn't exactly sure. He wasn't her type, at least not what she had thought was her type. But when she had been assigned to test him, to tempt him sexually to see if he would break and reveal his secrets, he had seemed so sweet that she actually found herself questioning her assignment and even asked to be taken off it.

She had been refused.

Sometimes Morrison is an asshole!

He was right, though. She couldn't exactly bail in the middle of her assignment because she had become sweet on the target. She had been thrilled when Chris had passed the test and refused her advances, despite using all of her feminine wiles.

And thanks to Kane, who had pushed the two of them together at the end, they were now a happy couple. It was a shotgun "wedding", her moving in almost right away since her apartment wasn't really hers—it had been part of the assignment. Chris hadn't minded, not in the least, and she had tried to make the transition for him from bachelor to committed relationship as easy as possible.

She felt they had the best of both worlds with her being a spy. Their time apart simply made their time together that much more intense. When Morrison had assigned her this mission as observer, she had jumped at the opportunity to get back out in the field, but all the moments where there was nothing to do but think, like these right now, she worried about her beloved Chris.

Langley is absolutely a prime target.

"They're making entry now," said one of the FBI agents inside the mobile command center parked around the corner from the house. She watched as one of the cameras showed the door being forced open with a battering ram, other views showing agents rushing into the front hallway as the same happened at the back. Local police cars and several FBI SUVs roared from their positions around the corners near the house, their squealing tires on the other side of the command post walls music to her ears causing her to twitch in her chair, every fiber of her being wishing she were out there, gun in hand, racing to apprehend the bastard responsible for so much horror.

But it wasn't to be, she merely an observer.

"We've got him!" came a voice over the comm as another voice announced the all clear. The command post roared to life, the massive vehicle moving forward then turning on to the suspect's street, coming to a halt moments later. The rear doors were thrown open and she followed several agents out, the evening sun low on the horizon. Her trained eye scanned the neighborhood, dozens of curtains held aside as scared and curious families watched the takedown. Others, more brave, or more stupid, stood on their porches watching.

Sherrie approached the suspect's house, the tactical team mostly outside now, securing the area as the agents moved inside to begin searching for useful intel. Down the street one set of neighbors had apparently had enough, their RV pulling away from the curb, leaving the neighborhood in its wake.

As she stepped inside she saw a man in handcuffs sitting uncomfortably in the corner of his wedge shaped couch looking scared, and if she didn't know better, entirely innocent.

There's no way this is the guy.

Tears streaked the man's face, he was beet red and looked on the verge of a panic attack. He was a massive man, probably approaching four hundred pounds, sporting an unkempt beard and head of knotted hair, some of it tied haphazardly in a ponytail. His light grey track pants were threadbare in several inappropriate locations, and his white C-3PO and R2-D2 t-shirt, with "These aren't the droids you're looking for" emblazoned underneath, was stained with some sort of pasta sauce in several places, probably aged to different time periods since his last load of laundry was done by his mother.

"What was he doing when you found him?" Sherrie asked the agent-in-charge, Tosh Wahlberg.

"Playing video games in his bedroom."

"Any other computers?"

"A few. Looks like a computer geek of some kind."

Sherrie turned to the man.

"What's your name?"

"Joe. Joe Cross."

"What do you do for a living, Mr. Cross?"

"I work at Burger Prince," he said, his eyes jumping from person to person, the sounds of his home being torn apart apparently disturbing.

"Doing what?" asked Special Agent-in-Charge Wahlberg.

"I dunno. Whatever Kerry tells me to do. That bitch has a hate on for me. All last week I was on toilet duty. That's just not fair! Have you seen some of the fat asses that come into our place? Can you imagine the mess some of those make? It's like they spread their cheeks so wide their asshole is on the seat and they shit right on it. It's goddamned disgusting! You should be arresting *them*."

"The 'fat asses'?" asked Sherrie, eying his massive girth and a prime example of a pot calling the kettle black.

"Damned right. And Kerry. Did I say that bitch has a hate on for me?"

He looked around at all the activity, appearing to regain some of his composure.

"Man, my friends aren't going to believe this shit."

"It's not the right computer!" yelled someone from upstairs.

"What?"

Wahlberg ran up the stairs toward the voice, leaving Sherrie alone with the suspect who continued to chatter about what was no doubt an online community of friends, Cross not striking her as the outgoing type.

Like my babe.

She felt a pang in her heart as she wondered if this could have been Chris if he hadn't have joined the CIA and instead wasted his intellect on gaming and burger flipping.

Not my babe!

She pulled out her Blackberry, unlocked it and held in the C key.

Dialing Chris (Office).

It rang once and was forwarded, ringing twice more before answered.

"Hello?"

Her caller ID was blocked, leaving her babe in the dark as to who called his cellphone, a number she knew he gave to almost no one. In fact, she couldn't remember anyone other than Kane calling it, or work. His parents always called the apartment, and he had no other friends.

"Hi hon, it's me."

"Hi!" came the cheery reply, then a lowered voice, as if he were surrounded by others. "Are you okay?"

"I'm fine, but I think something's wrong here. Could you have been wrong?"

"I don't think so, why?"

"This guy doesn't fit the profile, and I just heard somebody yell that it was the wrong computer."

There was a pause, then a quiet reply.

"Does he have wi-fi?"

Sherrie looked at Cross.

"Do you have wi-fi?"

Cross nodded.

"Doesn't everybody?"

"Is it secure?" she asked, knowing exactly where Chris was going with this.

"Nah. My mom could never remember the password and I got sick of logging her in, so I just made it public. It's not like I've got anything to hide."

"You live with your mother?"

"Yeah, what's it to you?" Cross wagged a finger at her and the other agents. "And you guys better have this house put back together before she gets back from her friend's house or she'll kick your asses."

Sherrie stifled a smile at the image as she ran up the stairs, the phone still pressed to her head.

"It's not secure," she told Chris, then told the room as she burst into the bedroom. "He's got an unsecured wi-fi network." She repositioned the phone. "Chris, what's the range on that?"

"Not much, a few hundred feet at best. It could be a neighboring house, a vehicle outside, hell, they could have a repeater sitting in the bushes."

"Wahlberg, check the surrounding houses and vehicles. It could be anywhere within a few hundred feet!"

"Shit!" exclaimed Wahlberg as he got on his radio, pushing past Sherrie as he rushed for the outside.

"What about an RV?" she asked, her mind beginning to race.

"Huh?"

"Nothing. Listen, are you in Ops?"

"Yeah, I'm still in OC3. We're monitoring your mission."

"Can you have them check for an RV leaving the area not even five minutes ago?"

"Yeah, just a second."

She heard muffled words at the other end as she rushed down the stairs and out into the early evening air, crisp and for the moment, non-nuclear. She flagged down Wahlberg.

"I need a vehicle."

Wahlberg said nothing, instead pointing at a nearby SUV, its red and blue lights still flashing, and tossed her a set of keys. She grabbed them out of the air and jumped in the vehicle, synching her cellphone with the onboard computer as she pulled away.

"Are you still there?" came a voice through the speakers.

"Yes, can you hear me?" she asked.

"Yeah. I'm going to jack you into the system. The Chief wants to hear you."

"He's there?"

"Yeah."

"Okay, go ahead."

She turned left, pretty sure she had seen a left signal light before she had entered the house. Some clicking then the sound from the speakers changed slightly, more of a hiss now being heard in the background.

"Agent White, you're now on live in OC3," said the voice of one of the techs.

"This is Morrison. Report."

"Sir, I'm going on a hunch. A large RV pulled away just as the suspect was taken down. I've got a feeling that our real suspect is in that RV, and they were jacked into our patsy's unsecured wireless network."

"Is that possible?" asked Morrison.

"Yes, sir," replied Chris. "He could easily tap an unsecured wi-fi, it would piggy back on its IP address. He can do that pretty much anywhere since so many people leave their networks unsecured."

"Wouldn't they need to be infected with the virus?" asked Morrison.

"No, their own machine is intentionally infected. They're only using the unsecured network to gain access to the Internet."

"Is there any way to get eyes on that RV?" asked Sherrie as she continued to drive, futilely looking for a vehicle with nearly a five minute head start. "I'm driving blind."

"Do we have any birds over the area?" came a woman's voice she didn't recognize.

"Negative. We'll have to tap into security and traffic cameras. Accessing now." There was a pause as the tech began his work, Sherrie pulling over to the side of the road, deciding it was best not to be racing in what might possibly be the wrong direction. "I've got a large RV two blocks away from the suspect's address five minutes ago, turning west. Sending coordinates now."

Sherrie's phone vibrated on the passenger seat. She grabbed it and hit the button to activate the navigation app, placing the phone in a cup holder. Cranking the wheel she turned around, tires squealing, horns honking in protest as she headed west.

"Roll units to that area now," ordered Morrison. "I want roadblocks, eyes in the sky—everything."

"Yes, sir."

Sherrie raced ahead, lights flashing, siren blaring, vehicles bailing out of her way as she chased a five minute old shadow, hoping for more recent camera images to be found by the experts back at Langley.

Suddenly there was a burst of static over her speakers and in her rearview mirror she saw a brilliant flash then a massive fireball blasted into the sky, the unmistakable plume with its bulbous head causing bile to fill her mouth.

"Sir, there's been another detonation," she cried as she continued racing forward, her eyes filling with tears. "Behind me, southeast of the city."

"What?!"

As she watched the fireball billow skyward the lights around her blinked then darkened, the streetlights fading to nothing, the traffic lights flipping to flashing red as taillights lit up the road ahead of her, many of the drivers simply slamming on their brakes and exiting their vehicles to stare at the horror behind them.

Sherrie barreled onward, wiping her eyes clear.

"There's been another nuclear detonation," she said, trying to keep her voice as calm and analytical as she could. "All power is out here."

"I've lost all traffic feeds," came the voice of the analyst.

"Shit!" muttered Morrison's voice over the speakers.

A sudden realization had Sherrie's foot lifting off the accelerator, her mind filling with a fog as her brain began to shutdown to protect itself.

"It's my fault," she whispered.

"What? Nonsense!" said Morrison, his voice firm as he apparently realized what was happening to his agent. "It's their fault, not yours. You were doing your job, just like anyone. They would have detonated that weapon no matter what. Now you keep doing your job, Agent, and that's an order! I want you to continue pursuit of that RV. We'll try to get eyes in the sky as soon as possible. Hear me?"

Sherrie slowly clawed her way back to reality, her mind beginning to process Morrison's words.

"Yes, sir," she whispered, her foot returning to the accelerator as she weaved through the light but mostly stopped traffic. She reached up and shoved the rearview mirror to the side so she didn't have to look at the hell behind her.

As she raced forward, often taking the center divide, she scanned the road ahead with the hopes that an RV would be stuck in the traffic, unable to weave in and out.

But that doesn't make any sense.

It was obvious that the terrorists had set off the weapon, most likely to aid in their escape. If that were so, then creating traffic chaos didn't make sense. It would only make sense if they were already either on a road that had little to no traffic, or completely off the roads, perhaps tucked away in a warehouse somewhere.

"Are there any warehouses or something around here, within five minutes of their last known location where they might hide? They have to have set off the weapon to cover their escape."

"Yes, there's several—"

"Wait a minute," interrupted Sherrie as she passed under a traffic sign indicating the airport was to the right. She did a shoulder check and cut across the several lanes to head to the airport, and as she careened onto the road she gasped.

"Oh my God!" she cried, her mind flashing images at her rapidly, of growing up, her childhood, the losses and joys, her martial arts triumphs, her being accepted into the agency, her finding love, and the realization that the emptiness she was about to leave in the cosmos was trivial, was insignificant, her contribution little to nothing in the grand scheme of things.

She would be a footnote in the history today's events would become.

As all of these images and thoughts flooded her mind, she cranked her steering wheel to the left, hammering on the gas, in a futile effort to avoid the Rocket Propelled Grenade streaking directly at her.

Operations Center 3, CIA Headquarters, Langley, Virginia

"Oh my God!"

A burst of static filled the room almost immediately after Sherrie's cry. Chris Leroux knew his girlfriend well, and could hear the terror in those last three words. Something had happened, something bad, and he knew he was powerless to help.

"What just happened?" demanded Morrison.

"We lost contact, sir," explained a tech, furiously hammering at his keyboard. "The cell signal was dropped. I've tried dialing back, but I'm getting nothing."

"Could the towers be down from the explosion?"

"Negative, sir. The tower she was connected to is still in service. The problem is at her phone."

"Maybe the call got dropped?" suggested Dimka from behind her desk on the elevated platform. "The circuits have to be getting overwhelmed with panicked civilians."

"And she thought to yell 'Oh my God!' just before her call was dropped?" said Morrison as he shook his head. "No, something happened to her."

Leroux gripped the sides of his workstation, the world swimming around him as he tried to focus on the screen in front of him. It was no use. The images and characters blurred into a mass of twisting, shimmering pools of colors as he felt his heart pound, his blood roar through his ears, and his mind begin to shut down as his unnoticed rapid breathing continued to quicken.

A hand grabbed his shoulder, jerking him back in his seat and he heard his name being called in the distance. Something struck his face, the sting bringing him back to reality with a rush of sensations finally culminating in Morrison's face staring into his, only inches away, his boss' hand on one shoulder, the other raised as if to strike him.

That's when he realized what the stinging sensation was he had just experienced.

He slapped me?

The thought kind of pissed him off. He held up his hand to block the next blow and pushed back from the workstation, putting a little distance between him and Morrison.

"Are you okay?"

Leroux rubbed his cheek and nodded, now noticing that he was dripping in sweat.

"You began to hyperventilate. Sorry for slapping you, but I need you in control of yourself. We've got a second nuclear detonation and we need to find these bastards."

Leroux nodded, his mind flooding again with thoughts of Sherrie and what might have happened to her, but this time he kept his breathing under control. It was his tear ducts that failed him. Hot salty tears scorched down his flushed cheeks. His breath caught in his throat and he held it, quickly wiping the tears away and halting the sob that almost escaped.

"I'm okay," he mumbled, returning his focus to the screen.

"Good," said Morrison, turning to the room. "Have units dispatched to her last known location. Find out whose vehicle she was in and whether or not it's got some sort of GPS link. Also try to track her phone. We have to assume she discovered something since she was nowhere near the blast zone."

The room jumped into a frenzy of activity, Leroux pulling out his own cellphone, discretely holding in the 'S' key, the phone immediately dialing the love of his life.

And going directly to voicemail.

Leroux's heart sank. The fact it didn't ring at all meant that the phone could not be detected on the cellular network, her phone was turned off or set to automatically go to voicemail, or worse, her phone had somehow been destroyed by whatever had terrified her.

He ended the call and looked over at Dimka, part of him hoping for an encouraging smile, even some bit of news, but instead what he saw shocked him.

She was crying.

And when she spotted him looking at her, she seemed terrified at having been caught, rather than embarrassed.

What the hell is going on here?

Charles de Gaulle National Intelligence Archive, Longjumeau, France

As more police cars screeched to a halt, blocking the gate, Kane quickly scanned their surroundings, his mind processing and eliminating options as they came to him. They could retreat and hole up in the building, but that would simply mean they'd be surrounded and eventually arrested after a long drawn out process. Which would delay the delivery of their vital intel.

They could try to negotiate with the police directly, but it would be of no use, and it would simply give reinforcements more time to arrive now that the situation was confirmed genuine.

He drew his Glock and pressed it against Alexis' temple. She immediately raised her hands as he positioned himself behind her, his free hand on the back of her neck, guiding her toward the van they had arrived in.

"BD, you drive, Niner in the back."

Niner jumped in the back of the van, leaving the rear doors open, wrapping his left arm around cargo netting, taking a knee and readying his weapon. Dawson climbed into the driver side, starting the vehicle as Alexis slid to the middle of the bench seat, Kane beside her with his gun still pointed at her head, clearly visible to the police at the gate.

"My mother sent a text. They have commandeered a vehicle. Go left out of the gate, I'll tell you when to turn right, about five hundred meters from here. They'll be waiting."

"Roger that," said Dawson as he put the vehicle in gear and slowly approached the gate.

"I thought they were supposed to stay at the hotel?" said Kane as he kept an angry expression on his face, glaring at the police officers.

"You obviously don't know my mother. There's no telling her what to do."

Kane leaned out the window and shouted in perfect French, "Let us pass or she dies!"

Dawson came to a stop, Kane pushing the weapon harder against Alexis' head.

"Please! Please do as he says!" she screamed, her performance Emmy worthy if not Oscar. The man in charge turned away from them, waving for one of the vehicles to be moved, shaking his head in anger at losing control of the situation so quickly.

One of the units blocking their path jerked backward and Dawson punched it, bursting through the roadblock and cranking the wheel to the left, giving the van all she had as they put some distance between them and the front gate.

"They're following us!" yelled Niner from the back. Kane glanced over his shoulder and saw Niner positioned so he could fire at any of their pursuers.

"Show them why they shouldn't. Non-lethal!" reminded Kane.

"You're no fun!" said Niner as his Glock opened up on the lead car, the first shot hitting the engine causing the driver to panic and swerve to the left, exposing the rear tire as the back end fishtailed. Niner's second shot took out the tire causing the back end to grip the asphalt suddenly, ripping the car into a vicious spin, bringing the entire procession to a halt.

"Turn right here!"

Dawson cranked the wheel, obeying Alexis' order, and as they made the turn Kane cursed. A police van was blocking their path, lights flashing. Dawson hammered on the brakes, already looking behind him for an escape route when Kane saw the doors open and two familiar figures exit.

"Stop! It's them!" he yelled as he jumped out of the van, helping Alexis down as Niner extricated himself from the back.

"In the back!" yelled Zorkin as he opened the rear doors. Two bodies tumbled out onto the ground and Kane was about to question the "no kill" orders when he saw them struggling against their bonds. Kane dove into the back and felt hands pulling him inside as Dawson and Niner followed. The doors slammed shut and moments later the passenger side door closed, the vehicle pulling away.

"Turn the damned lights off!" he heard Zorkin's muffled voice yell. West's reply was inaudible but elicited a laugh from his old friend. Within seconds the vehicle made a sharp right turn and over the next minute several more turns. A panel slid open separating the front from the back of what Kane could only describe as an oddly shaped paddy wagon.

"We're clear," said Zorkin, his breath short as his obvious excitement had taken over. "Any special requests for our next stop?"

"Let's ditch this vehicle ASAP and get back to the hotel so we can transmit this data. Hopefully that will give Langley enough time to stop any possible attack."

Zorkin's face clouded and his eyes darted away.

"What?" asked Kane, a gaping pit opening in his stomach as he already knew the answer.

"There's already been a detonation. We saw it on the TV while you were inside."

Bile filled Kane's mouth, a sense of horror overwhelming him at the thought of a nuclear detonation on home soil.

"Where?"

"Memphis."

Kane's head whipped to Dawson.

"Doesn't Red have family there?"

Dawson nodded.

"His folks."

Mike "Red" Belme was Dawson's second-in-command, and Kane knew he was also Dawson's best friend, Dawson actually the Godfather to Red's son Bryson. They were close. Very close. He could only imagine what Dawson must be going through worrying about his friend's family.

The van was silent, a cloud of gloom settling over them.

It was Kane that broke the silence.

"The best thing we can do now is complete the mission and prevent any more detonations."

"Agreed," said Dawson, his face again all business.

"Then we take revenge," muttered Niner.

"Hear hear," agreed West from the front.

Everyone involved dies.

Stewart International Airport, Outside Newburgh, New York

Vitaly Travkin strapped himself into his chair, turning it to face the front of the large retrofitted RV, locking it in place. The roar of the massive Antonov AN-124's engines quickly overwhelmed the soundproofing of their mobile headquarters, but as the plane gained altitude and the noise cancellation devices calibrated themselves, the inside quietened down to a workable level once again. The plane soon leveled off and he unlocked his chair, spinning back toward his work station, as did the other half dozen patriots in the RV with him.

They were the vanguard of the 'new' Soviet Union, their job to incapacitate the American economy and military forces around the world by holding it hostage. His grandfather, former Major General Levkin, had told him of the Crimson Rush plan while he and his mother visited once, and this was it only in part. There was no great invasion awaiting their success, and their plan was not to detonate all of the weapons at once. Their plan was terror. To create panic and to force America, on bended knee, to beg forgiveness and retreat within its borders.

And if it did so, Travkin and his team would sit by, lying in wait just in case the United States decided to interfere with the world again before Mother Russia was ready to counter Uncle Sam. And if America dared rear its head again, Travkin, or others like him, would detonate additional weapons.

But Travkin was confident the plan would work. They had figured no more than eight to ten weapons would be needed before the American public would demand their government give in. Life in America wouldn't change much since most of its citizens had no involvement in foreign affairs. Their economy would continue to lurch along under ridiculous structural deficits and massive multi-generational debt loads. In fact, they might actually save some money with the military cutbacks they could afford.

But in the meantime, Russia, with its massive oil reserves, would continue to grow their economy, continue to modernize their military, and once again begin to flex her muscles around the globe. And with Putin's continued consolidation of power, eventually Russia would return to the old ways of a party in charge, guiding its people to greatness. Not a communist party, but a hybrid pro-business, pro-capitalist, anti-democratic ruling elite that would stress security and military might over individual rights.

His chest swelled with pride when he watched tapes of the old parades through Red Square, of Sputnik beating the Americans to space, of Gagarin reaching the stars before any American, of the greatness that once was.

To imagine what it could be without having to support crippled states like before, with oil wealth rivaling any nation, was to feel goose bumps up and down your arms, the tingling almost orgasmic.

Though his grandfather doubted it would ever happen in his lifetime, Travkin was certain it would happen within his—the once proud CCCP adorning rockets and ships, tanks and airplanes, uniforms and buildings around the world again.

And the world would tremble in fear at the reawakened bear.

A debt free, massively capitalized nation, with a renewed pride in itself, and a military unrivaled the world over.

A screen flashed to his left and he tapped it, the image of his grandfather appearing, the old man wearing his old uniform with pride.

And a black eye and swollen lip.

"Grandfather! What happened?"

"It is of no consequence. There was an incident but I told them nothing. Be warned though, the Americans may know what Crimson Rush is, and may be getting close to finding you."

"Let them find us. There will be others to replace us."

His grandfather smiled.

"You remind me of myself when I was younger."

"I can imagine no greater compliment, General."

Levkin's smile grew more.

"Your mother will be so proud when she is informed of the critical part you have played in these events." He sighed. "I wish I were twenty years younger. I'd be there with you."

"Don't worry, General. We will do you proud, and you will live to see our country returned to its former glory, thanks to you."

Levkin nodded at his grandson, pride written all over his face. Then it turned all business.

"You were to deliver a status report ten minutes ago. What happened?"

"We were nearly discovered. The Americans raided the house where we had tapped the Internet feed so we were forced to leave. One of our tail cars spotted an FBI agent tracking us so we detonated the West Point weapon early to cover our escape, but unfortunately were forced to engage the agent. Their vehicle was completely destroyed and the occupant killed. Our departure was routine and unnoticed by the authorities."

"You're certain no one knows you're aboard the plane?"

"Absolutely. We loaded in a hangar and the plane left on an approved departure along with several others fleeing the detonation. No one will know it was us."

"Excellent. You're certain the agent pursuing you is dead?"

"Absolutely. There's no way anybody survived that explosion."

St. Luke's Cornwall Hospital, Newburgh, New York

Sherrie felt a dull hammering in her head, a fog separating her from a world out of reach, a world of echoes and strange noises and no memory of who and where she was. She focused on the sounds, at first mere distant murmurs, then as she slowly regained consciousness, voices, low and indistinct.

Then there was the pain.

It erupted with a fury that rushed her to a fully awakened state, her back leaping up and her eyes shooting open to a blurred, glassy world of stark white and moving forms.

"She's awake!"

She cried out in pain, unable to resist it anymore.

"Put her out, Goddammit! I'm still operating here!"

"Give me a moment," came a calm voice from behind her and suddenly a warmth—an exquisitely wonderful warmth—spread through her body and she dropped back onto whatever she had been lying on, a world of sparkling lights and fantastic colors tripping the light fantastic on the back of her eyelids.

And as she was about to completely give in to the wondrous sensations around her, she suddenly remembered there was something she needed to tell them, something too important to wait. She clawed against the warmth, trying to swim to the surface to relate her critical message, but it was no use.

The warmth was just too damned blissful.

Résidence Hôtelière de la Cerisaie, Longjumeau, France

"Why are you staring at me?"

Kane bit his tongue at West's expression of shock and denial as he looked away, his eyes looking for something else to fixate on other than his daughter, eventually deciding on the television showing the latest horrifying footage out of West Point Military Academy and Memphis on loops with talking heads providing near useless context.

"I'm sorry, I didn't realize I was," he mumbled, his face red with embarrassment.

"Be polite," tutted Adelle at her daughter. "After all, Mr. West did help save you all today."

Alexis frowned then turned her frustrations on Zorkin.

"Is that thing ready yet?"

Zorkin batted the air with his hand, dismissing her as he continued to copy the microfilm.

"Are you sure you know how to use that thing?" she replied.

"Listen, missy, I've been doing this since before your damned father was your age!" came the retort.

Jaws dropped.

Alexis turned beet red, her head whipping around at all the shocked expressions in the room.

"What? What are you all looking at?" she cried. "So I never met my father. Is it my fault he died before I was born?" She glared at her mother then West. "And why the hell do you keep holding his hand?" she fired. "You two can't seem to keep your hands—"

And then she froze, her own jaw dropping as she stared at West. The room became silent as the dawn of realization seemed to finally be creeping over the horizon.

"Done!" said Zorkin, spoiling the moment and tossing a USB key to Kane who caught it then inserted it into a laptop provided by Alexis. "I can't believe how difficult that was! I thought this was supposed to be the modern—"

"Why am I named Alexis?"

Zorkin shut up, finally cluing into the momentous discovery that was about to happen thanks to his outburst. Kane ignored it, instead uploading the files to Langley then quickly scanning the contents himself.

"What do you mean?" asked Adelle. "You know why."

"You said I was named after my father."

"Yes."

"But Alexis is a girls' name."

"Yes."

"So the male equivalent is Alex."

"Yes."

"And your name is Alex."

"Yes," replied West.

"Are you my father?"

The elephant in the room swelled as Kane struggled to focus on the intel streaming before his eyes. He looked up to see West nod then Alexis cry out, jumping from her chair and rushing out the hotel room door.

"I'll be back," said Adelle as she followed her daughter. West began to stand when she waved a finger at him. "You stay here."

West mumbled something that no one but he understood, then Kane cleared his throat, dialing Langley on his cellphone and putting it on speaker.

"This is Morrison. You're on speaker."

"Director, you're on speaker here too. I've got Mr. White and Mr. Green with me, along with Alex West and Viktor Zorkin."

"I've read all your files. With the exception of Mr. Zorkin, consider yourselves all sworn to secrecy as part of the National Security Act. Mr. Zorkin, I can't obviously place you under such restrictions."

"I am a patriot, Director, not a madman. Consider my services and discretion at your disposal."

"Very well. We've received your transmission and are reviewing it now. Have you had a chance to look at it?"

Kane nodded at the phone.

"Yes. We've got a lot of locations listed with deployment dates, partial radio frequencies—"

"What do you mean partial?"

"At least half of that portion of the microfilm has been damaged. Almost that entire column of data has been scratched out, almost as if deliberately."

"Goddamned French!" cursed Niner.

"We've also got activation and deactivation codes—"

"You've got deactivation codes?!"

"Yes, sir, but I'm not sure that's necessarily good news. From what I can tell, these codes can only be used after the device is already activated."

Dawson muttered a curse, shaking his head. "So what you're saying is that in order to deactivate the weapons, we need to activate them, risking them going off, then pray that the deactivation code works."

"Anything else of use?" asked Morrison.

"Well, we've got locations, but they're lat and long, down to the minutes, not seconds, so we'll know within about a square mile where the devices are."

"That's an awfully big area to search times one thousand."

"Looks like we're dealing with about five hundred devices according to the manifest. The rest were due to be deployed after the theft of the microfilm, and apparently those are all stored in warehouses in Russia."

The volume of Morrison's voice changed slightly as orders were barked.

"Deploy units to every one of those locations as you get them, and let the White House know that we need to have the Russians confirm they have those other five hundred weapons."

Kane continued to read the specs on the weapon as the conversation progressed.

"Anything else?"

"Not much, sir. There are detailed specs here so our guys should be able to disarm them once they find them, but that's about it. Oh, and whatever you do, don't cut the power in any of these areas."

"Why?"

"They're tied into the electrical grid with a limited battery backup. If power is cut, they'll immediately radio home, and if they don't get a response before the battery dies, they detonate."

"How long does the battery last?"

Kane shook his head.

"According to this, several days, a week at most."

"Which would be why we've never had any accidental detonations," said somebody else in the room at Langley. "We've never had a power outage in one of the weapons' locations longer than the battery could last."

"Christ, we've been damned lucky," muttered Morrison. "Anything else you can tell us at this point?"

"Negative. But I've only skimmed the data, you guys might have more luck. Where do you want us?" asked Kane, looking about the room.

"I want you in Moscow. The President has already added Levkin to the Termination List. As soon as we've got things secured here, he wants this man captured, interrogated, then dead."

"So do we," piped Niner.

"See if your friends in Moscow can help you. Morrison, out."

The line went dead and Dawson already had his own phone out, calling the "friends" in Moscow, Kane was certain. The door to the hotel room opened quietly and West rose. Kane looked to see a smiling Adelle then a meek Alexis enter the cramped quarters. Alexis' eyes and cheeks were red from crying, but she had a shy, tentative smile on her face as she approached West, arms dangling at her sides, shoulders drooped, chin down and eyes up, decades of womanhood wiped out leaving a child behind.

West said nothing, instead stepping around Kane's chair and taking his little girl in his arms for the first time as her shoulders heaved in sobs.

Kane rose as did the rest, stepping outside, a lump in all their throats at the tearful union.

Operations Center 3, CIA Headquarters, Langley, Virginia

"The President is giving a speech tomorrow to address what is going on, and to announce a change in official policy with respect to our national energy strategy," came the voice of the White House official briefing a large number of people tapped into the videoconference. Leroux was still in OC3, technically still in charge of the room despite Morrison being there, having taken a free chair at one of the workstations. Leroux was listening to the conversation, but his mind was preoccupied with something else.

Why was Dimka crying?

"The President will announce that all moratoriums on oil drilling will be lifted immediately, including Arctic drilling, as well as restrictions on shale oil fracking. The Keystone XL pipeline will be fast tracked, and all oil produced by companies in the United States will be reserved for domestic use only. The goal is to be oil and energy independent before 2020 with all of our oil being either domestic or Canadian sourced. This will be used to allow us to draw down our forces worldwide as we will no longer need to protect our foreign oil supplies. It is hoped that this will placate those responsible for the attacks."

Not bloody likely.

Suddenly something popped in Leroux's head.

If something happened to Sherrie, then they must have known she was following them!

Leroux reviewed the transmissions logs for OC3, quickly eliminating anything from the list that he could explain, the remaining few being personal cellphones and devices, with all but one device registered in the Langley network as being authorized.

Which means we have one unauthorized device in the room!

249

He sent a test ping to the device and it came back as active, another unauthorized transmission appearing in the log along with his authorized one.

"Unofficially we've grounded our aircraft, dusted off the rapid drawdown plans for our bases, and pulled our naval forces back from any unfriendly shores. At this moment in time, until we can stop the perpetrators of these heinous attacks on our soil, we must at least appear to be meeting their demands."

Leroux began decrypting the signals that had been sent from the unauthorized device, then nearly gasped out loud as the last message transmission appeared.

You are being followed.

Rage began to build as he realized it had to refer to Sherrie's pursuit of the RV. He glanced at Dimka, but she had positioned herself so he couldn't see her face.

Through the fog of rage he realized that Morrison was now talking.

"I've got news on just who might be behind this," he said. "We've been able to trace the money. It seems that a large amount was transferred to Islamov, who immediately transferred it to another account. It was bounced around to several more, but we found its final destination. The account belongs to a proxy company in the Cayman Islands. The source account also belongs to a proxy company, this one in the Bahamas. We raided the offices of both and were able to determine the owners behind them, and both were the same."

"You mean they sent themselves the money?" came a voice over the speaker.

"Exactly."

"Then the entire thing was a ruse right from the start!"

"It appears so. We believe the transfer was made to make us think Islamov and his people were behind this so we'd immediately blame Islamists for the attacks. This seems evident from the transmission they sent."

"If it's not Islamists, then who is it?"

"We've been able to trace both proxy companies back to former Major General Yuri Levkin. It would appear, ladies and gentlemen, that this man, a known Soviet era zealot who urges a return to the old days, is behind the attacks on our soil."

"So we're under attack by Russia?"

"There's no indication that Russia is officially behind this, however Putin and Levkin are known to be friends, and to regularly meet."

Leroux jumped slightly as the screen updated, indicating another message being transmitted. He quickly began to decode it.

"What are we saying here? Are we seriously saying that Russia could be tacitly behind these attacks?"

Morrison shook his head.

"At this point we just don't know. I would guess that at *most* Putin is aware of the attacks and hoping that Levkin achieves his goals, whatever they are, since we've been a thorn in the Soviet and Russian side for decades. Anything that hurts us helps them."

"Should we confront him? Let him know that we know?"

Morrison shrugged his shoulders.

"That's for the politicians to decide. I personally think we should keep it under our hats and use it to our advantage. Let them think we're still after Islamist terrorists, but quietly track down the Russians behind this."

Leroux stood up from his desk.

"Sir, I'm afraid it's already too late for that."

Morrison spun toward Leroux, the expression on his face suggesting shock at someone so low on the totem pole daring to speak.

"Explain."

"We have a traitor in the room."

Leroux looked at the decrypted transmission on his screen.

They know who's behind it.

"Explain."

Leroux picked up his own phone and dialed the number of the unauthorized device. Dimka jumped as a vibration was heard near her station. Leroux stepped over and grabbed her by the shoulder, spinning her around in her chair, a cellphone gripped in her hand, tears streaking her face.

He grabbed the phone from her and she collapsed on her keyboard, sobbing. Leroux flipped through the messages, confirming they had all been sent from her device, then handed it to Morrison as he joined them on the platform.

"What the hell is going on?" he demanded.

"She's been sending messages to someone the entire time," said Leroux through clenched teeth. "And she's responsible for Sherrie's death." He felt Morrison's hand on his shoulder, pulling him back slightly as the Director scrolled through the messages.

"Call security," he said, then, grabbing Dimka by the shoulder, he yanked her upright. "Explain yourself!"

Dimka was sobbing almost uncontrollably now, shaking her head, her face one of terror.

"Explain it to me or you'll never see the light of day again!" screamed Morrison, his voice filled with a rage Leroux couldn't recall ever hearing from anyone. It terrified him, causing an involuntary step backward and away from the source.

"They have my family!" she cried. Morrison let go of her shoulder and stood upright, pointing at the security team that had just arrived. "Lock down this room. Nobody in or out."

St. Luke's Cornwall Hospital, Newburgh, New York

The fog returned, the dull pulsing, throbbing noises a sea away cried out for her to return to the shores of the living. And she wanted to return. She hated it here. Wherever here was. Her mind was dim, a mere hint of her former self, but she knew she had to escape this sensory deprived void she found herself in for she had a message, an important message, that she had to tell someone.

The problem was she couldn't remember what the message was, or who she was supposed to tell.

Beeping surrounded her and she had the presence of mind to focus on it. It became clearer. Rhythmic, pulsating, its pitch steady and unwavering.

A heart rate monitor!

Then she remembered. The pursuit, the RPG, the explosion, the jump from the vehicle just as it was hit, and what she had seen as she blacked out on the pavement.

The sounds snapped into focus, crystal clear to her ears, and as she felt herself rush back to the shores of reality, as if yanked by a powerful force, a merciless force that reintroduced her to pain like she had never felt, her eyes shot open to reveal she was in some sort of hospital room, a privacy curtain hiding her from the horrors on the other side, patients moaning and crying around her, constant announcements over a PA system paging doctors, pounding footsteps in the hallways, chaos, hopefully organized, reigning out of sight.

The explosion!

She had forgotten about the nuclear blast. She must be in one of the hospitals now overwhelmed by what had happened. She looked down and saw a bandage covering her right thigh, pain throbbing from the area. Slowly sitting up, she examined herself and found only superficial cuts and bruises all over her body, and no other areas that seemed injured.

My face!

Terrified, she slowly, tentatively, reached up with both hands and then, counting to three, she shoved her face into her palms, then quickly began to feel over every square inch, finding nothing unexpected.

Breathing a sigh of relief, she wiggled her fingers and toes then closed her eyes, thanking God. She opened her eyes and cautiously touched the bandaged wound on her leg.

Nothing.

She pushed a little harder and gasped, a cry escaping before she could stifle it.

The curtain ripped open and a nurse entered.

"So you're awake."

Her tone was curt, almost rude.

Nice bedside manner.

"Where am I?"

"You're in the recovery room at St. Luke's."

Again, the reply was almost snapped at her.

"I need to get out of here, I have a job to do."

"You're not going anywhere, missy. There's two police officers outside to make sure of that!"

"Huh?"

"What, you thought you could just leave after what you've done?"

The woman's voice was almost hysterical now and Sherrie was getting a little confused if not pissed off.

"What are you talking about? What have I done?"

"What have you done? Are you kidding me? You and your people nuked West Point! And you? What was your mission? Where was your little car bomb supposed to go off? Some school? Some hospital? Didn't you do enough to my city? Enough to my country? If it was up to me I would have let you die, you piece of shit!"

The curtain moved again and the two police officers the nutbar nurse had mentioned appeared.

"Is there a problem here?" asked the sergeant.

"Yeah, this psycho is nuts," replied Sherrie. "I'm a federal agent with important intelligence regarding today's incident."

"Sure you are," spat the nurse. "You're a terrorist who accidentally blew herself up. You're a parasite on this great nation and deserve the death penalty for what you've done!"

"Would you get her out of here, please?" asked Sherrie. "She's not contributing."

The sergeant stepped forward.

"Are you done here?"

The nurse glowered at him, then Sherrie, then nodded, departing with a huff.

"Thanks," said Sherrie, propping herself up on her pillows. "I need to make a phone call. It's urgent."

"You'll get your phone call when you're processed at the station," replied the sergeant, turning to leave.

Holy shit! They actually think I'm a terrorist!

"Wait! Listen, I realize you have no reason to believe me, so I want you to do something. Just get on a phone, call four-one-one, ask to be connected to CIA Headquarters in Langley, then ask for Director Morrison. Tell him you've got an Agent Sherrie White here who needs to talk to him urgently otherwise there will be more attacks."

The sergeant's eyebrows narrowed and the expression on his face suggested a slight thaw in the coldness, and some definite doubt as to who she might be.

She calmed her voice, lowering it slightly. "Sergeant, I'm telling the truth. Do you really want to be the one who didn't let vital intelligence get into the right hands? Intelligence that might allow us to capture these guys before they detonate another bomb?"

The sergeant was completely facing her again, his right hand tapping on his gun grip, the other pulling at his hair.

He spun on his heel and left the room before Sherrie could say anything else.

Operations Center 3, CIA Headquarters, Langley, Virginia

Morrison turned back to Dimka as all eyes in the room focused on the exchange. Leroux had retreated to his chair, shocked at how he had confronted her. It wasn't in his nature to do something like that, but he had done it, without hesitation. He had discovered and captured a spy in their midst.

Wait 'til Sherrie hears about this!

A sudden overwhelming gloom surged over him as his feelings of concern, momentarily forgotten with the excitement of the past few minutes, enveloped him once again.

She's dead.

He mentally kicked himself for having the thought cross his mind. But he couldn't help it. They still hadn't heard from her. Her last few words were spoken in terror.

She's dead.

He glared at Dimka.

"What do you mean they have your family?" asked Morrison, towering over the still seated woman.

Dimka cried out, burying her face in her hands, then between gasps and sobs, she said, "They came three nights ago. Broke into our house, then told me that if I didn't cooperate they'd kill my husband and our two children!"

Leroux couldn't honestly say what he'd do if put in a similar situation. Would he turn traitor and try to save his family, or would he immediately tell his boss, hoping they could save the day without him betraying his country.

He didn't know.

He'd like to think he'd inform the authorities and let them deal with it, but then again, he wasn't a parent. He had no idea what that bond must be like.

"Why didn't you tell me?" asked Morrison, his voice slightly softer, but only slightly. He was clearly still pissed.

"I couldn't risk it."

"What do they know?"

"Everything."

"How? Just through this phone?"

"Yes."

"But how did they know you'd be assigned to a mission concerning them?"

She shook her head.

"I don't know."

"Maybe they're blackmailing others?" blurted Leroux, immediately regretting it as the Director spun around to face him.

"What?"

Leroux gulped, lowering his voice.

"Maybe she's not the only one."

Dimka seemed slightly encouraged by this, raising her face for the first time.

"That could be!" she said, excitement in her voice. "They said I might not even hear from them!"

Morrison shook his head.

"If we have a security breach this bad…"

His voice trailed off and Leroux found himself watching his boss' face change as the realization of how big of a problem they may be facing grew. He looked at Leroux, whose eyes darted away, then turned to Dimka.

"What do they know about the French operation?"

"They know it happened."

"And the results?"

"I never had time to transmit them."

"Okay, here's what you're going to do. You're going—"

"Sir!"

Morrison spun toward the voice below.

"What?"

"You're going to want to hear this!" said Conway, the analyst still helping Leroux with his project.

"Put it on speaker."

Conway nodded and hit a button at his station.

"You're on speaker with the Director."

"Sir, it's Agent White, Sherrie White, can you hear me?"

For the first time in his life Leroux knew what the angels must have sounded like at the birth of Christ. And it was beautiful. Her voice was like a dream that filled his heart with joy, all of the stress and horrors of the day disappearing as he realized the love of his life was still alive, and okay. His elbows hit his desk and he buried his face in his hands as his shoulders began to heave in relief.

She's alive!

A flurry of thankful prayers erupted silently, his eyeballs rolling up in his head in an attempt to look at the heavens.

He felt a hand on his shoulder, but didn't look, knowing it was Morrison.

"Agent White, I'm happy to hear you're okay. We've been worried."

"I was in a hospital undergoing surgery so I couldn't talk. I'm okay now. Listen, I have a vital piece of intel you need to know."

"Go ahead."

"Just before my vehicle was taken out by an RPG—"

"RPG?" yelped Leroux as his head shot up, his hands trying to wipe the tears from his face.

"Yes, RPG. Is that you, Chris?"

"Y-yes."

"It's so good to hear your voice. We'll talk soon. Director, I saw the RV entering a hangar where a large transport aircraft, probably an Antonov of some type, was being loaded. I think they're transporting themselves from city to city by plane!"

Morrison pointed at Conway.

"Find out if any Antonov's left Newburgh around the time of the detonation, and where they went."

"Yes, sir!"

"Agent White. Are you secure where you are?"

"Yes, sir, but I'm taking up a hospital bed that people in far worse condition than me are going to need."

Leroux could tell by her tone she wanted back in the game, but if she had just come out of surgery, there was no way he could see Morrison allowing her.

At least I hope not!

"I realize you want in on the action, Agent, but you've just been operated on. I authorize you to return to Langley by whatever means necessary so we can do a full debrief."

"Yes, sir!"

Morrison turned to Leroux.

"Take this conversation off speaker and isolate it to your headset. I'm sure you'll want to talk to her in private."

Leroux smiled, hitting a few keys on his keyboard.

"Can you hear me?"

"Yes! Yes I can!"

"Umm, can anyone else hear me?" He looked about the room, but nobody acknowledged his question. "I guess not." He lowered his voice. "It's so good to hear from you. I was worried sick."

"I'm okay. Just a leg wound, nothing serious."

"Thank God. What are you going to do now?"

"I'm going to discharge myself and get back to Langley. Hopefully you'll be seeing me in a few hours."

"Okay, I'll see you then."

"Love you."

"Love you too."

The call ended and he took a moment to gather himself as Morrison's voice droned unheard nearby. Hands clapped together, snapping Leroux from his reverie.

"Let's do this people, I don't want another detonation on our territory."

Everyone turned back to their terminals, leaving Leroux to wonder what the hell had just happened. Then he jumped from his seat, pointing at the monitor still showing his Malware hack mission status.

"Look!"

Heads spun toward him, then to where he was pointing.

Number of Positives: 2

Norfolk, Virginia

Vitaly Travkin pulled his phone off his hip, touching the display to open the text message that had just arrived from one of their coopted resources within the CIA. What the CIA didn't know was that the Russians had several moles within their headquarters, one of whom had been there since the days of the Soviet Union. A sleeper agent waiting an activation that would never come, had been activated only days ago.

And had responded, willing to cooperate despite the agency he had once worked for, the country he had once served, no longer in existence.

Travkin had no doubt the man had only responded out of curiosity, but once he had heard what was needed of him, and the ultimate goal of the mission, he had agreed immediately to help. His mission was simple. Make sure any operations relating to the crisis be routed through Dimka's Operations Center.

And he had succeeded.

Dimka was now their mole, providing valuable intel so they could remain one step ahead of any federal response. The beautiful thing about interagency cooperation was that everyone shared their intel, so it didn't matter what agency they penetrated, however CIA was preferred as they would most likely be involved in any external response that might impact General Levkin's safety.

French operation failed. Microfilm destroyed.

He smiled as he read the message.

"The microfilm has been destroyed!" he announced to those in the RV, eliciting a cheer from the men. He hit a few keys on his terminal to contact the General with the good news.

Nothing can stop us now!

Operations Center 3, CIA Headquarters, Langley, Virginia

Every display was alive with activity in Operations Center 3. Dimka was continuing in her role, Morrison wanting to have direct access to her in case she received intelligence from her family's abductors, and also should he need her to send a message to them. She was also very good at her job, everyone in the room seeming to accept that she had no choice but to cooperate, though Leroux still had some serious doubts about her choices and had no doubt there would be serious consequences when things were said and done.

Two displays showed feeds of the detonation zones, one showed his Malware mission status board, most of the others showing varying camera views of two operations going down right now.

The views on the left showed head cams from the FBI SWAT team about to take down the Antonov AN-124 that had left the Stewart International Airport outside of Newburgh only minutes after the detonation and landed at the Norfolk International airport in Norfolk, Virginia less than two hours ago. On the right were head cams from a second FBI SWAT team moving in on the RV traced by Leroux's program.

And down at the far bottom right, a lone display showed a camera Leroux knew belonged to Kane as he headed into the heart of the beast, a broadcast from the RV having been intercepted and traced to Russia. The Russian government had been contacted, told that if they didn't cooperate in a coordinated effort to capture the General, the United States would release the intelligence to the world along with several nuclear armed cruise missiles to eliminate the target, and that any Russian response would be considered an act of war.

The Russians had agreed and a joint Delta/CIA/Spetsnaz operation was underway.

"It's started," said Conway from his terminal. Leroux returned his attention to the camera images, his heart slamming against his ribcage, this the first time he had ever witnessed an operation like this.

It's almost like a video game.

He frowned at the thought.

With real lives at stake.

Norfolk International Airport, Norfolk, Virginia

Special Agent in Charge Max Turpin of the FBI motioned for his men to advance. Clinging to the left side of an empty fuel truck, they approached the Antonov from the rear, hoping they might gain access unseen, the intel they had being that the primary target, an RV, was no longer onboard. Minimal resistance was expected beyond the crew, but given the nature of what this group had done, they were feared to be highly trained mercenaries, most likely ex-Russian Special Forces.

Expect anything and everything.

The words echoed in his head from the briefing. Across the nation every talking head on television spoke of Islamic terrorists, every civilian eyeing their neighbors and coworkers warily if they even suspected they were Muslim. Mosques had already been attacked, Muslims were being beaten in the streets, targeted in classrooms and in public malls.

And up until the moment he had been told it was actually Russians behind the detonations, he hadn't felt one iota of pity for those being attacked. Now he just wanted to get this mission over with so the public could be informed of the truth so those not responsible in any way shape or form could be protected.

I wonder if they'll go after the Russians next?

He doubted it. They were white, looked like the average American, and were mostly Christian. In other words, too similar to the majority to target.

The fuel truck slowed slightly.

"Now! Now! Now!" he ordered through his comm, jumping off the side of the truck with his men, rushing toward the rear of the plane. He was in the lead, the sound of his men's boots hammering on the tarmac behind him filled his ears, the smell of aviation fuel his nostrils. It was mostly dark, the runway well lit to their left, the hangars and tarmac, along with the taxiways casting glows all around them, but the Antonov, a massive beast of an aircraft, was nearly dark, only a few lights on the undercarriage and the tips of the wings and tail lit. Long dim shadows were cast in varying directions from the stray lights in the area, but his men, all in black, were ghosts, his own arms, held out in front of him, his Glock gripped tightly, were almost invisible to him.

He flicked down his night vision gear and the area burst into a brilliant green, every detail of the cargo transport bursting into view as he continued to charge forward.

Suddenly his display lit up a brilliant greenish white, all detail disappearing. He cried out in pain as his eyes were overwhelmed, instinctively ripping the headgear away as he dropped to his knees. That's when he noticed the horrific sound erupting from in front of him. He scrambled backward, crablike, but it was too late. The Antonov had erupted into a massive fireball, expanding in every direction as the fuel ignited, eating every molecule of oxygen it could gain access to, shrapnel ripping through the air in every direction as the blast radius rapidly expanded.

The blast wave hit him, knocking him on his back, his head hitting the asphalt, bouncing several times as the Kevlar helmet did its job. A wave of heat, overwhelming, swept over him, sucking the breath right out of his lungs. He rolled over onto his front, covering his head with his hands, hunching his shoulders up to try and protect his exposed face as the flames roared over him. His eyes, squeezed shut, couldn't prevent him from hearing the screams of his men through the comm unit.

And then it was over, as quickly as it had begun. The pain in his body was excruciating, and as he tried to stand up he realized he couldn't, the searing pain unbearable. He managed to push himself to his elbows and open his eyes. He could see the rest of his team around him, some screaming in pain, some writhing in silence, others silent and still, their ordeal already over.

He collapsed to the ground, the pain too much, wishing he too was among the honored dead.

Granby Street, Norfolk, Virginia

Charlie Ventura, FBI Special Agent in Charge, had just given the order to take down the RV when he lost contact with the second team at the airport. It took several moments for a clear signal to come through, but it was already too late to abort their own mission.

The Antonov had exploded, most likely blown up by those onboard.

If these guys are suicidal, we've got no chance of taking them alive.

And they needed intel. They needed to know if they were the only team involved or if there were others like them. They needed to know where the bombs were, how to deactivate them, whether or not their command and control HQ was indeed in Russia where a transmission had been sent.

We need to know how to stop these goddamned attacks on our country!

He just wanted to kill them all, frankly. The only problem was he wanted to kill them *all*, and without knowing who deserved to be on that list, he had to at least capture someone to find out.

As they approached the rear of the RV, the traffic thankfully light, he kept their emergency lights and sirens off, wanting to get as close as possible so they could take out the tires and immobilize the vehicle before beginning a full assault, but with the airplane having been blown up, he was quite certain these guys were rigged to blow as well. For now his goal was containment.

Immobilize and contain.

And jam all their damned communications so they couldn't detonate another weapon. Ventura was critically aware of the situation, and the fact this RV was here meant for certain there was a weapon nearby, most likely targeting the naval base.

They can't be allowed to detonate the weapon.

269

"Begin jamming them," he ordered over his comm.

"Jammers activated," came the reply.

"Position to take out their tires."

His vehicle raced forward as another two surged by in the lane to the left, passing the RV on its left side. Suddenly what Ventura could only describe as gun ports opened in the rear of the vehicle and what appeared to be some sort of Gatling gun emerged.

"Jesus Christ!" yelled his driver as he swung to the left, the weapon opening up and eliminating the FBI vehicle behind them. Ventura watched in horror as the two vehicles on the left of the RV were taken out in similar fashion.

"Fall back!" he ordered, but it was too late. Three of his six vehicles were already in flames, and now, to his horror, the RV continued firing from the left and right sides of the vehicle, tearing fist sized holes through every vehicle and pedestrian it passed, those bullets fortunate enough to miss, shredding trees, asphalt, windows and facades.

It was mass murder.

"We need air support, now!"

Delta Team Bravo's Sergeant Major Mike "Red" Belme pointed at the RV below and Zack "Wings" Hauser, their specialist who could fly just about anything, guided the Black Hawk UH-60 to its target, banking to the right as they reduced their altitude and closed the distance. The carnage below was unbelievable, like something he'd expect to see in Iraq when most of that country was an active war zone.

But this was Norfolk, Virginia. A sleepy seaside port town.

Shit like this isn't supposed to happen in America.

Dozens if not hundreds of vehicles were aflame, their trail of destruction a glowing line leading straight to the source in the night time darkness. The trailing FBI vehicles that remained were holding their distance from behind and he could see local police units, their lights flashing, trying to set up road blocks ahead, not to stop the vehicle, but to prevent more traffic from being targeted.

It was horror on a Hollywood scale that at the moment he was almost numb to, he having just received word that his parents were confirmed dead in the Memphis detonation. He hadn't told little Bryson that his grandparents were dead, but he had told his wife, then left for the range, firing several hundred rounds from the biggest guns he could find.

Then word of this mission had come through and he had jumped at the chance.

A chance to kill those responsible.

"Take out the tires," he ordered over the comm, looking back to see Will "Spock" Lightman lean out with his door mounted M134 Minigun, it anything but "mini", capable of firing up to 6,000 rounds a minute. Taking aim and firing, he tore off the rear end of the RV, it swerving to the side as Spock adjusted his aim and removed the rear driver side tires from existence. Sparks erupted from the RV as metal met pavement, the vehicle immediately slowing allowing Spock to take out the front tire as well.

The vehicle ground to a halt, the cannons mounted on all sides continuing to belch their death. Wings swept down and toward the top of the RV, within moments hovering over top of it. Red leapt out, hitting the roof as did Atlas, Spock and Mickey, Wings immediately banking away. Using hand signals, Red sent Atlas and Mickey to the front of the RV to try and gain access from the door at the front passenger side. He and Spock made for a roof hatch on the rear of the vehicle, Spock quickly planting a C4 charge.

Red glanced over his shoulder and saw that Atlas and Mickey were out of sight.

"Bravo Two, Bravo Seven. Ready to detonate, over."

Red and Spock turned their heads, bending over to reduce their profile from whatever may come flying their way.

"Bravo Seven, Bravo Two, execute in three, two, one, execute!"

Spock's thumb pushed down on the remote trigger, the roar loud but not deafening, the two immediately whipping around, their Glock 22's gripped tightly as they approached the hatch. Red and Spock both pulled stun grenades from their belts and popped the pins, counting out to three then dropping them inside.

Several more explosions followed by screams erupted from the hole then Red rushed forward, dropping inside and hitting the floor in a crouch, weapon extended. He counted six live hostiles, along with Atlas and Mickey entering the front, the driver already taken out. One nearest Red raised a weapon and was eliminated by Spock from overhead as he swung into the vehicle.

The team rushed forward, pulling the men out of their chairs and tossing them onto the floor, making certain they couldn't reach any keyboards or self-destruct buttons before they regained their senses. Atlas put a hole in someone's head up ahead as he and Red advanced, Mickey and Spock zip tying the survivors as they moved forward. It took less than a minute and the vehicle was secure, the guns silenced, and four survivors captured for questioning.

One of the men surged to his knees, pushing his head toward a red button mounted beside a terminal near the middle of the RV. Red fired twice, the first hitting the man in the torso, altering his trajectory slightly and eliminating any muscles from contributing to the valiant effort. The second simply ended the man's life.

"Anyone else want to be a hero?" asked Red as he looked at the remaining three.

Silence.

"Who's in charge?"

Silence again, but one of the three, possibly the youngest, took a quick look to his left with just his eyeballs, giving Red enough information to know exactly who needed to be questioned.

He pushed the man to his knees with a boot shoved against a shoulder. A face glared back at him, defiant pride, even in defeat. Red had seen it before. It always broke in the end.

"I will tell you nothing."

"Feel free to think that for now. In fact, please don't tell us anything. You're going on the first flight to Gitmo, and before morning dawns, you'll be in more pain then you've ever imagined possible." Red dropped to one knee, lifting the man's chin with the barrel of the Glock. "You'll talk. They always do."

The man smiled at him, the smile turning into a sneer.

"I die so Mother Russia can live once again."

The man made a motion with his mouth that Red immediately recognized as the biting down on an implanted cyanide capsule, and as foam began to appear from the man's mouth, he laughed.

"There's nothing you can do now, American pig. I die by my own hand."

Red stood up and aimed his weapon at the man's smiling face.

"I don't think so. You killed my family, now I kill you."

He fired, opening a new hole in the man's head, freezing the smile in place and eliminating the gurgling from the man's throat that had become an annoyance.

That's for you, Mom and Dad.

Approaching Drovyanaya, Russia

Dylan Kane had to admit he never imagined he'd be in a situation like this during his career. Sitting with a couple of old Delta buddies—Dawson and Niner—while being transported into a combat zone, absolutely. Sitting across from a group of Russian Spetsnaz Special Forces? Maybe. Joint ops weren't unheard of.

But being transported in a massive Mi-24 Hind, in Russian airspace, for a mission on Russian soil, close enough for Moscow's air defense system to actually take interest?

Never.

But here he was, rushing toward an abandoned missile site less than two hundred miles outside of Moscow, one of three American "observers"—heavily armed observers—with two platoons of Spetsnaz operators. What would greet them, they had no idea. The latest satellite shots showed a dark, abandoned facility, as expected. But the last transmission sent from the RV in Norfolk was traced to this abandoned set of buildings, and it was their only lead.

All three strikes—the RV, the transport plane, and the abandoned missile site—were supposed to have occurred simultaneously, however Russian politicking had delayed their departure, the other events having taken place just ten minutes ago with at this point in time no valuable intel having been gathered.

Kane's fear now, and he knew it was shared by everybody, was that their element of surprise had been eliminated. Any commander worth their salt would be expecting an attack at any minute if two of his assets had been simultaneously taken out.

We could be walking into a turkey shoot. And we're the turkeys.

"There it is!"

Kane turned to see Colonel Chernov pointing slightly to the right through one of the windows.

"Any sign of activity?" asked Dawson.

"Negative. But that means nothing," replied Chernov. "Unfortunately we have the morning light. I would rather have done this at night."

"There was no way we could wait," replied Kane. "There's already a permanent glow over two American cities, we're not risking a third."

Chernov nodded then activated his comm.

"Prepare for insertion, one minute."

The team began to double-check their weapons and gear as the gunships raced toward the target, any hope of a stealthy approach impossible with the loud thumping of the propellers overhead. It made Kane long for the Jedi Rides the US Special Forces were blessed to have access to.

"First wave, begin assault," ordered Chernov. Kane watched as two gunships took the lead, heading directly for the facility as their helicopter and one other slowed, still advancing but allowing the first platoon to have about a thirty second lead on the insertion.

Kane pulled a small scope from his upper left pocket and held it to his eye, surveying the facility as the lead choppers touched down, spilling their highly trained operatives out the sides, the first chopper already lifting from the ground within seconds.

Suddenly an RPG streaked across the compound from the roof of one of the buildings, the warhead slamming into the first gunship, tearing the rear rotor off, the massive airframe dropping out of the sky like a rock, exploding on impact, secondary explosions from the weapons pods sending the first platoon to the ground for cover. Gunfire erupted from all around the men, quickly mowing down at least half the team as the rest ran for cover. Another RPG raced across the battle toward the second gunship, but it by now had enough speed and maneuverability for the pilot to avoid the unguided missile.

It opened fire, tearing apart the roof where much of the gunfire was coming from, missiles streaking from its weapons pods slamming into the façade, crumbling the building into a pile of concrete as the second wave choppers arrived on the scene, the side gunners opening fire blindly, spraying the surrounding buildings with massive rounds that tore apart anything in their paths.

Kane pocketed the scope, watching as the remaining five men on the ground regrouped, returning fire from behind the protection of the smoldering wreckage of their gunship and an abandoned troop transport. As the Hinds lay waste to everything in sight, the men on the ground focused on the command and control building, the rest, according to the plans provided by the Russians, merely support buildings—barracks, canteen, storage.

The hardened command structure was half buried into a hillside, its exposed front now a smoking, flaming mess as the Russians continued to hammer it with rockets and cannon fire.

"Remember, we need to get inside that thing," said Kane to Chernov, who frowned but nodded.

"Cease aerial fire, begin second insertion, only fire at soft targets."

Seconds later Kane's chopper touched down and he jumped out, rushing forward toward the abandoned transport and the cover it provided. Skidding to a knee, his shoulder checks confirmed Dawson and Niner were with him, Chernov and his platoon arriving unscathed. Weapons fire continued to rain down on them, but to Kane's trained ear, it sounded like only three, maybe four positions.

"I'm figuring four guns," said Niner, his back pressed against the front tire of the truck.

"Agreed," said Kane. He poked his head up for a moment, long enough to see muzzle flashes from two positions. "One shooter at my two o'clock, second window, second floor. Second shooter at my ten, right corner of rooftop."

"Roger that," said Dawson. He dropped to the ground, flat on his belly, his MP5K stretched out in front of him. "Cover me!"

Kane, Niner and Chernov's men jumped up, pouring fire randomly on the three buildings in front of them as Dawson rolled out into the open, sending several bursts of gunfire into the second floor window, the muzzle flashes stopping as he rolled back behind the truck, everyone ducking back down.

Chernov popped up and fired a single shot, dropping to a crouch.

"Second shooter eliminated."

The gunfire was sporadic now, the bullets still pinging off the rusted metal of the old transport. Kane poked his head up again but was immediately forced back down as he was narrowly missed.

"Someone almost punched my number," he said to Dawson with a grin.

"Better yours than mine," replied Dawson with a wink, popping up and firing several rounds. "Third and fourth shooters, ground floor of main complex, gun ports on either side of the main doors."

"Lovely," muttered Niner.

Kane turned to Chernov.

"Have the gunships hit the main doors on our signal!"

Chernov nodded, immediately passing on the order.

"Let's pop some smoke!" yelled Kane and within moments a dozen smoke grenades were tossed at the door, completely obscuring the entrance. The gunfire continued, but now blindly. "Hit them now!"

Chernov spoke into the comm and rockets streaked overhead almost immediately, slamming into the building. Kane rounded the front of the transport, rushing toward the right side of the door, Dawson, Niner and the rest of the Spetsnaz team following, splitting into two groups. Kane slammed against the wall, only three feet from the gun port, lead still pouring from the protruding barrel as it rocked left and right, aiming at nothing.

Kane flattened himself against the building, stomach against the concrete, then transferred his Glock to his left hand. Leaning over he poked the barrel inside and squeezed off an entire mag in various directions.

The firing stopped on his side.

Chernov preferred a more destructive route, instead tossing a grenade inside that was greeted with shouts of alarm then a massive concussive force and cries of pain from inside. Charges were set by the Spetsnaz team and the front doors of the command center were blasted open, the Russian platoon charging inside, only a few rounds fired before the all clear was sounded.

Kane and the Delta observers rounded the corner and Niner whistled.

"Christ, wasn't expecting this."

Inside was a marvel of Soviet era excess, a massive staging area carved out of the side of the mountain the size of a football field. Abandoned equipment was strewn about, but a dozen modern military and civilian vehicles were clustered around a large steel door about a hundred yards away.

A large steel door that was slowly closing.

"Shit!"

Kane sprinted toward the nearest vehicle, a Russian Humvee equivalent, and jumped inside, counting on it being more likely that the keys would be in a military vehicle than a civilian.

They were in the ignition.

He turned the key, the engine roaring to life. He slammed it in gear, hammering on the gas as he eased up on the clutch, the vehicle leaping forward. Cranking the wheel and shifting to second, he aimed for the massive door as the rest of the team realized what he was doing, following him on foot. The door was halfway closed now, and from the sheer thickness of it he knew there was no damned way they were going to be able to breach that without something equivalent to Thor's hammer.

Gunfire erupted from the other side, targeting him. He swerved slightly to the right and back to the left, patting himself on the back for choosing the military vehicle which was at least lightly armored against small arms fire. The team behind him opened up on the shooters, taking some of the pressure off him as he floored the accelerator, the door only a third of the way open, but he only yards away.

It's gonna hurt!

He slammed the brakes on just as he reached the massive door, wedging the mass of metal between the frame and the huge swinging door. Scrambling into the back seat, he pushed the rear door open and jumped out just as the front half of his vehicle was crushed, the vehicle slowly compressing as the motors worked against this new obstacle.

The door seemed to be winning.

You've got to be kidding me.

Pulling his Glock he hopped on the rear of the vehicle then over the roof, jumping to the other side of the door and into the command center itself. Gunfire greeted him as he hit the concrete floor, rolling as he took stock of what he faced. He pushed up from the floor, still spinning deeper into the complex and raised his weapon, taking a bead on one of the defenders, squeezing off two rounds, the first one missing, the second true, and as he hit the floor, rolling on his shoulder then back, pushing with his arms to keep some of the momentum, he finished by spreading his legs, halting his roll abruptly, firing on the two other targets before they could get a bead on him. Both dropped but not before a shooter, unseen, opened up on him.

He winced as he took a round to his left shoulder, pushing himself back into a roll as he tried to spot the shooter. More gunfire, tearing up the concrete beside him allowed him to hear where the shots were coming from. As his back hit the concrete, his arms extended above his head. His hands gripping his weapon, he raised his arms toward the ceiling and fired at his attacker crouched on a catwalk overhead. There was a cry followed by the satisfying view of his opponent falling off the catwalk, arms flailing, then the thump of the body slamming into the unforgiving concrete. Kane scrambled toward a small concrete staircase that seemed to go up only half a dozen steps as the rest of the team poured over his commandeered wedge and into the inner sanctum of the command center.

Chernov appeared first, taking a bead on Kane it seemed, his weapon belching lead as he rushed Kane's position. Kane rolled to the side, refusing to raise his weapon on Chernov, even if he were firing at him. If he were to die in a friendly fire incident, then so be it, but there was no way he was going to take out a comrade making a mistake.

But he wasn't hit, instead he heard glass shattering overhead, and as he rolled he spotted a man slumped over a control panel in a previously unnoticed booth. Chernov rushed up the few steps Kane had taken cover behind only moments before and kicked open the door, yanking the body off the console and tossing it onto the floor. Moments later the door began to open, the vehicle he had used almost sighing in relief as it expanded slightly.

Dawson grabbed him by the good shoulder.

"You okay?"

"Took a round to my shoulder," said Kane, glancing at it. Blood was oozing but not flowing, his fatigues stained, and the pain minimal unless he tried to move it.

Niner tore open the sleeve and took a look.

"You call that a wound?" he said with a grin, pushing Kane slightly. "You insult soldiers who have actually been wounded." Kane took a look and saw that he was only grazed, though still fairly deep. "You'll need some stitches. I can do it now if you want." The bobbing up and down of Niner's eyebrows and the all-too-eager shit-eating grin on his face had Kane turning down the offer.

"Just tape me up, we'll deal with it later," he said as Niner helped him to his feet and began administering to his wound.

"Got something over here!" yelled one of Chernov's men. "Looks like an elevator."

Kane began to walk toward the voice when Niner held him back.

"Hey, I'm operating here!"

Kane stopped, rolling his eyes at a smiling Dawson who was free to explore. Niner slapped the wound.

"Done."

Kane winced, rolling his shoulder to test it out, then nodded.

"Good work."

"I do my best under fire," replied Niner repacking his med kit. "Now let's go create some wounds of our own!"

The discovery proved to be a large elevator, the doors big enough to fit a good sized sedan through, with only two lights above, one indicating the Russian Cyrillic equivalent to Ground, the other of Basement. Chernov pressed the button.

There was a ding and the doors opened, revealing an elevator definitely big enough to fit a car, the design obviously meant to be able to transport a large number of people in a single load in the case of the ultimate emergency—nuclear war.

Chernov ordered the weakened first platoon to hold the ground as the rest boarded the elevator, Kane hitting the button for the basement, the doors closing moments later as Chernov's men left behind spread out, he had no doubt disappointed they wouldn't be about to get their revenge.

But Chernov was right to leave them above. They desperately needed intel, and trigger happy soldiers on a revenge fueled adrenaline rush were more likely to fire blindly, no matter how well trained they were, especially since they had no actual personal investment in the outcome. After all, these bombs were exploding on American soil, their traditional enemy. What did they care if a few more went off?

The elevator began to move, picking up speed rapidly.

"They're going to know we're coming," said Chernov. "My men will lead. As soon as the doors open, we'll pop smoke, exit, breaking left and right, finding cover and incapacitating anyone who resists. The goal is to take prisoners, and not damage the equipment, so be careful with your aim." He readied his Makarov as the elevator began to slow. "Masks."

Everyone pulled down their masks and goggles to protect themselves from the smoke, Chernov already popping one of the grenades and leaving it on the floor, the elevator quickly filling with smoke. Kane heard several more pins pulled as the elevator halted.

A ding and the door opened, the sounds of boots on metal advancing, gunfire already slamming into the rear of the elevator. Kane advanced at a crouch, stumbling over a body. He felt a hand pull him back to his feet, shoving him out of the elevator. He rolled to his left, the smoke clearing enough for him to seek cover.

"Activate the failsafe immediately!" echoed a voice over a speaker.

"Shoot anybody at a control terminal!" yelled Kane, jumping up and firing at the first person he saw, their head slumping into a keyboard. Shots erupted from around him, bodies dropping as those able to execute the order were quickly eliminated. Kane spotted Levkin running for a door at the opposite side of the control center, the smoke clearing to reveal massive projection screens and a dozen modern computers, this not the abandoned site the world was led to believe.

Kane raised his weapon and shot the man in the hip, dropping him to the floor, several Spetsnaz operators rushing to secure him.

"Are we too late?" asked Dawson as they all turned toward the screens.

Kane felt his stomach flip, his mouth water as his mind interpreted what was shown. A map of the world with dots spread across the globe, the vast majority in the United States, turning green, then down in the bottom, a countdown timer showing less than two minutes.

"There's hundreds!" exclaimed Niner. He pointed at the countdown. "Does that mean they only have two minutes before detonation?"

An automated voice sounded, and in Russian, a female voice announced, "Two minutes to self-destruct."

"Everybody out!" yelled Chernov as he grabbed Kane by the shirt, pulling him toward the elevator. Kane didn't need any urging, but broke free of the grip, pulling out his phone and taking several pictures of the displays before spinning on his heel and sprinting toward the doors as everyone, including a carried Levkin, boarded the elevator. Chernov held the door open, the button already pressed for the Ground floor, and as the last man cleared, he stepped back and the doors slowly rolled closed.

"Jesus, I hope this damned thing is as fast going up as it was coming down," said Niner, his sentiments silently agreed with.

But the elevator didn't seem to want to listen. It slowly began to rise, the speed increasing, but Kane couldn't tell if it was his imagination or reality that had him thinking things were going far too slowly considering the timeframe they were dealing with.

Chernov was already on his comm, the signal successfully traveling up the elevator shaft to the men above, ordering the choppers into position for an emergency evac, telling the men guarding the elevator doors to fallback and board the choppers as soon as they touched down.

"Umm, anybody think to synch that countdown with their watch?" asked Niner.

"Fifty-three seconds," replied Chernov.

Kane began a mental count in his head, the elevator finally slowing down at forty-five. The doors rolled open at forty.

The team guarding the door was gone, having followed their orders, and outside they could hear rotors thumping at full power as the Hinds awaited their cargo.

"Go! Go! Go!" yelled Chernov, Kane not needing any urging as they burst from the elevator and into the inner chamber. They raced for the massive door, it now wide open thanks to Chernov's good thinking earlier, otherwise they all would have had to climb over the now crushed vehicle Kane had commandeered.

The group sprinted across the massive assembly area toward the blown open doors, the morning sunlight spilling through the entrance as if signaling a paradise on the other side awaiting their blessed arrival.

Kane did a shoulder check and saw Dawson and Niner flanking him and Chernov bringing up the rear, four men carrying the injured and angry Levkin, each holding a limb.

They burst through the entrance and out into the sunlight, Kane blinking rapidly as he tried to regain focus, three Hinds appearing through the haze, the dust their blades were churning up not helping his eyesight. Kane broke to the right, heading for the farthest chopper, leaving the closest free for those in the rear carrying their prisoner. He jumped aboard, immediately seeking out the deepest corner and took a spot, out of the way as he pulled out his secure phone, quickly entering a message then transmitting it along with the photos he had taken should they not escape in time.

Levkin activated all weapons.

He looked up from his phone to see Dawson and Niner and several other Spetsnaz operators surrounding him as the gunship rose from the ground. He looked out, his mental count lost while he concentrated on his message.

But Niner hadn't.

"Five seconds!" he yelled over the roar of the straining engines as the massive bird painfully gained altitude, tilting forward to slowly increase speed.

Massive thumps sounded over the blades, and Kane looked down to see the entire area vibrating, the dust rising off the ground everywhere as a shockwave from below raised the surrounding earth several inches, then flames erupted from every opening, every building, as the explosion found any available escape it could.

Along with any hope of using the complex to deactivate the weapons.

Operations Center 3, CIA Headquarters, Langley, Virginia

Leroux almost jumped out of his chair as the klaxon sounded and the Defense Condition display updated to the brilliant red of DEFCON 2 indicating the Armed Forces were ready to deploy within six hours.

And the United States was only one step away from nuclear war.

But who the hell are we going to attack?

There was no doubt now that it was Russians behind the attacks, but the question was whether or not the attacks were condoned by the current government, and if they weren't, did they have knowledge of the attacks? From the mood of the now crowded Operations Center 3 it was obvious all wanted to strike back at somebody, but there was division on whether or not a retaliatory attack on the Russians was justified.

"I say hit a few of their naval task forces. They're military targets, on the open seas, with no risk of civilian casualties. They need to be punished now to send a message to the world that we won't be messed with!"

"Enough!" yelled Morrison, ending all discussion instantly. "We'll worry about striking back later. Right now we need to figure out how to stop these bombs from going off!" He paused, letting his words sink in. "Now, how much time have we got?"

"From the pictures our agent transmitted, it appears they activated a failsafe mechanism that triggered a self-destruct on the facility, and transmitted activation codes to the remaining weapons," said Don Eppes, one of their experts on the Russians, fluent in the language.

"What does the map show?" asked a voice over the speaker.

"At the moment of the picture being taken, it showed over five hundred devices around the world, about half of them green, a quarter red, the rest black. We're assuming that green means activated, red means that the activation failed, and black means dead weapons."

"How many of these are on our soil?"

"Almost four hundred, with half of those green."

"Two hundred weapons," muttered Morrison.

It was mind numbing. Too much for Leroux to listen to. Instead he tried to block the question and answer session. It was a waste of time, either repeating things they already knew, or asking the wrong questions. It didn't matter whether it was ten or ten thousand weapons, the only question that mattered was how to stop them.

"Have we notified our allies?"

"Yes, the photos have been transmitted along with the microfilm intel, and a note that the intel had been in the possession of the French since 1982."

"That should go over well."

Already the petty bickering is taking over.

Something was nagging at him. At first he thought it was why they didn't just control the weapons from their command center in Russia instead of the RV here, but after pondering it for only a few seconds, he realized they couldn't risk any transmissions being tracked back to Russia since they were trying to frame Islamists for the attacks.

It was something else. Something that had been said earlier, a possible solution to their problem. They had bombs ready to detonate, with no indication of how long their countdowns would be, but they had to assume they were short. Thanks to the intel from the microfilm they knew some of the radio frequencies they were using, so if they could get the others to somehow transmit, they could locate the transmission, then use the general coordinates they had from the microfilm to cross-reference the deactivation code, and transmit back on the same frequency to deactivate the weapon.

But how the hell do you get them to transmit back?

"What's the status on the deactivations?" asked Morrison.

Conway turned from his terminal.

"We've transmitted the deactivation codes that we have radio frequencies for and all weapons that were indicated green on the photos have signaled back a code. We're assuming that code is an acknowledgement that they have deactivated. Recovery teams have been dispatched to all locations to deactivate the pinpointed weapons, and to evacuate any areas that we can't deactivate."

"But we have no idea how long their countdowns are."

"Affirmative. We have to assume fairly short though."

Morrison looked up at the ceiling, his hands on his hips.

"Kane, can Levkin talk?"

"Yes, sir."

"We need to know how much time we have."

"Understood."

A scream blasted through the speaker before the transmission was cut off, the room silent for only a moment before speculation rampaged freely again.

And a thought continued to nag at Leroux. The deactivation codes were working when sent on the proper frequency. They couldn't risk just blanketing all frequencies with all of the codes as failsafes were probably built into the devices against such a thing and were liable to set off the weapons. The idea had been suggested early on and thankfully dismissed just as quickly.

"Sixty minutes from the failsafe transmission!" came Kane's voice over the speakers.

"Confirm, sixty minutes?"

"Yes, from the moment of the transmission."

"Does somebody have an updated time?" asked Morrison.

"Forty-two minutes, thirteen seconds remaining," said Leroux without looking up, he already having programmed the computer with a countdown of the transmission.

"Put that up on the screen."

Leroux hit a couple of buttons and moments later his Malware display was replaced with the countdown timer.

"How the hell are we supposed to evacuate over a hundred sites in forty minutes?"

"We can't," said Morrison, his voice already resigned to defeat.

"Whatever you do don't cut the power."

Kane's words echoed through his head and Leroux's heart leapt as he jumped to his feet.

"Why don't we just cut the power?"

Approaching Parker Dam, Arizona

Lieutenant Rick Messina looked out the window of the Black Hawk helicopter he and half his men were in, the rest in a second chopper just behind them. The mood had been somber since the moment word of the Memphis detonation had arrived, the realization of how important their jobs actually were and that this was not some veiled exercise or wild goose chase chilling.

And his current destination had him in a near panic.

They were heading for Parker Dam to help evacuate the locals, it being a confirmed site for one of the hidden nukes. It hadn't gone off yet, and his last briefing half an hour ago suggested there was no reason to suspect it would, but all sites across the country were being searched and evacuated if possible.

I can only imagine what they're doing at places like Grand Central Station in New York!

Their mission was relatively easy compared to many of the other units having to deal with highly populated areas. Here they were dealing with a few thousand, almost all with vehicles, most out of the estimated blast radius, but downriver of the dam, therefore vulnerable to flood waters should the dam burst.

Guilt racked him over and over again.

Get to campground ASAP!

He had sent the text message thinking he was saving their lives, and instead he had sent them into one of the few danger areas in Arizona.

I've killed them.

He shook his head and gripped his thigh hard to ward off the tears that threatened to spill over his eyelids.

290

They're perfectly safe. Just execute your orders and get them out of there.

Repeated texts failed to reach them, coverage never good in the area, and Angela most likely asleep. He tried again, almost all of them trying to communicate what they knew with loved ones as soon as word had been received that the list had been made public. Communication between buddies in the various units had confirmed the few locations in Arizona, and those had been sent out via text almost immediately. Now with the mass evacuations occurring across the country, the locations had been provided to the public to try and save as many lives as possible. The problem was too many people were asleep.

He leaned forward and looked at the pilot.

"Can this thing go any faster?" he asked over his mike.

"Not if you want to get back," was the reply.

"To hell with getting back. We just need to get far enough from the river. Worry about getting back later!"

There was no reply but the helicopter dipped slightly and he could hear the engines strain a little harder, the pilot apparently agreeing with his thoughts.

We have no more time!

Operations Center 3, CIA Headquarters, Langley, Virginia

The door to OC3 opened and Leroux barely glanced, his eyes glued to the screen showing the national power grid as it rapidly darkened. It had taken a Presidential order to get the private companies to shut down and a guarantee to pay for any damages that might result. A few had apparently resisted with a second message sent from the White House that anyone disobeying the order would be arrested and charged under anti-terror laws quelling any dissent except to express the worry that they might not be able to turn things back on.

Nobody cared.

It was more important to stop the weapons from detonating than pick up the pieces later.

"Shutdown complete," came a voice over the speaker.

A figure moved to Leroux's left and he felt a hand on his shoulder. He assumed it was Morrison, still providing comfort, but when he looked up he could see Morrison standing five feet away. He turned to look at who was touching him.

"Sherrie!" he cried, jumping up and hugging her, not caring who saw them, or more accurately not able to control the impulse to take her in his arms regardless the consequences. She returned the hug, tight, and he felt her shoulders heave several times as she silently sobbed.

"Transmissions beginning to be received from disconnected weapons."

He freed her from his grip and smiled at her, both their eyes filled with tears as they turned, his arm draped over her shoulders, holding her tight. They watched the display showing the known locations begin to light up as the weapons sent their call-home signal to see if the Soviet Union had collapsed and if the failsafe, as described by Levkin, should be employed.

Leroux shook his head as he thought of the failsafe, its aim clear—to destroy the apparent victor in any Armageddon that may have occurred, its designers presumably so arrogant they felt nobody should have the planet if the USSR couldn't.

"Deactivation codes being transmitted to live weapons."

On the screen a counter showed over 514 weapons deployed, 442 in the United States. The 'Believed Active' counter sat at 279, with the 'Believed Dormant' counter at 163. The counter showing 'Call Back Transmissions Received' was rapidly increasing, already at over 30, with the 'Deactivation Codes Transmitted' running at less than half the rate, only at 13.

But it was the 'Presumed Deactivated' counter that sat stubbornly at zero that had everyone's attention. Leroux held his breath, unknowingly, his grip on Sherrie increasing to the point where she shifted her shoulders, bringing his attention to what he was doing.

He looked down.

"Sorry."

Her eyes never left the screen.

The counter ticked to 1.

"We have our first presumed deactivation."

Cheers erupted from the packed room as the counter then flipped to 2, all the other counters increasing rapidly as the weapons dialed home for instructions, and those instructions were transmitted by the victors in a war lost decades ago.

Leroux began to breathe slightly easier as the deactivated counter continued to spin up and the indicator of 'Presumed weapons still active' counted down toward zero.

Presumed.

That was the problem they were facing. They were making the assumption that the weapons on the pictures Kane had taken that were black were actually dead already, safe to find and deactivate at a later time.

But what if we're wrong?

The counter rapidly dropped, and after less than ten minutes was down to just one remaining weapon.

"What's the status on that last weapon?" asked Morrison.

"It's dialed home, sir, but it's not acknowledging receipt of the deactivation code."

"What does that mean?"

"It means it's still active and will detonate in less than three minutes."

"Send the code again!" yelled Morrison.

"I have, sir, several times. It won't acknowledge receipt."

"Location?"

"Parker Dam, Arizona."

River Island State Park, South of Parker Dam, Arizona

Angela Messina woke to confused sounds around her. It was still nighttime, and a quick look at her watch had her really confused. Camp rules basically banned any noise at this hour, all-night partiers frowned upon and usually self-policed by the other campers.

But this was different.

This was the sounds of people packing up and vehicle engines roaring to life.

This was panic.

Her heart began to race as she unzipped her sleeping bag then crawled forward to unzip the tent. She scrambled outside, flashlight in hand, and gasped as she rose.

The entire camp seemed awake, tents being torn down, bags tossed into the back of trucks and those apparently in the know early, already pulling away.

She rushed over to the kids' tent and unzipped it, grabbing their legs and shaking them.

"Wake up!" she yelled.

Her son woke first, sitting up and rubbing his eyes.

"Get your sister up and get dressed. Now!"

"Why?"

"Because I said so!" she yelled, his eyes popping open wide at her outburst, his head rapidly bobbing in acquiescence. Angela left the tent and ran toward one of the vehicles being loaded.

"What's going on?" she asked the woman she recognized from the evening before, her name escaping her.

"It's all over the news. There's a nuclear bomb at the dam!"

Angela nearly blacked out, the thought of her children all that kept her from collapsing right then and there. She looked at her SUV parked nearby then the tents and their gear and made a split second decision.

To hell with packing.

She ran back to her tent, grabbed her cellphone and car keys, then as she crawled out, she found her two kids standing outside their tent, gaping at what was going on around them.

"Let's go, now!" she said, running toward the SUV.

"What's going on?" asked the kids in unison, but she ignored them, instead unlocking the doors with the fob and climbing into the driver's seat, starting the engine as she yelled for the kids to get inside. As soon as doors were shut and she confirmed with a shoulder check that both were in the backseat, she put the vehicle in gear and peeled away from their parking spot.

"What about the tents?"

"Forget the tents. We have to get out of here!"

"What's going on, mom?" asked her daughter, beginning to panic as they were cut off by another vehicle, everyone now stuck in a long line of vehicles barely inching forward.

She looked in her side view mirror and the entire horizon behind her flashed with a brilliant light that lit everything around them in every direction, impossibly long shadows bending toward the ground, then shooting up into nothingness once again as the intense light faded, replaced with a fireball, brilliantly orange, red and yellow against the night sky.

The kids were looking back at the explosion, crying now, as even they realized the seriousness of the situation. But she was certain they didn't know the half of it.

If that took out the dam, the Colorado is about to flood, and we're dead.

"Let's go!" she yelled at the vehicles ahead of her, too many brake lights, too many turned heads looking at the explosion. She looked to her left and saw a gradual rise that crested several hundred feet above. She hit the button switching the vehicle to four-by-four mode then cranked the wheel to the left, hammering on the gas. She quickly shot up the rise, taking out the small brush in her way, swerving to avoid several larger trees, fortunately sparse.

She crested the rise and found herself on a flat expanse leading to the highway, clogged with traffic, but at least moving in the right direction. She hammered on the gas, rushing across the cleared area, then wedged herself into the flow on the 95 heading south, away from the dam, but hugging the river the entire way.

We need to find a way off this!

But to her left, all she could see were unforgiving hills, unpassable.

She slammed her fists into the steering wheel as they crawled along, 210 billion gallons of water beginning its rush down the Colorado River.

Rick Messina looked at the gridlock below as hundreds of vehicles tried to escape along a road that followed the exact path of the impending flood. And it appeared the traffic wasn't able to pick up much speed as desperate residents continually forced themselves on to the roads rather than be left waiting for a break in the non-stop traffic.

The good news was that the word had obviously gotten out. The bad news was that it was every man for himself out there.

They need to head inland, away from the river!

His phone vibrated in his hand and he looked at the call display.

Angela!

He answered.

"Are you okay?"

"No! Oh my God, no! Don't you know what's going on?" she cried.

"Yes. Now I need you to stay calm. Where are you?"

"We're on the highway, heading south."

"Are the kids with you?"

"Of course the kids are with me! What the hell kind of—"

"Stay calm." Messina motioned for the map to be handed to him. "Do you know where you are?"

"We just left the campground and are stuck in traffic."

His finger found the campground and traced the road.

"Okay, have you reached the gas station yet, the one on your left?"

"No, but I see it up ahead."

"Okay, just after that is a dirt road on the left. Take it, follow it a few hundred feet past some trailers, then it splits. Take the left split, then follow that as far as you can. That'll take you through the hills and away from the river. Just keep going and eventually you'll reach a high point where you can stop."

"Okay, I see it, I see it!" cried Angela. "I'm turning now!"

Horns honked and tires screeched and Angela remained silent for several moments, the whimpers of his children obvious over the hands-free kit his wife was using.

"Are you okay?"

"Yes, we're on the road!" she said, then in typical Angela fashion paused. "What the hell kind of road is this? Are you sure this is a road?"

"It's more like a trail. How's your gas?"

"Full."

"Then just keep going!"

"Sir, you've got to see this," came the voice of the pilot over his headgear, at the moment only over one ear. He turned and looked out the front of the chopper and gasped. A massive wall of water, several stories high at least was pushing down the Colorado, the banks burst on either side as what remained of the town of Parker Dam rode the crest of it, debris ranging from houses to vehicles being carried along.

"Hon, I've got to go. You keep going ahead and you'll be safe."

"What about you?"

"I'm in a helicopter. Don't worry about me. When this is over I'll find you."

"Okay, I love you."

"I love you too. Love you kids!"

"Love you too, Dad!" they yelled in unison, the terror in their little voices still obvious.

He ended the call, stuffing the phone back in his pocket.

"We're too late here," he said over the comm. "Let's go downriver and see if we can do any good there."

"Roger that," replied the pilot, banking and sending them down the river and away from the impending wall of unleashed natural fury, the world's deepest dam no longer, and the unnatural reservoir, held by force behind a massive wall of concrete, suddenly freed, trying to reclaim the territory it once held.

"What's that?" yelled one of his men, pointing out the side of the helicopter. Messina looked down, not seeing what the corporal was seeing until a search light suddenly focused on a vehicle stopped on a side road, a woman waving with both arms at them.

"Can you get us down there?" asked Messina.

"Yeah, but you'll have less than two minutes before that water is on us."

"Do it."

The helicopter lowered and when they were just a few feet from the ground Messina and two of his men jumped out, hitting the ground then running toward the woman, her screams for help barely audible over the pounding of the blades.

"Help me!" she yelled as they reached her. "I have a flat tire!"

The roar from the approaching water was deafening and Messina looked to see the dark mass, lit only by the stars and moon, approaching rapidly, the pilot's estimate of two minutes way off.

"Let's go!" he yelled, grabbing the now frozen women by the arm. She wouldn't budge.

"Pick her up!" he ordered, his two men grabbing her and carrying her to the chopper, rolling her inside as they climbed in after her. The wall of water was so close mist could be felt, the thunderous approach louder than the chopper.

"My baby!" she screamed as she suddenly snapped out of shock.

"What?"

"My baby! She's in my car!"

Messina, half in the chopper, spun, and with one last glance at the wall of water, jumped back down and raced toward the car as fast as he could. He slammed into the side, unwilling to lose any time in slowing down, then pulled open the door and found the baby in a car seat. He quickly unsnapped her then pulled out the tiny bundle, probably only weeks old, then turned toward the chopper.

The roar of the wall of water was all encompassing now, overwhelming his senses as he sprinted toward the helicopter now rising from the ground. He saw one of his men hooked into a harness, leaning out the side of the helicopter, his hands extended as Messina raced toward them, the baby cradled in his arms.

A quick look to his left and he knew he had no more time. He said a silent prayer and raised his right hand, the baby tightly gripped in it, then as if going for a touchdown pass, fired the baby as hard as he could toward the outstretched arms of his fellow guardsman, but as the baby hurtled through the air he realized with a deadening of his senses that his throw was short.

The corporal who had first spotted the woman, and who was now in the harness, jumped from the chopper, arms outstretched, rapidly dropping toward the baby, catching her as she began her descent, his arms quickly drawing her in and cradling her against his chest as his comrades above pulled them both to safety, the helicopter rising above the impending threat.

As Messina breathed a sigh of relief reality once again came back into focus and his head spun to the left just as the wall of water slammed into him with so much pressure he almost blacked out immediately from the shock. And as he scrambled helplessly to stay alive, he realized it was no use, and instead turned his attention to more important things as he was battered to death by the debris and the rocky bed of the Colorado.

Thank you God for saving my family.

And he only hoped that whatever sins he had committed in this world would be negated by his one final, selfless act, that resulted in a mother and her precious daughter escaping the onslaught.

And Lieutenant Rick Messina, Arizona National Guard, husband and father of two, finally succumbed, one of the final recorded victims of a Cold War long forgotten.

Operations Center 3, CIA Headquarters, Langley, Virginia

There was silence throughout the Operations Center as the realization that there had been a detonation set in, reports from the ground scant, the only information that had reached them so far was that the dam had failed.

The only saving grace was that by the time the wash from the collapsed dam would reach any substantially populated area, it would have dissipated enough to do little if any damage.

But it signaled one other thing.

Possibly.

If all the weapons were set to detonate at the same time, then the others should have gone off by now as well. And none had. Which meant the crisis might actually be over.

But Leroux refused to let himself relax.

"Any word on other detonations?" asked Morrison.

"Negative. No other detonations reported as of yet."

As of yet.

"How long do we wait?" asked Sherrie, her voice barely a whisper.

"We don't," replied Morrison. "We continue forward, locate each and every one of these weapons, deactivate them, make them safe, then find every single person involved, and bring them to justice."

Justice.

Right now Leroux just wanted them all dead. That would be justice. After all, it was the method of justice most employed by the USSR, the very empire these crazed lunatics were trying to restore. It would be fitting justice to slap them in some third world style gulag in Alaska, awaiting trial, then just shoot them all after torturing them for the names of their comrades.

Comrades.

It made him sick. Why would anyone want to bring back the old USSR? But then he realized that it was already happening, and most Russians were either cheering it, or tacitly supporting it, those who spoke out labelled agitators and tossed in prison.

And if the West wasn't careful, they could once again face an enemy even more powerful than before, with massive reserves of money and dozens of countries heavily dependent upon its oil and natural gas reserves, not the least of which were most Northern European countries.

Would America stand alone if the gas taps were turned off, leaving its traditional allies in the cold?

Leroux shuddered at the thought and hoped that the events of the past few days would at least open the world's eyes to the dangers such a future might bring.

Sherrie squeezed his hand.

"Are you okay?"

He nodded.

"I was just wondering if there's another Cold War, would we still have the will to fight it."

She frowned.

"These are different times, but I like to think we would."

Leroux nodded, unsure if he shared her confidence.

Alex West Residence, Black Forest, Germany

Alex West sat in his favorite chair with a clear view of the front door, tea on his knee, a smile on his face, happier than he could ever remember being. Adelle sat in the next best seat, Alexis the third, and poor Viktor Zorkin was relegated to the worst seat in the house, his back to the door.

But none seemed to mind, all smiles and laughter, Alexis having taken to her father quickly, already calling him 'papa', something that melted his heart every time he heard it.

And he and Adelle had rekindled their romance, something he was pleased could still happen at seventy-five without blue candies. They were slower in their old age, but with gun-toting KGB no longer chasing them down, they could be forgiven for taking their time and enjoying each other's offerings.

"It will take some time to track them all down," said Zorkin as he sipped his tea. "Perhaps years."

"I'm not sure who could be left beyond underlings," said Alexis. "General Levkin is dead, all of the men at his complex are dead, and his men in America are either dead or captured."

"Don't forget the money, my dear," said West. "Somebody fronted an awful lot of money for this endeavor."

"Follow the money," agreed Adelle.

The sound of a car pulling up outside had West and Zorkin reaching for their weapons, urging the women to stay behind them, but instead they too pulled their own.

"I count two," whispered Zorkin.

"No, three," said Adelle.

"Definitely three," agreed West, though he couldn't be certain, but if he were going to be wrong, he was going to go with his beloved's answer.

There was a knock at the door.

"Enter," said West. "Slowly."

The door opened and a pair of hands appeared first, empty, then the smiling face of Kane.

"Are we interrupting anything?" he asked as he entered, followed by the two Delta operatives Dawson and Niner.

"This is cozy," commented Niner, the fact the room was never designed for seven painfully obvious.

"I didn't expect to see you again," said West, standing and offering his chair.

Kane waved it off.

"No, you keep it. We're only here to say hi and to pass on the thanks of our government for your help. We've got a flight to catch this evening out of Frankfurt."

"Can I get you anything?"

"No, that's okay. I'm just really here for one thing."

"What's that?"

"I seem to remember owing someone an arm wrestle."

Zorkin jumped from his seat, looking for a place to meet the challenge.

And finding no surface not covered in some remembrance.

"It appears we are defeated by a packrat," he muttered. "Perhaps it's for the best."

"The best?" asked Kane.

"Yes, I wouldn't want to embarrass you in front of your friends."

Kane laughed and Niner leaned in.

"Are you going to take that from an old man? Kick his ass!"

The room erupted in laughter as Kane shook his head.

"I think maybe it's best to leave some questions unanswered."

Niner leaned forward again.

"How about the hood of the car?"

Zorkin leapt from his chair again and rushed for the door.

"Time to teach this young bastard a lesson!"

Zorkin disappeared, followed by a laughing Kane and his friends, leaving West, Adelle and Alexis behind.

"Mom, how did you ever get out of the Soviet Union after you were captured?"

Adelle smiled.

"Perhaps that's something you should ask your dad."

Siberia, USSR
April 14th, 1982

Adelle Bertrand shivered, curled up into a ball in the back of the military transport. Her teeth chattered from the cold and her fingers were so numb she was beginning to worry about frostbite. Her face was swollen from the beatings, and she didn't want to think of what had almost happened.

Even though they were trained to shut down, to compartmentalize, weeks or months of repeated rapes was something nobody could recover from, no matter how good the training.

But Zorkin had saved her, intervening and making sure she was put into the right hands, honorable hands. She had still been beaten. Still tortured. Still interrogated for weeks.

But *that*, she was trained for, and could recover from.

The vehicle suddenly braked, skidding to a halt on the frozen, snow-covered roads, cursing from the front cabin erupting from the two men tasked to transport her. She listened to the sound of the passenger side door opening, yelling, then several pops, more shouts, and two more pops, the distinctive sound of a muzzled weapon unmistakable.

The engine still idled ahead of her, but the sound of feet crunching on snow rounded the side of the vehicle, stopping at the rear. The canvas flap was tossed aside and a flashlight was shone in her face. A shadowy figure climbed inside then walked toward her, kneeling beside her, a hand reaching out.

She shrank away, not wanting to be touched by anyone.

"Adelle, it's me."

The voice was familiar, but in the darkness she could see nothing. She remained silent as she tried to place the voice, but the engine and howling wind made it impossible.

The flashlight left her face and shone on the man's face and she cried out in joy, leaping forward into his arms.

"Alex!"

He held her tight, and though she was in pain, terrible pain, she didn't say a word as her cracked ribs screamed in agony at his crushing embrace.

It was the most wonderful feeling she could imagine.

"What are you doing here?"

He smiled as he cut her bonds.

"I could ask you the same question."

She rubbed her wrists as he began to open a bag he had with him.

"How did you find me?"

He handed her a warm winter jacket which she pulled on immediately, her fingers too numb to zip it up.

"Here, let me get that," he said as he zipped it for her. "A note was slipped under my door with this location and a date and time."

"Who do you—"

"I think we both know."

"Zorkin."

West nodded as he fitted a warm toque to her head.

"Good thing he's on our side sometimes," said West as he helped her from the back of the truck.

When they both were standing at the rear of the vehicle Adelle grabbed his neck, pulling him down to her, her frozen lips pressing against his as he returned the kiss, the embrace not one of lust, but of a passion now beyond the primal.

She broke the kiss and looked up at him, tears in her eyes.

"I think you love me."

He smiled and wiped away a tear that had escaped.

"I admit to nothing, but then again, you are a highly trained spy, so you should be able to tell."

She smiled, pushing away from him but still holding his hands. Assessing his eyes and his smile, she nodded.

"You love me."

It was a statement of fact. Not a joke, not a guess, not a wish. A fact.

West smiled.

"Lady knows best."

He pointed to the front of the truck.

"Now, how about we get out of here, we've got a sub to catch."

Adelle let West help her into the truck, West climbing into the other side after dumping the bodies into a ditch and covering them with snow. As the vehicle began to move forward, glorious heat spilling into the cab, she looked at the man she knew she loved and wondered what their future might bring.

Whatever it is, I know it will be wonderful.

THE END

ACKNOWLEDGEMENTS

I grew up an Air Force brat living in many places, the longest in West Germany, spending many of my formative years, eight through fifteen, living and breathing the daily reality that was the Cold War. We lived off base, "on the economy" as it was known, so we could experience German culture while we were there. We lived on the second floor of a house—its own separate apartment—in a town called Hugsweier, with our German landlords living on the main floor.

The two families became extremely close, and my parents still visit annually.

Herman and Erica were fantastic people, and I have over the years come to think of them as my German grandparents and their daughter as a sort of sister. Herman unfortunately passed away some years ago, and I hope soon that life will stop interfering with my plans to get back to my old stomping grounds so I can see the rest of my extended family soon.

These were fantastic times, exciting times, and terrifying times. The military base we were stationed at was a prime Soviet target. In a nuclear exchange, we knew we were toast within minutes. Even if the war stayed conventional, we were still a prime target. We had bomb drills at school, not fire drills. We lived under constant terrorist threat, whether it was from groups like the home grown Red Army Faction (also known as the Baader Meinhof Gang) or Middle Eastern terrorists, it never ended. The searches, the armed guards, the Armored Personal Carriers at the gates to go to school, not to mention the armed escorts on the school busses.

Exciting. Terrifying.

One of the many things I have come to realize now that I've spent more than twenty-five years back home is that the average person has no concept of how good we have it here. 9/11 was a wake-up call, but little has happened on home soil since then. We don't go to sleep at night with tanks on our streets, soldiers in our workplace, children practicing bomb evacuation drills, and an enemy, only hundreds of miles away, who wanted to kill us.

And with the Soviet Union defeated, a new generation of Europeans no longer know that fear either.

And it is all thanks to those Cold Warriors who held back the Russian bear for decades, eventually winning in the end, so future generations wouldn't know the fear the USSR and its allies in the Warsaw Pact represented. It is a generation of soldiers who were willing to die to defend our way of life, but thankfully were never forced to.

But because few shots were fired, these veterans are quite often forgotten, overlooked in favor of our vets from two world wars, Korea, Vietnam, and more recently Iraq and Afghanistan where actual battles that make great movies occurred. But these Cold Warriors, like my father, are veterans who joined a volunteer military to defend us, with little thanks or recognition, against a military arguably mightier than any we have ever faced in history or since, armed with nuclear, biological and chemical weapons, as well as a massive sophisticated conventional force far more terrifying than the average civilian knew.

I'd like to thank these Cold Warriors, these veterans—and there are millions of them—for their service and sacrifice.

And my German family, for making one military family feel so much at home, *Vielen dank*!

On a *much* lighter note, there are people to thank for their contributions to this book, the writing of which was a far less noble endeavor than fighting the Cold War, I assure you! I'd like to thank Brent Richards for teaching me how to headbutt someone without knocking yourself out,

Klaus Rößel for the German translation and Felicitas Grant and Mechtilda Dowd for the double-check. For advice on the Black Sea and boats in general, I'd like to thank Richard Jenner. As well, the real Chris Leroux for some gaming info, and the real Rick Messina who has been a great friend and supporter for many years—sorry I killed you, dude! Of course I'd like to thank my wife and daughter and parents, as well as all my friends for their continued support, and you the fans who have made all this possible.

And to those who have not already done so, please visit my website at www.jrobertkennedy.com then sign up for the Insiders Club. You'll get emails about new book releases, new collections, sales, etc. Only an email or two a month tops, I promise!

ABOUT THE AUTHOR

 J. Robert Kennedy is the author of over one dozen international best sellers, including the smash hit James Acton Thrillers series, the first installment of which, The Protocol, has been on the best sellers list since its release, including a three month run at number one. In addition to the other novels from this series, Brass Monkey, Broken Dove, The Templar's Relic (also a number one best seller), Flags of Sin, The Arab Fall (also #1), The Circle of Eight (also #1) and The Venice Code, he has written the international best sellers Rogue Operator, Containment Failure, Cold Warriors, Depraved Difference, Tick Tock, The Redeemer and The Turned. Robert spends his time in Ontario, Canada with his family.

Visit Robert's website at www.jrobertkennedy.com for the latest news and contact information.

The Protocol

A James Acton Thriller, Book #1

For two thousand years the Triarii have protected us, influencing history from the crusades to the discovery of America. Descendent from the Roman Empire, they pervade every level of society, and are now in a race with our own government to retrieve an ancient artifact thought to have been lost forever.

Caught in the middle is archaeology professor James Acton, relentlessly hunted by the elite Delta Force, under orders to stop at nothing to possess what he has found, and the Triarii, equally determined to prevent the discovery from falling into the wrong hands.

With his students and friends dying around him, Acton flees to find the one person who might be able to help him, but little does he know he may actually be racing directly into the hands of an organization he knows nothing about...

Brass Monkey

A James Acton Thriller, Book #2

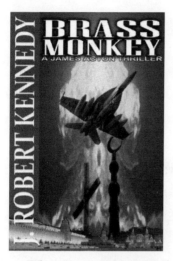

A nuclear missile, lost during the Cold War, is now in play--the most public spy swap in history, with a gorgeous agent the center of international attention, triggers the end-game of a corrupt Soviet Colonel's twenty five year plan. Pursued across the globe by the Russian authorities, including a brutal Spetsnaz unit, those involved will stop at nothing to deliver their weapon, and ensure their pay day, regardless of the terrifying consequences.

When Laura Palmer confronts a UNICEF group for trespassing on her Egyptian archaeological dig site, she unwittingly stumbles upon the ultimate weapons deal, and becomes entangled in an international conspiracy that sends her lover, archeology Professor James Acton, racing to Egypt with the most unlikely of allies, not only to rescue her, but to prevent the start of a holy war that could result in Islam and Christianity wiping each other out.

From the bestselling author of Depraved Difference and The Protocol comes Brass Monkey, a thriller international in scope, certain to offend some, and stimulate debate in others. Brass Monkey pulls no punches in confronting the conflict between two of the world's most powerful, and divergent, religions, and the terrifying possibilities the future may hold if left unchecked.

Broken Dove

A James Acton Thriller, Book #3

With the Triarii in control of the Roman Catholic Church, an organization founded by Saint Peter himself takes action, murdering one of the new Pope's operatives. Detective Chaney, called in by the Pope to investigate, disappears, and, to the horror of the Papal staff sent to inform His Holiness, they find him missing too, the only clue a secret chest, presented to each new pope on the eve of their election, since the beginning of the Church.

Interpol Agent Reading, determined to find his friend, calls Professors James Acton and Laura Palmer to Rome to examine the chest and its forbidden contents, but before they can arrive, they are intercepted by an organization older than the Church, demanding the professors retrieve an item stolen in ancient Judea in exchange for the lives of their friends.

All of your favorite characters from The Protocol return to solve the most infamous kidnapping in history, against the backdrop of a two thousand year old battle pitting ancient foes with diametrically opposed agendas.

From the internationally bestselling author of Depraved Difference and The Protocol comes Broken Dove, the third entry in the smash hit James Acton Thrillers series, where J. Robert Kennedy reveals a secret concealed by the Church for almost 1200 years, and a fascinating interpretation of what the real reason behind the denials might be.

The Templar's Relic

A James Acton Thriller, Book #4

The Church Helped Destroy the Templars. Will a twist of fate let them get their revenge 700 years later?

The Vault must be sealed, but a construction accident leads to a miraculous discovery--an ancient tomb containing four Templar Knights, long forgotten, on the grounds of the Vatican. Not knowing who they can trust, the Vatican requests Professors James Acton and Laura Palmer examine the find, but what they discover, a precious Islamic relic, lost during the Crusades, triggers a set of events that shake the entire world, pitting the two greatest religions against each other.

Join Professors James Acton and Laura Palmer, INTERPOL Agent Hugh Reading, Scotland Yard DI Martin Chaney, and the Delta Force Bravo Team as they race against time to defuse a worldwide crisis that could quickly devolve into all-out war.

At risk is nothing less than the Vatican itself, and the rock upon which it was built.

From J. Robert Kennedy, the author of six international bestsellers including Depraved Difference and The Protocol, comes The Templar's Relic, the fourth entry in the smash hit James Acton Thrillers series, where once again Kennedy takes history and twists it to his own ends, resulting in a heart pounding thrill ride filled with action, suspense, humor and heartbreak.

Flags of Sin

A James Acton Thriller, Book #5

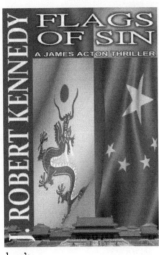

Archaeology Professor James Acton simply wants to get away from everything, and relax. A trip to China seems just the answer, and he and his fiancée, Professor Laura Palmer, are soon on a flight to Beijing.

But while boarding, they bump into an old friend, Delta Force Command Sergeant Major Burt Dawson, who surreptitiously delivers a message that they must meet the next day, for Dawson knows something they don't.

China is about to erupt into chaos.

Foreign tourists and diplomats are being targeted by unknown forces, and if they don't get out of China in time, they could be caught up in events no one had seen coming.

J. Robert Kennedy, the author of eight international best sellers, including the smash hit James Acton Thrillers, takes history once again and turns it on its head, sending his reluctant heroes James Acton and Laura Palmer into harm's way, to not only save themselves, but to try and save a country from a century old conspiracy it knew nothing about.

The Arab Fall

A James Acton Thriller, Book #6

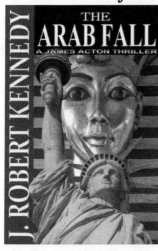

The greatest archeological discovery since King Tut's tomb is about to be destroyed!
The Arab Spring has happened and Egypt has yet to calm down, but with the dig site on the edge of the Nubian Desert, a thousand miles from the excitement, Professor Laura Palmer and her fiancé Professor James Acton return with a group of students, and two friends: Interpol Special Agent Hugh Reading, and Scotland Yard DI Martin Chaney.

But an accidental find by Chaney may lead to the greatest archaeological discovery since the tomb of King Tutankhamen, perhaps even greater. And when news of it spreads, it reaches the ears of a group hell-bent on the destruction of all idols and icons, their mere existence considered blasphemous to Islam.

As chaos hits the major cities of the world in a coordinated attack, unbeknownst to the professors, students and friends, they are about to be faced with one of the most difficult decisions of their lives. Stay and protect the greatest archaeological find of our times, or save themselves and their students from harm, leaving the find to be destroyed by fanatics determined to wipe it from the history books.

From J. Robert Kennedy, the author of eleven international bestsellers including Rogue Operator and The Protocol, comes The Arab Fall, the sixth entry in the smash hit James Acton Thrillers series, where Kennedy once again takes events from history and today's headlines, and twists them into a heart pounding adventure filled with humor and heartbreak, as one of their own is left severely wounded, fighting for their life.

The Circle of Eight

A James Acton Thriller, Book #7

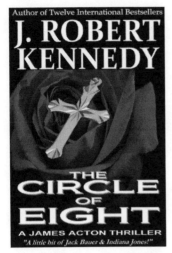

Abandoned by their government, Delta Team Bravo fights to not only save themselves and their families, but humanity as well.

The Bravo Team is targeted by a madman after one of their own intervenes in a rape. Little do they know this internationally well-respected banker is also a senior member of an organization long thought extinct, whose stated goals for a reshaped world are not only terrifying, but with today's globalization, totally achievable.

As the Bravo Team fights for its very survival, they are suspended, left adrift without their support network. To save themselves and their families, markers are called in, former members volunteer their services, favors are asked for past services, and the expertise of two professors, James Acton and his fiancée Laura Palmer, is requested.

It is a race around the globe to save what remains of the Bravo Team, abandoned by their government, alone in their mission, with only their friends to rely upon, as an organization over six centuries old works in the background to destroy them and all who help them, as it moves forward with plans that could see the world population decimated in an attempt to recreate Eden.

The Circle of Eight is the seventh installment in the internationally best selling James Acton Thrillers series. In The Circle of Eight J. Robert Kennedy, author of over a dozen international best sellers, is at his best, weaving a tale spanning centuries and delivering a taut thriller that will keep you on the edge of your seat from page one until the breathtaking conclusion.

The Venice Code

A James Acton Thriller, Book #8

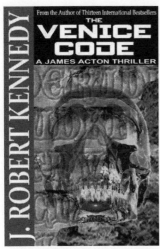

A SEVEN HUNDRED YEAR OLD MYSTERY IS ABOUT TO BE SOLVED. BUT HOW MANY MUST DIE FIRST?

A former President's son is kidnapped in a brazen attack on the streets of Potomac by the very ancient organization that murdered his father, convinced he knows the location of an item stolen from them by the late president.

A close friend awakes from a coma with a message for archeology Professor James Acton from the same organization, sending him along with his fiancée Professor Laura Palmer on a quest to find an object only rumored to exist, while trying desperately to keep one step ahead of a foe hell-bent on possessing it.

And seven hundred years ago, the Mongol Empire threatens to fracture into civil war as the northern capital devolves into idol worship, the Khan sending in a trusted family to save the empire--two brothers and a son, Marco Polo, whose actions have ramifications that resonate to this day.

From J. Robert Kennedy, the author of fourteen international best sellers comes The Venice Code, the latest installment of the hit James Acton Thrillers series. Join James Acton and his friends, including Delta Team Bravo and CIA Special Agent Dylan Kane in their greatest adventure yet, an adventure seven hundred years in the making.

Rogue Operator

A Special Agent Dylan Kane Thriller, Book #1

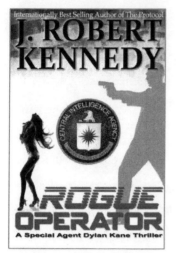

TO SAVE THE COUNTRY HE LOVES, SPECIAL AGENT DYLAN KANE MIGHT HAVE TO BETRAY IT.

Three top secret research scientists are presumed dead in a boating accident, but the kidnapping of their families the same day raises questions the FBI and local police can't answer, leaving them waiting for a ransom demand that will never come.

Central Intelligence Agency Analyst Chris Leroux stumbles upon the story, and finds a phone conversation that was never supposed to happen. When he reports it to his boss, the National Clandestine Services Chief, he is uncharacteristically reprimanded for conducting an unauthorized investigation and told to leave it to the FBI.

But he can't let it go.

For he knows something the FBI doesn't.

One of the scientists is alive.

Chris makes a call to his childhood friend, CIA Special Agent Dylan Kane, leading to a race across the globe to stop a conspiracy reaching the highest levels of political and corporate America, that if not stopped, could lead to war with an enemy armed with a weapon far worse than anything in the American arsenal, with the potential to not only destroy the world, but consume it.

J. Robert Kennedy, the author of nine international best sellers, including the smash hit James Acton Thrillers, introduces Rogue Operator, the first installment of his newest series, The Special Agent Dylan Kane Thrillers, promising to bring all of the action and intrigue of the James Acton Thrillers with a hero who lives below the radar, waiting for his country to call when it most desperately needs him.

Containment Failure

A Special Agent Dylan Kane Thriller, Book #2

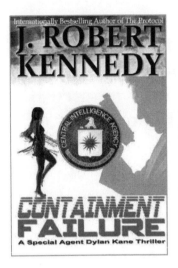

THE BLACK DEATH KILLED ALMOST HALF OF EUROPE'S POPULATION. THIS TIME BILLIONS ARE AT RISK.

New Orleans has been quarantined, an unknown virus sweeping the city, killing one hundred percent of those infected. The Centers for Disease Control, desperate to find a cure, is approached by BioDyne Pharma who reveal a former employee has turned a cutting edge medical treatment capable of targeting specific genetic sequences into a weapon, and released it.

CIA Special Agent Dylan Kane has been given one guideline from his boss: consider yourself unleashed, leaving Kane and New Orleans Police Detective Isabelle Laprise battling to stay alive as an insidious disease and terrified mobs spread through the city while they desperately seek those behind the greatest crime ever perpetrated.

The stakes have never been higher as Kane battles to save not only his friends and the country he loves, but all of mankind.

In Containment Failure, eleven times internationally bestselling author J. Robert Kennedy delivers a terrifying tale of what could happen when science goes mad, with enough sorrow, heartbreak, laughs and passion to keep readers on the edge of their seats until the chilling conclusion.

Cold Warriors

A Special Agent Dylan Kane Thriller, Book #3

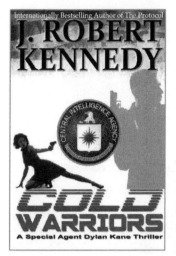

THE COUNTRY'S BEST HOPE IN DEFEATING A FORGOTTEN SOVIET WEAPON LIES WITH DYLAN KANE AND THE COLD WARRIORS WHO ORIGINALLY DISCOVERED IT.

While in Chechnya CIA Special Agent Dylan Kane stumbles upon a meeting between a known Chechen drug lord and a retired General once responsible for the entire Soviet nuclear arsenal. Money is exchanged for a data stick and the resulting transmission begins a race across the globe to discover just what was sold, the only clue a reference to a top secret Soviet weapon called Crimson Rush.

Unknown to Kane, this isn't the first time America has faced this threat and he soon receives a mysterious message, relayed through his friend and CIA analyst Chris Leroux, arranging a meeting with perhaps the one man alive today who can help answer the questions the nation's entire intelligence apparatus is asking--the Cold Warrior who had discovered the threat the first time.

Over thirty years ago.

In Cold Warriors, the third installment of the hit Special Agent Dylan Kane Thrillers series, J. Robert Kennedy, the author of thirteen international bestsellers including The Protocol and Rogue Operator, weaves a tale spanning two generations and three continents with all the heart pounding, edge of your seat action his readers have come to expect. Take a journey back in time as the unsung heroes of a war forgotten try to protect our way of life against our greatest enemy, and see how their war never really ended, the horrors of decades ago still a very real threat today.

The Turned

Zander Varga, Vampire Detective, Book #1

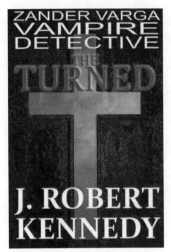

Zander has relived his wife's death at the hands of vampires every day for almost three hundred years, his perfect memory a curse of becoming one of The Turned—infecting him their final heinous act after her murder.

Nineteen year-old Sydney Winter knows Zander's secret, a secret preserved by the women in her family for four generations. But with her mother in a coma, she's thrust into the front lines, ahead of her time, to fight side-by-side with Zander.

And she wouldn't change a thing. She loves the excitement, she loves the danger. And she loves Zander. But it's a love that will have to go unrequited, because Zander has only one thing on his mind. And it's been the same thing for over two hundred years. Revenge.

But today, revenge will have to wait, because Zander Varga, Private Detective, has a new case. A woman's husband is missing. The police aren't interested. But Zander is. Something doesn't smell right, and he's determined to find out why.

From J. Robert Kennedy, the internationally bestselling author of The Protocol and Depraved Difference, comes his sixth novel, The Turned, a terrifying story that in true Kennedy fashion takes a completely new twist on the origin of vampires, tying it directly to a well-known moment in history. Told from the perspective of Zander Varga and his assistant, Sydney Winter, The Turned is loaded with action, humor, terror and a centuries long love that must eventually be let go.

Depraved Difference

A Detective Shakespeare Mystery, Book #1

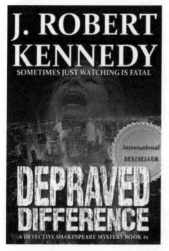

WOULD YOU HELP, WOULD YOU RUN, OR WOULD YOU JUST WATCH?

When a young woman is brutally assaulted by two men on the subway, her cries for help fall on the deaf ears of onlookers too terrified to get involved, her misery ended with the crushing stomp of a steel-toed boot. A cellphone video of her vicious murder, callously released on the Internet, its popularity a testament to today's depraved society, serves as a trigger, pulled a year later, for a killer.

Emailed a video documenting the final moments of a woman's life, entertainment reporter Aynslee Kai, rather than ask why the killer chose her to tell the story, decides to capitalize on the opportunity to further her career. Assigned to the case is Hayden Eldridge, a detective left to learn the ropes by a disgraced partner, and as videos continue to follow victims, he discovers they were all witnesses to the vicious subway murder a year earlier, proving sometimes just watching is fatal.

From the author of The Protocol and Brass Monkey, Depraved Difference is a fast-paced murder suspense novel with enough laughs, heartbreak, terror and twists to keep you on the edge of your seat, then knock you flat on the floor with an ending so shocking, you'll read it again just to pick up the clues.

Tick Tock

A Detective Shakespeare Mystery, Book #2

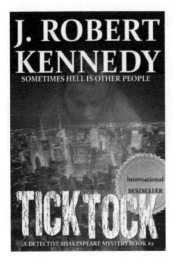

Crime Scene tech Frank Brata digs deep and finds the courage to ask his colleague, Sarah, out for coffee after work. Their good time turns into a nightmare when Frank wakes up the next morning covered in blood, with no recollection of what happened, and Sarah's body floating in the tub. Determined not to go to prison for a crime he's horrified he may have committed, he scrubs the crime scene clean, and, tormented by text messages from the real killer, begins a race against the clock to solve the murder before his own co-workers, his own friends, solve it first, and find him guilty.

Billionaire Richard Tate is the toast of the town, loved by everyone but his wife. His plans for a romantic weekend with his mistress ends in disaster, waking the next morning to find her murdered, floating in the tub. After fleeing in a panic, he returns to find the hotel room spotless, and no sign of the body. An envelope found at the scene contains not the expected blackmail note, but something far more sinister.

Two murders, with the same MO, targeting both the average working man, and the richest of society, sets a rejuvenated Detective Shakespeare, and his new reluctant partner, Amber Trace, after a murderer whose motivations are a mystery, and who appears to be aided by the very people they would least expect—their own.

Tick Tock, Book #2 in the internationally bestselling Detective Shakespeare Mysteries series, picks up right where Depraved Difference left off, and asks a simple question: What would you do? What would you do if you couldn't prove your innocence, but knew you weren't capable of murder? Would you hide the very evidence that might clear you, or would you turn yourself in and trust the system to work?

From the internationally bestselling author of The Protocol and Brass Monkey comes the highly anticipated sequel to the smash hit Depraved Difference, Tick Tock. Filled with heart pounding terror and suspense, along with a healthy dose of humor, Tick Tock's twists will keep you guessing right up to the terrifying end.

The Redeemer

A Detective Shakespeare Mystery, Book #3

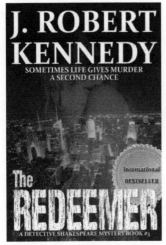

SOMETIMES LIFE GIVES MURDER A SECOND CHANCE

It was the case that destroyed Detective Justin Shakespeare's career, beginning a downward spiral of self-loathing and self-destruction lasting half a decade. And today things are only going to get worse. The Widow Rapist is free on a technicality, and it is up to Detective Shakespeare and his partner Amber Trace to find the evidence, five years cold, to put him back in prison before he strikes again.

But Shakespeare and Trace aren't alone in their desire for justice. The Seven are the survivors, avowed to not let the memories of their loved ones be forgotten. And with the release of the Widow Rapist, they are determined to take justice into their own hands, restoring balance to a flawed system.

At stake is a second chance, a chance at redemption, a chance to salvage a career destroyed, a reputation tarnished, and a life diminished.

A chance brought to Detective Shakespeare whether he wants it or not.

A chance brought to him by The Redeemer.

From J. Robert Kennedy, the author of seven international bestsellers including Depraved Difference and The Protocol, comes the third entry in the acclaimed Detective Shakespeare Mysteries series, The Redeemer, a dark tale exploring the psyches of the serial killer, the victim, and the police, as they all try to achieve the same goals.

Balance. And redemption.

15077859R00207

Made in the USA
Middletown, DE
22 October 2014